MAGGIE FINDS HER MUSE

MAGGIE FINDS HER MUSE

Dee Ernst

ST. MARTIN'S GRIFFIN
New York

First published in the United States by St. Martin's Griffin, an imprint of St. Martin's Publishing Group

MAGGIE FINDS HER MUSE. Copyright © 2021 by Elizabeth Ernst. All rights reserved. Printed in the United States of America. For information, address St. Martin's Publishing Group, 120 Broadway, New York, NY 10271.

www.stmartins.com

Designed by Donna Sinisgalli Noetzel

Library of Congress Cataloging-in-Publication Data

Names: Ernst, Dee, author.
Title: Maggie finds her muse / Dee Ernst.
Description: First edition. | New York : St. Martin's Griffin, 2021.
Identifiers: LCCN 2020045320 | ISBN 9781250768339 (trade paperback) | ISBN 9781250768346 (ebook)
Classification: LCC PS3605.R75 M34 2021 | DDC 813/.6—dc23
LC record available at https://lccn.loc.gov/2020045320

Our books may be purchased in bulk for promotional, educational, or business use. Please contact your local bookseller or the Macmillan Corporate and Premium Sales Department at 1-800-221-7945, extension 5442, or by email at MacmillanSpecialMarkets@macmillan.com.

First Edition: 2021

10 9 8 7 6 5 4 3 2 1

This is for Gene . . . my happily ever after.

MAGGIE FINDS HER MUSE

Chapter 1

*In which I enter full panic mode and
dispose of unwanted clutter*

*Here lies Maggie Bliss, who died a slow and tortured death
by total impostor syndrome after failing to write the final book of
the Delania Trilogy.*

I stared at the words I'd just typed, then said them out loud.
They sounded perfect for my tombstone. I'd have to save this
little nugget, just in case. But where? Send it to my daughter?
Probably not. The last thing she needed was *another* therapy
moment. My ex-husband? He'd always been good at paper-
work, but we had been divorced for twenty-three years, so . . .
no. My agent was a logical choice, but it might raise a few red
flags. After all, he thought my writing was going along just fine.

Maybe I could print it out and frame it, with careful instructions attached.

Wherever it ended up, the good news was that the next time
my editor, Ellen, sent me one of her hourly texts asking if I was

writing about Delania, I could, for the first time in six months, truthfully answer *yes*.

I was all alone in my office as I said the words, and it was a good thing. Every author in the world knows in their heart of hearts that despite the fame, awards, accolades, and devoted followers, at any moment we could all become incapable of putting together even the simplest of sentences. If another writer had heard those words, she would have pulled down the leg of her sweatpants, poured us both more coffee, and helped with the punctuation.

But if anyone *else* had heard me, well . . . people would be disappointed. Even upset. There were the readers, literally millions of them, who didn't know or care what impostor syndrome was. All they knew was that they had read the first book of the Delania Trilogy and were eagerly awaiting the second. To them, there was no question there'd be a third book. After all, this *was* a trilogy. Those readers had questions. Expectations. They were invested. They wanted a great big The End. If I didn't write one, well, can you imagine what would happen to me?

Then there were my agent *and* my editor, who both insisted that this third book was going to bring my career to the next level. They had invested a great deal of time, energy, and money in my work over the years, and this was going to be the payoff. Yes, they'd also be upset.

It's not like I didn't know how this trilogy ended. Of course I did. Bellacore (call me Bella) LoModeria, twenty-six, five ten, flat stomach, ample bosom, and green-flecked eyes, had given up on love and wasn't looking for a man. Not any man. Not even . . .

Lance. Sergeant David Rupert Lancaster, thirty-four, six feet two inches of rock-hard muscle, and surprisingly smooth skin despite the constant stubble on his firm and often clenched-in-frustration jaw. He knew that Bella was the woman for him and was going to do everything he could to make sure she knew it too. Theirs was a love that was never meant to be. Theirs was a passion that could not be denied. Theirs was a story destined to bring tears of joy and heartbreak and, ultimately, happily ever after.

All I had to do was finish writing it.

And therein lay the problem. For all my plotting and charts, maps and good intentions, I was two months away from my deadline and hadn't written a single word.

Except for this epitaph, which I found to be both pithy and profound.

Listen—writer's block happens to all of us. And usually writer's block was not a big deal for me because I always took a bit of time between books. But I had signed the biggest deal of my twenty-plus-year career for a trilogy that would bring to life the tortured love between a beautiful ex-supermodel-turned-foreign-rescue-worker and a hard-bitten ex-Navy SEAL determined to protect her in war-torn, made-up Delania.

The first book started slowly, but word of mouth drove impressive sales. The second book of the trilogy was due to be released in early June, less than two months away. Already the buzz was intense. Presale numbers alone had earned me the third-place spot in *People* magazine's Best Summer Reads list, a slot on *Good Morning America,* and book tours across the country.

That was the kind of success that might let me quit teaching creative writing classes every fall, which I did because I could not yet support myself solely on my writing. Yes, I know . . . writers are supposed to be rich. The truth is that most of us are *not* consistently on the top of the bestseller lists and are not in the same tax bracket as Stephen King. If I lived somewhere other than northern New Jersey, I could scrape by on book royalties alone, but I wasn't about to move to Iowa just for a more reasonable cost of living.

And then there was the Cable Network Option. That's right, an option for the Delania Trilogy to be made into a miniseries produced by a Very Important Actress/Producer. An option that would give me not just quit-teaching money but . . . dare I say it . . . *beach house* money.

I'd wanted a beach house since the first time I'd set my tiny two-year-old feet in the ocean. I remember it clearly: the sudden cold of the water, the sharp tang of salt in the air, the sand crunching between my toddler toes. *This is what I want,* I thought then. I want to live *here*.

I hadn't changed my mind over the past forty years. And the option was finally going to make it real. But thanks to *Game of Thrones,* which had to have its finale written on the fly because the author had not finished the last book, nobody was going to sign anything until the final book was on my publisher's desk.

So . . . everything I had ever hoped for as a writer was right there. Sitting in front of me. Waiting.

All I had to do was finish the damn book.

Correction. *Start* the damn book.

I met Greg Howard seven years ago at a cocktail party given by Drew University, which was where I'd been teaching my creative writing course for years. Greg was a writer of political nonfiction and would be giving a writing seminar there for the first time in the spring, and the cocktail party was to welcome him aboard. I took my time with him, carefully weighing the cost of a relationship. After all, he was younger than I and, quite honestly, a bit intense.

But I pursued him because he was, for all intents and purposes, my perfect alpha male: strong and sexy, exciting, with an air of danger about him. He had, in the course of his career, survived being held at gunpoint, stranded in the middle of the Amazon, and taken hostage by a small but determined guerrilla band somewhere in Africa. He was also charismatic and bright and engaging, funny and . . . well, let's be honest again here . . . passionate. As in, the mere touch of his lips on the back of my neck was enough to turn my knees to jelly. One of the reasons I was so good writing about mind-blowing sex was because whenever Greg was around, that's what I got, pretty much whenever I wanted it. Did that make me shallow? No. We spent even more quality time out of bed. But I have to say, the thought of those fingers and that mouth of his tended to make me gloss over his greatest and most fatal flaw:

His ego.

He had won a Pulitzer and a National Book Award, and had been asked to speak before Congress and the UN. He had groupies. And he loved it. He had never, in all the time I'd known him, shown the least bit of hesitation or self-doubt about anything he'd done. He was absolutely confident in all his choices.

That's sexy.

But it was also starting to take a toll. I recently had begun to feel a bit tired of always being the second-most important person in the room when we were alone together.

We had been living together for almost four years. Well, living together when he was actually in New Jersey, teaching his seminar. But that was only for six months of the year. He spent the rest of his time on the road, in one hellish country or another, researching his books. And when the research was done, he went up to his remote cabin in Maine to write. Alone.

Since his writing seminar was every spring, he was currently in New Jersey. On the day I wrote my epitaph, he had come home at some point in the early afternoon, probably when I was staring out the window or scrolling the internet or doing anything other than actually writing. I came downstairs to find him pulling things out of the refrigerator.

As writing is a lonely profession, I was grateful to have Greg around to discuss whatever problems I faced while working.

Although I was not about to throw myself at him, sobbing with frustration, begging for help, I felt that desperate.

"Hey, how was your day?" I asked, moving in for a kiss.

He backed away. "You're still in your writing clothes," he said.

That was true. I was in sweatpants and my sleeping shirt and may or may not have bothered to brush my teeth. I know I hadn't brushed my hair.

"I've been trying to work," I explained.

He looked around, scowling. "Where's the food?"

I stepped back. "The fridge is full of food. Can you be more specific?"

He narrowed his eyes. "All the food for tonight?"

Oh . . . crap. "Ah . . . that's tonight?" I asked. Every semester he invited all his students to the house for an informal dinner, and tonight was the night. "I forgot. I'm sorry, but you know I've been preoccupied with this book. Which I really need to talk to you about. Could you maybe just push it back to next week?"

"I can't just *push it back*. Those kids will be here in four hours. What are you going to feed them?"

"Wait . . . what am *I* going to feed them? These are your dinners, not mine. Take them to a restaurant. Tell them it's a potluck this year and have everyone bring a dish. You have a PhD, Greg. You escaped a cartel's compound in the Philippines and an ISIS stronghold in Pakistan. I'm sure you'll figure something out." I ran my fingers through my hair, hit a snag, and tugged. "What I really need right now is to talk to you about my book."

He shook his head at me, reminding me of my father when I would come home with a bad report card. "Maggie, I count on you to do this every year. You didn't get my email? I sent it this morning, reminding you."

I closed my eyes briefly. "Really? You sent an email? I'm supposed to be your partner, not your social secretary."

"If you were my partner, you would have remembered."

"If you were *my* partner, you would have noticed that I've been distracted and in a semi panic for the past few months. You know that I have the third book to finish, right?"

He nodded.

"And don't I usually try to talk to you about tricky plot points?"

He nodded again. He rarely had any suggestions. In fact, I'm fairly certain he barely paid attention. But he always put on his *I'm listening* face.

"When was the last time I asked you anything about this new book?"

He frowned.

"Exactly," I said. "I haven't written a word. At all. In months. And have you even noticed? I mean, has it crossed your mind that I should be writing and I'm not, and maybe, just maybe, you should ask me why?"

He ruffled his short sandy hair. "I've been distracted too, Maggie. You know that."

"Yes, and I know exactly why because I love you and am

interested in your work. I know that *your* deadline has been pushed up, *your* department is undergoing another reorganization, and *you're* having trouble getting a visa to wherever the hell you're going next. I know all that because I ask you every day what is going on in your life."

"Are you suggesting I'm not just as interested in *your* life?"

"I'm beyond suggesting, Greg." I exhaled loudly. "Do you have *any* idea what's going on with me? Because I've been trying to tell you for the last five minutes, and you don't seem the least bit interested."

He pushed his hands into the pockets of his jeans. "Now, Maggie, it's really not the same thing, is it? I mean, my work . . . well . . ."

I could feel weeks, no months, no, maybe *years* of resentment start to bubble up. "Yes, your work. Let's talk about your work, Greg. It takes you away from us, from me, for half the year. The other half of the year you have speaking engagements and calls to testify in Congress and lectures to give, in addition to your all-sacred class schedule, also taking you away from me. And when you *are* here, I'm automatically expected to be on call for your social obligations. Whereas I plan every conference, signing, or engagement around your schedule."

He rolled his eyes. "I can't help it—"

"Yes, Greg, you *can* help it. You could say no once in a while. You could bring me with you to your conferences and meetings. I'd love to go with you. And your time in Maine . . . do you know that I've never seen the inside of the Maine place?"

"Because I work there."

"Yes, and I work *here*. And I manage to work around what-ever it is you happen to be doing at the time, no matter how dis-tracting it is, because you never bother to temper your activities around the fact that I am, in fact, working." I stepped closer. "Except I haven't been working, Greg. At all. And I have two months to my deadline, and I'm finally in total panic mode, and why don't you care?"

He shook his head. "Maggie, let's face it: My work is just more important than yours."

And . . . there it was. What I'd been stewing and steaming about for so long that I couldn't remember when I *hadn't* been stewing and steaming. "Really, Greg? More important? Then why doesn't it pay any of the bills around here?" I could hear the timbre of my voice ratchet up.

"Money isn't everything, Maggie," Greg said calmly.

"You're right, Greg. It isn't. But money did send those text-books *you* promised to that school in Colombia. *My* work paid for that. And that nice BMW you drive?" I stood very close to him, and we were eye to eye, and I may have been scream-ing. "If your work is so friggin' important, where's the friggin' money, Greg?"

He stepped back and I could see a calm regret in his eyes. "There are so many other ways to measure value, Maggie. I'm disappointed that you could be so shallow."

"And I'm disappointed I've spent all this time living with a man who would freely take whatever I gave him and never once consider the time and effort I put toward getting it in the first place."

We stared at each other. He looked almost uncomfortable. Then—

"That doesn't solve the problem of what we're going to feed my students tonight."

That did it. "I don't give a rat's ass what your students eat tonight. And I don't care what *you* eat tonight either. Tonight or any other night. I am having a career crisis, and all you can think about is what to do about *your* problem."

He threw up his hands in obvious frustration. "There are people coming over, Maggie!"

But I was on a roll. "Your coming first has been the basis of our entire relationship. I've gone along with it because I always believed that if I had a real problem, you would put your own needs aside and help me out. Well, that moment is here and now, and you're not stepping up to the plate. So I think the best thing you can do right now is start packing up all your stuff and get out of here."

I didn't hear his answer. I didn't even see if his face registered astonishment, anger, or just woeful acceptance. I turned, walked up to my office, and, quite loudly, slammed the door.

I felt such anger. No, not anger—rage. And resentment, and frustration, and disappointment. Not just at him and his complete failure to be the man I wanted and needed, but at myself for being so blind as to see that he had never been that man, and he never would be.

I loved him, or at least I had. The past few months had brought a definite cooling-off between us, and not just physically. I'd felt myself moving further and further away from him until I barely recognized *what* I was feeling. Which was why I also felt profoundly relieved. Love was not enough. I'd learned that from Alan, my ex-husband. I was on the brink of something for myself that was too important to walk away from, and if he wasn't willing to at least try to understand, then I was finally done trying to make the two of us work.

I heard a gentle knock on the door. "Go away, Greg," I said. The last thing I needed was his puppy-dog eyes and his wandering hands and his hot breath in my ear. . . .

"Maggie, don't you want to at least talk about this?"

"Yes. Talk."

"Through the door?"

"Why not? I can hear you perfectly."

I heard his sigh of frustration. His way of winning arguments usually involved slipping his hands under my clothes, but with a solid door between us, he had no edge and he knew it. "I'm sure you'll feel differently in the morning, after you realize how childish you're being."

That may have been the wrong thing for him to say. I picked up the large brass ampersand that served as a bookend and threw it at the door.

Greg always was a smart man, so he left. I don't know what he told his students, nor did I care. When he came home, much later, he slept in the spare bedroom. He was gone when I woke the next morning.

In my books, when the heroine breaks up with her significant other, she spends sleepless nights wracked with regret. I slept like a baby. Or like someone who just stepped out from beneath a shadow that had grown way too long and dark.

The next morning I called my agent, Lee Newcomb.

"You what?" he almost yelled, and he was not a yeller. "You don't have *anything*? My God, Maggie, we have already had two deadline extensions. You know how tight this schedule is. You have to turn in the first draft in less than ten weeks or the publication date will be pushed back, and that would be deadly. We need to do this."

Yes, *we*. Lee and I were a team, which is why he was the one I always turned to if I had book issues.

"I know, Lee. I need to jump-start my brain. You need to help me."

I could picture him in his office, an old brownstone in Hoboken, New Jersey, on the top floor of his elaborately decorated townhouse. His office was gray, spare, and elegant, much like Lee himself. He spent hours on the phone and would always get up and pace around the room while talking. He claimed it was the only exercise he got.

"Does Ellen know?" he asked.

"Are you kidding? No, Ellen doesn't know," I snapped. "I've been lying to her for months."

"You could have asked for help a little earlier, you know? Like, four or five months ago? Jeez, Mags, what's going on?"

I was in my office, once the smallest bedroom, which had

floor-to-ceiling bookcases, a cushy sofa for deep thinking, and an antique campaign desk worthy of Hemingway himself.

"I don't know, Lee. I'm just stuck."

"Is this a midlife crisis kind of thing?"

I snorted. "I wish. I think I'm past a realistic midlife point by now."

"Pish."

"No, really. I'm forty-eight. How many ninety-six-year-olds are there?"

"More than you'd think. But—your book. What can I do? What do you need?"

"Oh God, why hadn't Greg said that?" I moaned. I was huddled into the corner of the sofa, sipping hot tea and staring out the window at the large pond across the street. It was late April and spring was bursting out pretty much everywhere. Ducks were paddling happily. Songbirds were singing, carefree in the cool air. Somewhere deep underwater, fish were swimming. Everyone was having a perfectly marvelous time. Except me.

"What about Greg?" he asked.

"We're not together anymore. Well, technically, I guess we are, but that's only until he packs up all his stuff and moves out, which could take weeks, and there's going to be all that tension and angst, and you know how I hate tension and angst in my life. . . . How am I going to write this book, Lee?"

"Come to Paris with me and Martin."

I was not expecting to hear *that*. "But, isn't your Paris trip, like, a pilgrimage? Isn't there's an aging relative there somewhere, and a vineyard?"

"The aging relative died years ago and yes, we go to the vineyard, but we begin and end in Paris. We have a housekeeper at the Paris apartment, Solange, who will love you and take excellent care of you while Martin and I are gone. The apartment is huge, four bedrooms. Only one bath, but that's Paris. You'll be in the most romantic city in the world with two gay men who are on an unlimited budget. And besides, isn't your daughter over there somewhere?"

My daughter, Nicole, was the product of my brief marriage, and she was indeed, over there somewhere. She had moved to France a little over a year ago upon deciding, after several false starts in several expensive graduate programs, not to mention at least six jobs that lasted barely a few months each, that what she really wanted to do with her life was to be a translator of things English to things Breton. I didn't know that Breton was even a language, but it made sense for a French major with a minor in art history. "She's in Rennes. It's west of Paris. In Brittany."

"I bet she'd love to spend some quality time with you."

I pushed myself up off the sofa and moved closer to the window. Were those two ducks . . . screwing? "I think if she had really wanted to spend quality time with me, she wouldn't have moved so far away in the first place."

"Paris, Mags. The city of lights. Art, history, and more hot men than you can shake a stick at. Two sticks. I bet your little romantic brain will kick into overdrive. You have a passport?"

"Yes, but . . ."

"We leave Sunday night. I'll send you the link for our airline reservations and you can try to get the same flight. You'll probably have to pay through the nose, and you may only be able to get first class, but you can write the whole thing off."

"What about my book launch?" I asked.

The launch of the second Delania book, *Fire in the Blood,* included a book tour, interviews, and television and radio spots. It was also barely eight weeks away.

"Get in six solid weeks of writing, then you can fly back and do whatever you need to do to get ready for the book launch." Lee said. "That's plenty of time for you to pound out a first draft, and that's all we need. I will call Ellen and tell her you're going into seclusion to finish the last bit of the book. That way she won't text you every day."

"Try three times a day," I said.

"Well, let's face it: There's a lot on the line here, and as it turns out, she has every right to be concerned."

I stared out the window, thinking. "I have nothing to wear in Paris."

"Bring lots of black and gray and one fabulous scarf. That gorgeous Ferragamo one you treated yourself to a few years ago. And good shoes."

"I'm too short for Paris," I argued, but I could feel myself sinking into the whole idea.

"Too short? What are you talking about?"

"According to the standard height and weight chart, I need to grow three inches taller."

"We'll work on that when we get there," Lee soothed. "There's chocolate in Paris."

I chewed my lower lip. The ducks had finished their little display of uninhibited affection and now swam in opposite directions. "Yeah?"

"And éclairs."

"Send me the link. I'll think about it."

I hung up the phone. Yes, the ducks were now on opposite sides of Burnham Pond. More birdsong. A few annoying bursts of yellow, as the daffodils had begun to bloom.

Paris might be exactly the change I needed. But before I left, there were a few details that needed taking care of.

I had two best friends, and I always texted them together.

> M: Threw Greg out. Still can't write so going to Paris Sunday. Can we drink?

Their response was simple. Tomorrow. Brunch. Eleven thirty at The Office.

That's what best friends are for.

One of the oldest tropes in romance writing is the naive college student falling for her dashing older professor, who teaches her everything from what wine to drink to how to have a mind-blowing orgasm in less than three minutes. The thing about clichés is that they become clichés because they happen so often. Take Alan and me. I was a college student and had already decided on a career as a writer, but needed to take a pesky math course to fulfill my graduation requirements. I waited until my junior year and then, at the age of twenty, tried to learn what I never paid attention to in all of high school: algebra.

Algebra, by the way, had numbers *and* letters. Since I was in love with letters, I thought algebra would come easier to me than, say, regular math.

I was wrong.

It took me only two weeks to realize I was never going to understand algebra, and that put me in a real bind. Because I had waited so late to take the required math class, if I dropped it, I wouldn't have room in my schedule until the last semester of my senior year, creating a very real possibility of my not graduating at all if I managed to flunk it. So I had to pass. With a healthy GPA, I was willing to take a D. I just could not afford an F.

My roommate looked at me, arched her eyebrow, and muttered, "Maybe you need to find out who you have to sleep with around here to pass Algebra I."

Turned out that I needed to sleep with my own professor, Alan Goddard. Tall, handsome, and totally unaware that most of his female students would have gone to bed with him even if he didn't control their grade. I was, I must confess, perfectly willing to do whatever I needed to do to get the grade necessary to put the algebraic nightmare behind me. Ten minutes into our first one-on-one conversation, where I was pleading supreme ignorance of all things mathematical and asking for advice, tutoring, remedial instruction . . . anything . . . he smiled, told me to calm down, and offered me herbal tea. I accepted. Two hours later, he asked me to dinner. I accepted. Then he asked me back to his place.

I accepted.

I passed the class. Not because we ended up married the very next semester but because I was so in love with him that I actually paid for a grad student to sit with me twice a week and help me understand what the hell was going on in class.

We had a short, passionate, short, tempestuous, short, roller-coaster marriage that ended after three years, right after Nicole's second birthday. He was a decent, caring man, so Nicole had a loving relationship with him. Alan and I even, at some point, became friends. And why not? He remained charming and handsome, and while I couldn't imagine ever living with him again, I had always enjoyed his company. We'd shared holidays and all the usual benchmark events in our daughter's life until her college graduation three years ago. I hadn't seen him since, although we still exchanged cards commemorating our divorce day.

After said divorce, he moved to Pennsylvania and became a dean at a small, very prestigious university. I started teaching English at the local high school while scribbling stories, and I ended up writing romance novels under three different pen names as well as my own.

Nicole began reading when she was just three years old and grew into a brilliant but extremely complicated young person. At the beginning of her junior year in high school, I sent her to a psychologist to try to figure out why someone so smart could have so many problems handling social situations.

The word Asperger's finally emerged, and everything in her life suddenly fell into place. All those boundaries she had set for herself, the lines that no one dared cross without causing tantrums and tears, were not just lines drawn by a moody, rebellious teen. They marked the pathways she needed to move through a world that was profoundly different from her own inner world. I stopped pretending I knew what was best for my only child, and our relationship became easier, friendlier, and almost normal.

I had not seen Nicole since she'd come home at Christmas, but we spoke every Monday. That was when she called me. I didn't call her, but if there was anything urgent that I needed to speak with her about, I'd send a text and she'd get back to me. Her life was one of schedules and routine, and I made it a point to never interrupt unless absolutely necessary. If she were any other adult child living in another country, perhaps the idea of a surprise visit would be met with absolute delight.

But not my kid.

So I sent her a text, asking her to call when convenient, which was apparently at six thirty the next morning.

"Mom, hello. Didn't we just talk the other day?"

"Hi, Nicole. Yes, I know, but I have a surprise for you."

I waited for her anticipation and excitement to jump out from the rectangle of my cell phone. It did not.

"What surprise, Mom?"

"I'm going to Paris!"

Still no excitement, now coupled with no joy. "Why are you going to Paris, Mom?"

"Because I'm having a problem with this book I'm working on, and Lee thought I should go there to get inspired. I've never been to France, you know. I'll be staying at his flat, working, and since I'm there . . . aren't you done with classes soon? Maybe you could meet me?"

Come on joy, come on joy . . . "Actually, I'm done with classes. And finals. And I already have plans to be in Paris."

"Oh? How lovely. We could spend lots of time together."

"I'll be with Dad," she said slowly.

I drew back and stared at the phone. What did she just say? "Alan is going to be in Paris? He hates to travel. He hates to fly. And if I remember correctly, when you told him you wanted to study in France, he spent weeks trying to talk you out of it."

Across the ocean, she said something in French to somebody, and I listened with patient ignorance. My daughter never *just* had a phone conversation. She was always doing something else, going somewhere, cleaning, cooking, whatever.

"Yes, well," she said, back to me and in English. "Heather arranged it, apparently, and now they've split up, but since he already paid for everything, he's coming alone. He has a two-bedroom flat in Le Marais, and I'll be staying with him. And he'll be meeting Louis."

So, who was Heather, exactly? How had she gotten Alan to agree to go to France? Apparently they'd broken up, but when? And as a result, Alan was actually traveling alone to France? *And* meeting the boyfriend that Nicole had been so careful not to mention too many times?

I just plowed on, hoping I could eventually catch up. "I

don't mind seeing Alan, you know. Or meeting Louis, for that matter. I can spend time with all of you. How do you feel about spending time with all of *us*?"

There was a very long pause. She was either giving my question a great deal of thought or emptying out an entire chest of drawers.

"It's fine," she said at last. "Let me know when you arrive. Do you know where you're staying?"

"Not a clue, but I'll send you the address. I'll be there Monday."

"Okay, Mom. See you then. Love you."

She clicked off before I could say *love you more,* but she already knew that.

Even though I arrived for brunch a few minutes early, Cheri Robinson was waiting for me, and Alison Wazinski was literally at my heels through the door. We ordered Bloody Marys without a word to each other, perused the menus in silence, and placed our orders. I looked from one to the other.

"What?"

"We're *waiting,*" Alison said.

I took a gulp of my drink. "Greg and I finally just . . ."

"Well, it's about time," Cheri said. She'd divorced her husband five years ago and was slowly rebuilding her life, quite successfully. She was my age, built like a fireplug, and her hair was in long cornrows, some of them bright pink. "I have been waiting for you to ditch that man for months now. Let's face it, you've been emotionally checked out since Christmas."

"Cheri," Alison chided. "I thought we agreed . . ." Alison had been married for over thirty years and had four children, six grandchildren. A gray braid fell down her back, her freckled face had never known a makeup brush, and I was sure *Original Earth Mother* was tattooed on her back.

Cheri waved her hand. "I've got my nephew's birthday at two. I can't sit here all day and wait. So, you threw him out. Good. Now, what's this about Paris?"

I sat back. "Wait. Emotionally checked out? How can you even say that?" I was arguing with her even as I admitted to myself she was right.

Cheri raised her eyebrows. "When was the last time you two had sex?"

I shrank back in my chair. She had a point there. Greg and I hadn't exchanged more than a good-night kiss in weeks. "Well . . ."

Alison made small clucking noises. "We've known you for a long time, Maggie." And they had. Alison and I had side-by-side classrooms when I first started teaching over twenty years ago. "We've seen this before. We know the signs, and have we ever been wrong?"

Cheri took a gulp of her drink, licked her lips appreciatively, and took a bite of her celery stalk. "We called that guy Jackson? Remember him?"

Jackson. Right. He was a mistake for sure. "Well, okay, maybe him, but . . ."

"And Thomas? Toothy Thomas the dentist? We told you after the first three dates he was a waste of time," Alison said, looking rather smug.

"And when you broke up with that editor? The short one with the mustache? I was only two weeks off with that one," Cheri said. "And you'd been with him for a *long* time."

"Three years," I muttered.

"Besides," Alison said, "Greg was never good enough for you. None of those men were. Now, tell us about Paris. Will you be able to see Nicole?"

I dragged myself away from trying to analyze every relationship I'd had in the past twenty years. "Yes. She's done with school. She's going to be in Paris. Alan is there, visiting. And I think I'll meet Louis."

"Alan? How nice. I always liked Alan," Cheri said. She was my next-door neighbor when I first bought the condo, and her son was Nicole's age. She'd been at all Nicole's birthday parties and had therefore met Alan on several festive occasions.

"And where are you staying?" Alison asked.

I explained Lee and his Paris flat.

Cheri whistled appreciatively. "Staying for free? Lucky you. I'd visit Paris every year if I could afford it. You'll love it."

"I'm there to write," I said. "So the usual rules apply."

The usual rules were that when I was writing, I stayed completely off social media. There were also no phone calls, texts, or transmission of silly cat videos to distract me. Those were the rules my friends understood and had agreed to years ago.

Alison shook her head. "Oh, I don't think so. You'll be in Paris."

"But I'll be writing."

"This is different," Cheri said.

"How?"

"Because it's Paris, that's why," Alison said.

"I'll still be writing," I told them.

"But," Cheri said, "you could be there for weeks. I get that you stay off of Facebook and even Twitter. Those are major time sucks. But Instagram? Aren't you going to post all your photos to Instagram?"

"I won't be taking any photos," I said. "Listen to me: *I'll be too busy writing.*"

Cheri made a face. "Fine. But what about us? You can't cut *us* off completely. What if there's serious news about Nicole?"

"Or Alan?" Alison countered. "Or, who knows . . . you could meet someone."

"I'm there to write," I insisted. "No distractions. At all."

I looked up. Cheri and Alison were both giving me the evil eye.

"All right," I said. "Texts only, Sundays only. Unless my condo burns down or there's someone in the hospital."

Cheri tut-tutted. "I don't think so. Paris, remember?"

"Okay. Any day is fine."

"Morning or evening?" Cheri asked.

I shook my head. "Now you're asking me to figure out time difference, and that's something I refuse to do on an empty stomach. I'll text you when I have time, and you guys do the same. That way, if anything exciting does happen . . ."

"You're in Paris," Alison said. "Of course something exciting is going to happen."

"I'm there to *write*," I repeated. I turned to Alison. "No cat videos," I said. Then I tilted my head at Cheri. "And nothing political."

She reared back. "I beg your pardon?"

"I mean it. I don't care what Congress does or how many sea turtles need surgery because they ate plastic straws. I can't afford distractions." A plate of huevos rancheros was set in front of me and I sighed with happiness.

Cheri snorted. "Oh, honey. You want to talk about distractions? The food in France . . ."

I dug into my eggs. "Seriously? This is huevos rancheros. The best thing ever. How much better could the food possibly get?"

Cheri rolled her eyes. "Just wait."

Chapter 2

I arrive in Paris, and it does not suck

Some of my writer friends can, with barely three hours' notice, pack a carry-on suitcase with a variety of clothing items that can be combined in one way or another to make twenty-three different outfits, complete with matching accessories. They also manage to fit in three pairs of shoes, a lightweight jacket, and a dashing rain hat. There is always room in their carry-on for the wallet, keys, laptop, e-reader, and very important, possibly top-secret files, as well as makeup, fabulous jewelry, and a portable hair dryer. They arrive at the airport just in time to get on the shortest line, breeze through security, and drink a delightful glass of champagne before takeoff. Once on board, having been randomly upgraded to first class, they enjoy their perfectly smooth flight to wherever, where they deplane refreshed, smiling, and full of energy.

I am not one of those writers.

If you saw my Pinterest board for travel, you'd think I'd

mastered how to dress for any season in any country, how to say twenty-five essential things in fifteen languages, and how to avoid motion sickness, jet lag, and being swindled by charming strangers. Sadly, I mastered none of those things, in spite of all my pins.

Packing was always a trial, even though I had lists and more lists, not to mention videos that I'd watched with a religious devotion in an attempt to pack my suitcase without everything emerging looking like it had been crammed in a paper bag for three days. I usually open my suitcase to find I've taken five pairs of identical black pants, three T-shirts, a ten-year-old down vest from Lands' End, and forgotten my underwear.

Since I really didn't know how long I would be in Paris, packing was even more excruciating than usual. There was the usual pile of clothes, and I tried carefully tucking in at least twelve different bottles of beauty products, ranging from anti-aging serum to undereye cream to lip-plumping lotion. I could barely lift the suitcase, it was so weighted down by my insane desire to see Paris looking like a twenty-year-old. I finally gave up and left all the products in a pile on the bed. Then I kept the Uber waiting fifteen minutes while I tried to close the damn suitcase before pulling out the first five items on the top. I arrived at the airport with barely two hours to spare, got in the slowest line imaginable, and got pulled out of security even though I was TSA PreCheck. I finally raced through the terminal to my gate, only to find my flight had been delayed three hours.

I texted Lee. He and Martin were at the bar. Where else

would they be? They were both of a generation that firmly believed that every situation had a matching cocktail. I finally found Lee sitting in a quiet corner, laptop open, while Martin read *The Wall Street Journal*. They both looked happy to see me as I collapsed into the chair between them.

"Hello, Mags. Care for a drink?" Lee said, leaning over to kiss my cheek. Martin lowered the paper enough to give me a wink and a smile.

I nodded, and when the waitress appeared, I ordered a very dry martini with two olives. Yes, I know you're not supposed to drink before a long flight, but I'd found the vodka gave the Xanax a quicker liftoff. And I loved olives.

"You look harried," Lee noted.

I sighed. "I couldn't close my suitcase, so I just started pulling things out. I think I left all my bras in Morristown."

Martin lowered the paper, his eyes dancing. "Well, *that* should certainly work well for you in Paris." Martin was from Jamaica and still had that lovely lilt in his voice. I had no idea how old he was because he was bald, his gleaming scalp showing no signs of gray. He was short and compact, as opposed to Lee, who was tall and gangling with wild white hair and eyebrows that might have been spawned by the late, great Andy Rooney.

Lee glared. "She's in Paris to *work*, Martin. The woman has to write one hundred twenty thousand words in the next six weeks, and she's going to start as soon as we land." He looked at me sharply. "Unless you've already begun? Did my lecture spur you to action? Have you spent the last two days typing frantically?"

I shook my head. "I've spent the last two days avoiding Greg while he started packing his things. That involved locking myself in the guest room and binge-watching *The Great British Baking Show,* seasons two and three."

Martin let the paper drop and whistled appreciatively. "That's a lot of television."

I nodded and reached as my martini arrived. "Yes, I was up until two in the morning craving treacle puddings and shortbread." I took a sip and let the vodka calm my jangled nerves. "And fantasizing about Paul Hollywood."

Martin leaned over and chuckled. "I do a lot of that myself."

"You watched people *bake*?" Lee said, somewhat incredulously. "Is that all you did?"

I shook my head. "No, don't be silly. I had a terrific brunch with my two best friends, Cheri and Alison. We were mourning the loss of Greg. It was kind of like a wake, but with Bloody Marys and huevos rancheros."

"Bravo," Martin muttered.

"I also stopped the delivery of *The New York Times* and called my plant-watering person. Oh, and this morning? I pulled all of Greg's things out of the office and stuffed them into the trunk of his car." I smiled at the memory. With all his books and awards out of my floor-to-ceiling bookcases, I could finally display my four RITA awards, my six Romantic Times Reader's Favorite awards, and all the bestseller lists I'd cut from various sources and had framed. "I was going to do the same for his clothes, but there wasn't room, so I just left them in the middle of the garage."

Lee gasped. "You didn't!"

I polished off the rest of my martini in one long gulp. "Oh, yes, I did." I set the glass down and breathed deeply. "And it felt great."

"Good," Martin sniffed. "I never did like him."

"You never met him," I pointed out.

"True," he conceded. "But I heard all the stories. And I have seen pictures of him. I mean, he does look pretty hot, and he does have a certain air of celebrity about him, but it seemed that he never appreciated you."

I shook my head. "He did not. He told me my work wasn't as important as his. And when I pointed out that my work paid all the bills, well, he got huffy." I sniffed and carefully ate one of the olives. "I hate a man who huffs." I ate the second olive. "So. Tell me about Paris. Where are we staying?"

Lee stopped glaring at Martin and focused on me. "When my mother died, I inherited a flat in Paris that had originally belonged to her aunt, my great-aunt Helene, as well as the family vineyard out in Provence. I also inherited the housekeeper at the flat who, according to the will, can live there until her death. Solange takes care of things—dusts and makes sure all the bills get paid and keeps all the family silver polished. We'll be heading for the vineyard out in Provence the day after we arrive, by the way. It was planned before I invited you to come with us. You'll have to do without us for a bit."

"We should cancel," Martin advised. "We need to show her Paris."

Lee smacked his palm on the glass tabletop. "No, we will

not cancel. She is there to find her muse and get to work, not be shown around."

"But she's in France for the first time," Martin pressed. "She should probably come out to the country with us."

"No she should not. She should find a place to plug in her computer and *write*." Lee glared at me. "That is your plan, right?"

"Well," I said, "yes. That and seeing Nicole."

"Naturally," Martin said. "Lee, be reasonable. She has to see Nicole."

"And maybe I could meet Louis."

Martin's eyebrows shot up. "Louis? As in, a *beau*?"

I nodded. My daughter was brainy and beautiful and, since her first high school crush, had viewed most men with complete disregard. The fact that she'd mentioned Louis more than five times in the past six months led me to think that perhaps, finally, she'd found . . . someone. I hadn't questioned her about him, of course. Not even when she'd been home at Christmas. Any perceived interest on my part would be enough for her to throw him right out the window.

"I think so," I said. "I'm pretending to be completely disinterested. You know how she is. But I did suggest that since I was going to be there an introduction might be in order, and she didn't drop the phone and run away screaming, so who knows?"

"How exciting. You must meet him," Martin said. "Isn't that exciting, Lee?"

"Not as exciting as writing one hundred twenty thousand words of sex, love, adventure, and more sex," Lee grumbled. "This is a *working* vacation."

I stiffened up and narrowed my eyes at Lee. "You tempted me with the promise of art, history, and two gay men on an unlimited budget. Not to mention more hot men than I could shake a stick at to help kick my romantic brain into overdrive. How am I supposed to find hot men if I'm chained to my computer in an apartment, and guarded by an ancient house-keeper?"

"Exactly," Martin said. "She needs to be out, seeing things, eating wonderful food, looking at beautiful people." He grinned. "Without her brassiere."

I grinned back. "That's my plan."

Lee glowered. "You know that if I have to ask for this dead-line to be extended, I will be very cross."

I patted his hand. "Lee, I promise: I will write."

He glared at me, then Martin. "I certainly hope so." He glanced at his watch. "Good. We have lots of time. Let's get another drink."

When we arrived in Paris, it was the next afternoon. Someday I'll understand all about different time zones and how they work; I had always just imagined it was all a bit of magic. We sauntered though customs and stopped for coffee in the airport. There was no real coffee, not that I recognized anyway. It was bitter, strong stuff with steamed milk. Lee explained that this was café crème and promised I'd learn to love it. It jolted my brain awake, which was a good start.

"Where can we get a cab?" I asked.

Lee shook his head. "We take the Métro. You need the complete Paris experience."

I followed with a smile pasted on my face. I hated any form of transportation that involved going *under* something. Underground, underwater, whatever. I did everything I could to avoid the New York subway system. In traveling from New Jersey to New York, common sense made taking a bus through the Lincoln Tunnel an obvious choice over the G. W. Bridge, but I closed my eyes the entire time while I was trapped underground, then under the river, inches from certain death.

And driving to New York City? In a car? Yes, I knew people did it, but only the very crazy ones.

But the Paris underground station was bright and clean, filled with well-dressed people standing quietly. I felt the tension leave my shoulders. Very nice.

"Now," Lee said, "let me tell you how to navigate France without being an Ugly American."

Martin sighed and rolled his eyes.

"Will there be a test?" I asked sarcastically.

"No, but if you don't pay attention, believe me, you will fail. First of all, when you enter a shop or café, look at everyone and say hello. Bonjour is best, but hello will do. You must greet everyone you see."

"Oh, come on, does anyone really care—"

He held up a hand. "Yes. Here, they care. It's a simple thing, Maggie. Smile and say hello."

"Got it."

"Don't tip."

"What, never?"

"Never. Here everyone makes a living wage, and a tip would be an insult."

"What about a cab?"

Lee turned to me, his thin, lined face a mask of despair. "Mags, did you not *hear* me? Why is it that you refuse to listen to anything I say? I'm your agent. I have your best interest at heart, in all things. Do. Not. Tip."

I looked past him to Martin. "He's cranky?"

Martin flashed a smile. "Always."

We emerged from the depths of the Métro directly in front of the Arc de Triomphe. I had to admit, I stopped dead still in the middle of the sidewalk to stare.

I had seen it in pictures hundreds of times, but in real life, the monument was stunning, graceful, and dignified, soaring above worn stone pavers. It was surrounded by a circle of traffic, and beyond the bustle of cars was a band of trees, barely leafed out in bright spring green. And people—the obvious tourists, pointing and taking pictures, and the equally obvious Parisians, walking purposefully, eyes ahead, going about their everyday lives amid the splendor.

Lee nudged me on. "We walk right down here," he said.

Martin shook his head. "Give the woman a second to be a tourist."

So I stood there in the early Paris spring afternoon and gawked like a Trekkie at Comic-Con. Lee had to physically take me by the elbow and pull me gently down the street and away.

"That was beautiful," I said excitedly, pulling my suitcase, my tote bag over one shoulder. "People get to see that every day?"

Lee shook his head. "No, they only take it out on Mondays and alternate Thursdays."

We were walking down a wide, cobblestone street. "Where are we now?"

"Victor Hugo Avenue," Martin said. "Lee, why don't you give her some genuinely useful advice?"

"Like what?" I asked.

"Like, you'll want to spread butter on everything, then sit there making yum-yum noises while you chew," Martin said.

I filed that away. I had been known to actually make yum-yum noises while I ate, so this advice seemed pertinent.

"You can buy excellent wine here for around four euros a bottle. Don't ask the clerk if the price is wrong," Martin continued. "It isn't. Also, people will cut in front of you in line. All the time. Just smile. Don't look aghast and make a loud comment in English, because the French don't care if someone cuts in line, and most of them understand English and will think you're terribly crass."

I hated line cutters so filed this away as well.

We entered a large traffic circle. "This is Victor Hugo Place," Lee announced. "We're almost there."

I found myself grinning. There were cars, beautiful people walking, cafés were open, the air was clear, and the noise was not too deafening. I would have been perfectly happy to sit in the nearest chair and just watch for hours, but Lee kept nudging me along. We turned down a side street, walked past a florist, a gift shop, and a small restaurant, and finally stopped in front of two large wooden doors, intricately carved, with small arched windows at the top and one large, brass knob.

"We're here," Lee said, shaking out his key ring and sliding an impressive-looking key into the narrow slot.

I looked up at the doors in wonder, holding my breath. "This looks like the entrance to Moria," I whispered to Martin.

He grinned. "Almost."

We walked into a small lobby with a twelve-foot ceiling and marble floor.

"This way," Lee said, nudging again. "Stop gawking. You'll be living here. You can stare later. Right now I have to piss like a racehorse."

Martin and I waited for the elevator with the luggage while Lee raced up the narrow stairs.

"What floor?" I asked.

"Second. He'll make it in time. He always does."

The elevator arrived, barely large enough to hold Martin, the suitcases, and myself. "This, by the way, is the *lift*," Martin told me, firmly pushing the button.

I nodded. "Got it."

We stepped out into a small hallway, a door to the left, a

door to the right, and the staircase in front of us. The door to the left was ajar, and Martin led the way in.

All the ceilings were tall, with ornate moldings and complicated chandeliers. The floors were smooth hardwood covered by faded oriental rugs, and the front room had floor-to-ceiling windows overlooking the street. I practically ran to them and stared out.

"Martin, this is gorgeous." I glanced around. There was a second parlor, exactly mirroring the room I stood in, even down to the fireplace mantel. There were bookcases everywhere, very eclectic art, and comfortable, overstuffed furniture next to simple but delicate antiques. In the second parlor, a long farm table was surrounded by midcentury, transparent acrylic chairs.

"If I lived here, I'd never leave," I told him.

Lee appeared, smiling. "I know. This is where we'll retire, I think. Although the villa in Provence is kind of eye-popping as well. Ah, Solange, meet my dear friend, Maggie Bliss. Mags, this is Solange Varden."

I was expecting a stooped, cronelike housekeeper, one suited to a fairy tale. Or perhaps a tall, stiff Mrs. Danvers type. Solange was neither. She was old, no doubt, easily over seventy, and she did nothing to disguise her age. But she was tall and slender, with snow-white hair in a short, severe cut, brushed up and away from her high forehead. Her eyes were wide and pale blue, her nose thin and perfectly straight. She was stunning. She crossed the room in three strides and gave me a hug, kissing me on both cheeks.

"Welcome to Paris, Maggie. I have read all your books, and

I just love them. I imagined you to be older, for some reason, but you are probably close to my son Max's age. How lovely." Her face sharpened, as though she'd just thought of something. "Are you working on the last of the Delania books? I so love that series. You must tell me what's going to happen so I can lord it over my book club!" Her English was heavily accented but perfectly understandable, her smile bright and natural.

"I have no idea what happens," I blurted. "That's why I'm here."

She looped her arm through mine. "Come, let me show you your room. It belonged to Helene. Usually Martin and Lee claim it, but since they are leaving tomorrow, they can have the guest room. Besides, this is Paris, and you may have the need for a large, beautiful bed. It overlooks the courtyard, and there is a small balcony. You will be inspired."

I peeked into a few tall, half-open doorways before we came to my room. It was spectacular, and not just because of the massive canopied bed dressed in layers of pillows and soft throws. There was also a small fireplace with a marble mantle, and the chair in the corner appeared to have a rather tattered but still easily identifiable mink coat thrown over it. I just stared, thinking that if I couldn't be inspired by this place, I had no business calling myself a writer ever again.

"You will write wonderful things here, yes? Lee, bring the girl's suitcase, please. She must unpack. Do you need a bath? Lunch? I have wine—"

"I'm good, thank you, Solange. This is lovely."

Lee rolled my suitcase up to the bed. "Martin and I are leaving in the morning, but we can go out this afternoon and show you the neighborhood."

"May I come with you tomorrow?" Solange asked.

Lee frowned. "I thought you didn't want to go up with us."

"I didn't, but it's my sister's birthday. I forgot."

Lee tilted his head. "I didn't think you liked your sister."

"I don't. That's why I forgot." She shrugged and turned to me. "But it is her seventy-fifth, and that is a big number. So, I should go."

Lee nodded. "If you wish, Solange." He looked at me. "She worked at the vineyard as a child; all her family is there," he explained. "She only moved to Paris when her son was born, and stayed here with my great-aunt Helene." He frowned at me. "You won't mind being alone?"

"Not at all," I said, and I meant it. Having this large, charming apartment to myself sounded like heaven.

Martin, standing in the doorway, made a noise. "Not with Jules," he said shortly. "I refuse to drive all that way with Jules."

Solange made a face. "Oh, Martin, how can you say that?"

I looked around for Jules. Younger companion? Ancient uncle?

Lee nodded. "Martin is right. He farts too much, and last time he peed all over the back seat of the rental and it cost me three hundred euros."

Solange sighed and turned to me. "How they abuse him," she said. "And he is so lovely."

"Ah," I cleared my throat. "Who is he?"

Solange broke into a smile. "My bulldog. You would look

after him for me? It will only be a few days. He just needs to be walked three or four times a day, fed every evening, and—oh, here he is now!"

There was a click-click along the wooden floors as Jules turned the corner. I am not gonna lie here: Jules was ugly. I was never a dog lover, but always enjoyed other people's pets, and even found beauty, grace, and real personality in dogs. But Jules was fat, waddled on stubby legs, and drooled. And as he shuffled into the room, he woofed rather nastily at me, then farted. Very loudly. And yes, it stank.

"Oh, Jules, such bad manners," Solange cooed as she bent to pick him up. She walked over and thrust him at me. "Meet Maggie, darling. She'll be taking care of you for a few days."

Jules did not look impressed. I reached out and took him and tucked him under my arm. He was a French bulldog— what else?—small and compact. He wheezed as we bonded. After twenty seconds, I handed him back.

"No problem."

He farted again.

Lee shook his head and left the room, muttering. Solange bent her head to Jules's and murmured in French as she left. Martin flashed a grin.

"Welcome to Paris, Maggie."

I unpacked, shook out my clothes, hung them in a tiny armoire, and took inventory. I had four pairs of pants, all black. Since three of those were made of some sort of knit, they would more accurately be described as leggings. Or sweatpants. One button-down white shirt, four long-sleeve T-shirts, a pair of jeans, a football jersey to sleep in, and a beige cardigan sweater with pockets that looked exactly like the cardigan Mr. Rogers used to wear. I had a pair of pretty blue kitten-heel pumps that I knew were comfortable enough to actually walk in, black ballet flats, my Minnetonka moccasins, and the gray slip-ons by Toms I'd worn on the plane. I had seven pairs of identical white cotton panties and two bras.

I seriously under packed for Paris. In the short walk from the Métro to the flat, I had passed hundreds of women, all better dressed than I. They also, how can I put this, *looked* much better than I.

I had to admit that when I turned forty, I went into a bit of a sulk. I stopped getting facials and manicures, getting my hair done, and dressing up every morning. After all, old age was just around the corner, and after that was death, so why bother? Shortly after that I'd met Greg, and he didn't seem to care what I looked like. I realized that was probably because he was too worried about what *he* looked like, and as long as I was willing to worship and adore him, my appearance didn't matter.

"I need to shop for clothes," I announced as I entered the living room. "I mostly packed writing clothes." Lee and Martin were both lounging in front of the fireplace, Martin reading a newspaper, of course, in French.

"If you're here to write, then you only need writing clothes," Lee pointed out.

Martin lowered the newspaper and glared at Lee. "Don't be absurd. She'll need to walk the dog and go out for coffee."

I slumped into a chair. "I can wear my writing clothes for that sort of thing, I suppose. I was talking more about going out somewhere—you know, to a museum or someplace nice to eat."

Lee shook his head. "Maggie, as much as I hate to admit it, Martin is right. You can't wear those rags you wear to write out of the apartment. In fact, you can't even wear them to take out the garbage. We'll take you somewhere and let you get a few things."

Martin stood and stretched. "We should go out and give you a tour of the neighborhood before exhaustion sets in and you want to sleep for a whole day. Let's go."

I looked down at what I was wearing. My outfit was slightly wrinkled from the flight, but still looked neat enough. Gray twill pants, a navy cotton pullover, and the Ferragamo scarf. "Am I well-dressed enough to go shopping?"

Lee kissed my cheek. "Barely. Let's go."

The neighborhood around Place Victor Hugo was charming—the buildings were all old and beautiful, the shop windows artful and inviting. The people on the street were impossibly chic: the women sleek and stylish, the men groomed and sexy. There were three separate bakeries; a chocolate shop; cafés that served wine with every meal, including breakfast; a mini grocery store; a major grocery store; and a few women's boutiques. We returned to the apartment with bags of clothes and food and wine.

Solange roasted a perfect little chicken surrounded by carrots and potatoes that tasted completely different from what I was used to. I kept giving Lee *Are you sure?* looks until he threw a piece of baguette at me.

Martin pointed at me with his fork. "After about five days, you will dread going back home if for no other reason than because you'll have to eat tasteless food again."

Solange shook her head. "My poor son. He lives in New York now, which is supposed to be such an amazing food town, but he can't find a decent leek to save his life. Sometimes he comes back here to Paris just so he can shop for produce."

"What does he do?" I asked, trying to be polite even though I was getting very sleepy and wanted nothing more than to push myself away from the table and crawl into bed.

She shrugged. "He banks. That's all I know. He lives in New York, and he has a place in London. He travels quite a bit."

Lee sipped his wine. "Max works for the World Bank. He's brilliant and very successful."

Solange shrugged again. "If he were so successful, he would not have gone through three wives." She leaned toward me. "No grandchildren. Can you imagine? I asked him for *one* thing. . . ."

I smiled sleepily, and Martin took my fork out of my hand. "You're going to drop forward into your plate. Go. Sleep. We'll leave you detailed notes about how to survive without us."

I first went to the bathroom to wash my face. The toilet, a

wooden affair that was flushed by pulling a handle that dangled from a tank eight feet above, was in a small closet with its own window. The bathroom proper had a sink the size of a soup bowl with separate spigots for hot and cold water. The tub was surrounded by dark-green tile and rested on a platform that was reached by climbing a small step. I imagined a shower but made do with a splash of cold water.

I grabbed my phone, took a picture of my bed, and sent it to Cheri and Alison. I tried to figure out what the time would be in New Jersey. It was almost seven in the evening here, and with a six-hour time difference, it would be around midday in Jersey. Would they even read it? Alison had retired from teaching but volunteered at several places, so she might answer right away. Cheri had her own real estate office, so if she was with a client . . .

The response was immediate.

> A: OMG are you sleeping there???
> C: She'd better do more than SLEEP in a bed like that. Howz the food? amiright or amiright?
> M: I need to sleep. First meal memorable. Just wanted you to know that I landed and it's all good. I'll be writing from now on so don't expect much

Next, I texted Nicole the address and received your basic "K" back. I saw that Greg had left me six messages that I deleted unread, and noted that my eye doctor appointment in June needed to be rescheduled. I set down the phone, lay down, and was asleep three minutes after my head hit the pillow.

Tuesday morning, my first morning in Paris, began well enough. I had breakfast with Solange, who explained that Lee and Martin were getting the rental car, a process that apparently could take hours and might possibly involve an illicit exchange of cash and/or threats of blackmail.

"Martin has a license, but getting a car in Paris is like screwing your wife. In theory, it's as simple as pie. But if the wife is in a bad mood . . ."

We drank café crème, which she made herself without an elaborate machine for brewing the coffee and steaming the milk, and ate toasted slices of baguette scraped with the thinnest layer of butter and strawberry preserves.

It was heavenly.

Solange then began telling me what I needed to know: how to work the washing machine, where to walk the dog, where to buy the best bread, what not to eat at the café down the street, how to jiggle the key if the lock seemed stiff—little details that I knew I should pay attention to. She then handed me a few handwritten sheets that Lee and Martin had worked on the night before: More tips on how to spend a few days in Paris without turning the entire population against me personally and U.S. citizens in general.

I promised to read them later in the afternoon. I should have sat down to read them that very moment.

Martin came in half an hour later. Lee had the car and was circling the block. Solange immediately ran into her room and came out with a black tote bag. Martin grabbed the two carry-ons and followed her out into the hallway, blowing kisses and calling out a few more vague instructions on how to not make a fool of myself in the most beautiful city in Europe.

I stood at the front window and watched as a small black car slowed down just enough for Martin to throw the cases in the trunk while Solange climbed into the back seat. Martin looked up, saw me, and waved. He jumped in and the car sped off.

Alone at last.

I ate more bread and butter. The windows were open, letting in the spring breeze and the muted noise of the street. I sat and admired the tall ceilings and lovely woodwork. Then I changed out of my football jersey and into something more conducive to getting some work done: black leggings and a pink T-shirt. I opened more windows, ate more bread and butter, and set up my laptop. My screen saver was a collage of homes, all of them with lots of windows overlooking an ocean. This was the pot of gold at the end of my rainbow: the beach house.

I opened a folder with more pictures of beach houses, then the folder of *interiors* of beach houses, then went on Realtor.com and found a dozen homes in Virginia that were right on the water and looked just lovely. I couldn't afford any of them. Yet.

I sighed, clicked on another folder, and spent the next few

hours reading the very detailed summary I'd put together of the first two Delania books.

Why, you may ask, would the person who spent three years *writing* the first two Delania books need to read a detailed summary? Well, to be honest, my memory was terrible. I barely remembered the number of my seat on the plane ride over, despite having committed it to memory, and that was just yesterday. Something I'd written two or three years ago was as familiar to me as the Paris Métro map. Besides, Delania was an entirely fictional place, which meant I had no frame of reference outside what I'd created. So I needed some sort of touchstone, something to go back to so that I could sit down with confidence and start writing the greatest last book in a trilogy ever conceived by mortal man. Woman. Whomever.

After those few hours, I decided to step out and around the corner for a little something-something to eat. Preferably slathered with butter.

I looked for Jules. He was stretched out in the middle of the hallway, snoring. Solange told me that he needed three or four walks a day, but didn't specify when. Since he was sleeping so soundly, I bypassed the leash, grabbed the key off the counter, and exited the apartment.

Outside the air was cool and the sky looked like rain, so I decided to just run to the mini grocery, pick up a few things for dinner, perhaps a bottle or two of wine, and maybe some chocolate. Since the chocolate shop was closest, I went in there first.

I remembered what Lee had told me and smiled brightly

at the salesclerk, said hello, and then bent over the glass case. I heard a faint *bonjour* in response, but it barely registered. The display in front of me was beautiful. So beautiful that I wondered, just for a second, if I'd be able to actually eat any of the cunningly crafted pieces in the sleek glass case. I finally pointed to a tray of tiny chocolate squares, each adorned with a single hazelnut and a swirl of caramel.

"Hello again. Six of those, please."

I now realized that the clerk, dressed in black and an immaculate white apron, was staring at me with a mixture of faint distaste and outright curiosity. I glanced down, expecting to find a hole in my shirt, or perhaps a coffee stains somewhere. Nothing. It was just my general appearance that was causing her expression.

Right. I wasn't supposed to go out in writing clothes.

Damn. I smiled bravely, dug into my pocket for a few euros, took the box out of her hands, and backed out of the shop. I turned and crashed into three impeccably dressed young men, their trousers creased perfectly, their shirtsleeves rolled up just so, their shoes buffed to a high shine.

I apologized and practically ran back to the flat.

Once there, I set my chocolates down and changed into one of my newly bought-in-Paris cashmere sweaters and the least wrinkled of my pants—the gray twill. Then I took off the pants, found the ironing board, and pressed them to within an inch of their cotton-rayon lives. I slipped on my ballet flats, put on a bit of lipstick, and ventured out again.

The first wine shop I found was not the one Lee had taken

me to the night before, but a bottle of wine is a bottle of wine, right?

Wrong.

"Hello," I dutifully said upon entering.

The clerk came out from behind the counter and bowed. "Bonjour, madam. How may I assist you?"

I hadn't paid much attention to what Lee had said when asked the same question the previous night. I should have, because what was *I* supposed to say? So I just took a deep breath and let it fly.

"I have a bottle of wine in my flat, I forgot the name, but it's very good. It's a nice, inexpensive white, a little fruity, but not too sweet. Floral undertones. The label is blue."

An expression not altogether pleasant flickered across his face. "Ah, thank you, madam. How helpful it was that you remembered the color of the label rather than the name of the wine, as that is the way we organize our selections. Excuse me while I see what I can find in our *blue* section." He turned and walked to the back of the store, through a small doorway, and was gone.

"Idiot," I muttered, pushing my way out of the shop. I was sure there was at least a bottle left back at the flat. I'd finish it, then bring the empty bottle with me the next time.

Back outside, I pulled out my phone. I wasn't going to wander all over the neighborhood looking for the Paris grocery store, the Monoprix, especially since I was already unsure how to get back to the flat. Lee had insisted I enter the address into my phone last night, and I was grateful to see I was only three minutes away. And four minutes from the grocery store. I set off, clutching my red Coach wristlet, determined to shop efficiently. Once I got there, however, all bets were off. This was a much larger store than the one we'd been to the night before for cheese and crackers. The produce section alone set my heart racing.

I was not a very good cook. I'd managed most of my dinner parties by carefully following recipes or providing extravagant takeout. But I loved food, the picking out and eating part of it, and I spent almost two hours cruising up and down the store aisles. There were vegetables I'd never seen before. Those I did recognize were not large, shiny, and perfect, but rather looked like they'd just been picked by the friendly neighbor next door. The meat was not all pale, uniform pink: the beef was deep red, the chicken pale gold, and the pork sausages went from almost white/gray to bloodred/black.

I spent almost twenty minutes looking at all the sausage.

Then there was the cheese. I cannot even begin to describe all the cheese, and apparently you could sample any or all of them.

I wanted to just pitch my tent there and be done with it.

I was careful not to put everything that I wanted into the cart because that would have meant getting two additional carts. I used prudent judgment and managed to splurge on just five cheeses. And strawberries. And gelato. I also chose a few premade meals that looked amazing, and some cute packets of crackers.

This, so far, was the best shopping experience of my life.

I thought I was doing fairly well. I'd ignored the scrutiny of the security guard who, at one point, actually peeked around a corner display to watch me sniff parsley. The other looks I'd received from my fellow shoppers, I knew, were about my clothes, which I realized were not good enough for this grocery store in this neighborhood, but—lesson learned.

Then I had to check out.

The clerk took all the items from my cart, scanned them, weighed them, and set them to the side. I paid with my card—no problem there. Then I stood and waited for my purchases to be bagged.

Then I stood a minute longer.

The clerk motioned for me to step aside. Apparently there was a person behind me. I knew that—what about my groceries?

"Pardon," I said, smiling, although by this point I was pretty tired and, since I was also hungry, rather bitchy. "What about my stuff?"

He looked at me as though I were crazy. Didn't he understand what "stuff" meant?

"Aren't you going to bag my groceries?" I asked, perfectly polite.

The woman behind me shouldered her way in front of me. "Americans," she spat. "We don't bag things here. You bring your own."

"What?" I looked around. "My own what? Bags?"

Why, yes. Everyone else held some sort of container—a cloth tote, a basket, a canvas sack. Everyone was bagging their own. Everyone but me, because all I had was a chic but utterly useless Coach wristlet.

I almost sat in the middle of the floor and cried. Luckily a young woman tugged on my sleeve and pointed—there were tote bags for sale, right there on the end. I grabbed two, went to the back of the line and, after paying for them, packed away everything I had just bought, still waiting patiently for me at the end of the counter.

I left the shop, looked at my phone, and practically ran back to the flat, jiggling the key in the lock and running up the stairs rather than waiting for the lift.

Once inside, I took several deep breaths, unpacked, and ate an entire container of chocolate gelato with a tablespoon. I stepped over Jules three different times going back and forth from the kitchen to the bathroom, to the living room, to the bedroom to change back into my sweatpants, and then back to the living room.

Finally, my rinsed strawberries at my side, I sat before my laptop. I was ready. I could do this.

I heard a faint woof.

I opened three files that contained three of my most promising starts.

Another woof, a little louder this time.

Sighing, I got up and went back into the hallway.

Jules had finally moved. He was pacing by the front door, his nails making annoying little clicks on the hardwood floor.

He needed to be taken out for his afternoon walk.

Of course he did.

Chapter 3

*In which I find a naked man
in the bathtub*

When I first started out as a writer, I owned a type-writer. It was noisy, and mistakes were a pain to correct, and I always forgot to change the ribbon, but there was a certain satisfaction in stopping what I was writing, reading it over, re-alizing it was total crap, then ripping the sheet of paper out, crumpling it up, and tossing it to the floor. If nothing else, at the end of my workday, I could look around and get a satisfactory count of all my false starts.

Sadly, that doesn't happen when writing on a laptop. All my false starts were saved, usually in a file that identified what scene I wrote and how many times I wrote it. For example, Mondayinjeep.one.

By ten o'clock that evening, I'd gotten up to Mondayinjeep.twentysix.

I was a total failure as a writer. I'd never again put down more than three words in a row that were worth a cursory glance from anyone, let alone a discriminating reader of romance. I collapsed back in my chair, head hanging backward, feeling sorry for myself and wondering what kind of career opportunities there were for fortysomething women who wanted to work in their pajamas.

I finally opened the bottle of wine and poured myself a very generous glass. I texted Nicole, who immediately called back.

"Hey, Mom. How was the flight?" She was a bit breathless as she spoke. She was probably doing sit-ups.

"Fine, honey, thanks. Do you know the address? Are we close?"

"You're in the eleventh arrondissement. Right off the Place Victor Hugo. I know it. Very chichi." She managed to make one of my favorite concepts sound boring and a little sad. One reason we don't talk much. "I'm in Le Marais, actually, but we're fairly close. Should we meet tomorrow? Somewhere in the middle?"

"No problem. Just tell me where, and make sure its someplace I can find on my phone. I know how you love those quaint local places, but they can be hard to find." Once, while she was living in Brooklyn, we were to meet up at a small Vietnamese restaurant she knew of that, she claimed, was the real thing. Not only could I not find it, I couldn't even find the right block. I stood on a corner for fifteen minutes waiting for her to come and get me, during which time I was propositioned. Twice.

"How about the Musée d'Orsay? Do you think you can find it? It's fairly big, and there are lots of signs."

I loved my daughter, I really did, but some days she was a total bitch. "I'll try, dear. If not, you can look for me as I throw myself off a bridge into the Seine."

She was quiet, then, "Which bridge?"

I closed my eyes and when I opened them, my wineglass was empty. Just like magic. "What time, Nicole?"

"Noon." A pause. "Although Daddy and I have a bit of catching up to do."

She'd seen him at Christmas, which is when she'd last seen me, but I knew that Alan did not get the same weekly phone call I did. "Do you want to spend some more time alone with him? I'll meet you later."

"That would be great, Mom. Three-ish?"

"Three-ish is doable."

"He's looking forward to seeing you, by the way."

I smiled. "I'm looking forward to seeing you both. Bye." I set down the phone and thought about doing a bit more writing. I then found half a baguette in the kitchen and ate it, smeared with butter, and drank what was left of the wine, which was pretty much the rest of the bottle. I took the last splash in the glass with me down the hall to the bedroom. I pulled off my clothes and put on my sleep shirt. Then I crawled into bed.

I awoke with a vague feeling I had forgotten something. I

squinted at the clock. Almost 6:00 a.m. Was I supposed to get up for some reason? My head was spinning, so I fumbled on my dresser and found my trusty Aleve, took two or five with whatever was left in the wineglass, and went back to bed.

At eight o'clock, when I woke again, I remembered Jules. I had to walk the dog. Lee had given me free rein of this amazing apartment in the middle of Paris, and all I had to do in return was walk an ancient bulldog. I strained my ears, listening. Yesterday, the click of his nails as he paced up and down in front of the door signaled his desire, as did the gentle woof. I didn't hear either and had a nightmarish vision of my finding him lying on his back, all four of his stubby legs sticking up in the air. I scrambled out of bed to practically trip over him as he lay farting peacefully in the middle of the hallway.

Thank God.

Now, if I could make it to the bathroom and flush the toxins out of my mouth, I thought I might feel almost human again.

I crossed the hallway to the toilet in its own little room. I peed for about five minutes, then took the short walk down the hall to the *other* part of the bathroom. I narrowed my eyes and zeroed in on the sink. It seemed extremely far away, but maybe that was because I couldn't seem to move my feet very quickly. Not hungover, exactly, just adversely reacting to a bit too much wine in my system. I finally reached the sink and leaned against it, sighed in relief, and turned on the water. Those two damn spigots again, one hot, one cold. How was I supposed to get warm water onto my face? I cupped my hands, hoping a little from each side would meet and mingle.

I splashed my face. Almost. I tried again, and heard a deep, quiet voice speak.

"Madam?"

I kept my eyes closed and fumbled for the towel I knew was hanging there. There was a man in the bathroom. My fingers closed on the towel very slowly, and I gripped it tightly.

Why was there was a man in the bathroom?

The flight-or-fight reaction kicked in. How fast could I run to get out of the bathroom, get down the hall, unlock the front door, get down the stairs, and out onto the street?

I wiped the water out of my eyes so I could open them. There was a marble figure of a cherub on a shelf right next to the mirror. Was it heavy enough to do any damage if I hit him over the head? Could I grab it, swing around, and knock this interloper square on the head, rendering him helpless and immobile until the police arrived?

My eyes shifted from the cherub to the mirror, and I could see exactly where the voice came from.

The bathtub.

And the man sitting in it.

I turned around very slowly. "What are you doing in the bathtub?" I managed in a hoarse whisper. I spoke English, of course, because I hadn't learned those twenty-five useful phrases, and even if I had, I didn't think "What are you doing in the bathtub?" was one of them.

He answered in English. "Taking a bath."

"No, I mean, what are you doing in *this* bathtub? In this flat?"

"I live here," he said reasonably.

"No, you don't," I said, getting a bit indignant. "Lee and Martin live here."

A glint of humor lit up his very blue eyes. "So does my mother, Solange. You are . . . ?"

"You're Max?" Oh, thank God he wasn't some crazed murderer. A crazed murderer taking a bath before killing someone didn't make much sense, but my brain was still a bit wine-logged.

Now that both flight and fight were off the table, I took a breath and looked at him more carefully. He just missed being handsome, with a mouth a little too wide, a nose a bit too thin, and a chin that jutted just a smidge too much. He did have beautiful blue eyes under dark and rather wiry brows and silver hair that swept up and off his high forehead, just like his mother. His shoulders and chest looked about right for a man in his fifties: gray chest hair and smooth skin. As the tub was elevated, I could barely see that the water came up almost, but not quite, to his waist.

"Yes, I'm Max. You are a friend of Lee and Martin, then?"

"Yes," I explained. "I'm a writer. I'm here in Paris looking for my muse."

"Ah. I see. And do you expect to find your muse in this bathtub?"

I realized where my eyes had been straying and forced them back up to his face. Oh, dear God. Now he thinks I'm not just a complete idiot but a sex-starved pervert as well. In my defense,

I could see nothing of great interest in the water because of the bubbles.

Which suddenly struck me as very funny. "A bubble bath?"

His mouth twitched. "I have dry skin."

Perfectly logical.

I backed away from the cherub, my need for a weapon gone. I suddenly realized that I was wearing my Joe Montana football jersey, faded and worn to almost a ragamuffin degree. While I was thankful that I wasn't naked, as all my curves tended to slope downward, and the only toned or sleek body parts I had left were the tops of my feet and the back of my neck, I wished, just for a moment, that I owned a black, almost-see-through negligee. And that, owning such an object, I had remembered to pack it.

"You probably want to finish your bath," I said. "I'll just leave and walk Jules."

"I already walked Jules."

"Thank you. Then I'll get us some bread?"

His mouth twitched again. "I've already brought up some bread."

"Good Lord, how long have you been here?" I asked.

He openly smiled. "Just about an hour. I'm a very fast worker."

I really wanted to lean over and take another peek into the bathwater to see if, in fact, there was any physical proof of that, but instead I chose to turn and leave, closing the door, quite firmly, behind me.

"I suppose you made coffee?" I yelled through the door.

I heard a deep chuckle. "No, not yet. Please, why don't you find the French press and make us a pot?"

At least I could do something to elevate my status from an unfashionable peeping Tomette to a reasonable human being.

Now, what in the hell was a French press?

Every romance writer worth their salt knows what happens when a man and a woman who have never met before encounter each other in a bathroom when one is in the shower or tub and one is not.

Whoever is in the shower is blissfully unaware of the existence of the person walking in on them. After all, why shouldn't they be alone? They feel they have a perfect right to be there, and they usually do.

As for the person walking in . . . well, they usually have a perfectly good reason to think that *they* are also alone and also belong there.

This is a classic Meet Cute. The following pages would include dropped towels, torn shower curtains, and various degrees of nakedness. She was lean and supple, with skin like silk and limbs all toned and sleek. Or not—she could be round and plump, with dimples in all sorts of adorable places. But whatever the body type, she would be either exactly what the hero has always wanted in a naked woman, or the exact opposite of what he's always wanted until that very moment.

He would be tall and lean, with washboard abs and a hardened jaw, and, if he happens to be the one getting wet, the drops would run down his muscled chest in such a way that our plucky heroine would forget for a second that she has no clothes on because all she'd be thinking is, *Boy, do I want some of that!* Or, she'd be thinking, *Oh my God, he's a barbarian.* One of them would end up thinking . . . ah, perfection. The other would be thinking . . . never in a million years.

Or, as in this case, one of them would run off to google how to make coffee in a French press while the other was probably wondering if all American women slept in scruffy football jerseys.

I decided I could probably manage to make a pot of coffee without doing too much damage. After the disaster of yesterday, I knew I needed a good French-coffee-making outfit. I almost googled that as well, but decided that cashmere was the answer. I pulled on my jeans and another of the sweaters I'd bought the first day, brushed my hair quickly, and then found the lone bottle of tinted moisturizer that had survived the preflight health-and-beauty-aid purge. I put on some lipstick, found my ballet flats, and put some silver hoops in my ears, and went out to make coffee.

Jules hadn't moved an inch, so I stepped around him and went into the kitchen.

For a space barely as big as my walk-in closet back home, it had a great many storage spaces that were very hard to see into, so I had just found the coffee when I heard a gentle cough behind me.

"Perhaps, I could make the coffee?" he asked.

I felt my shoulders slump. "I'm used to a Keurig," I explained, turning and pushing the bag of whole beans into his hands. "Sorry."

Max smiled. "Don't worry. Why don't you sit down?"

Excellent idea.

I felt unsettled. He was dressed in beautifully pressed blue jeans and a perfectly tailored button-down shirt, pale blue with a faint darker stripe. He wasn't my type at all, but there was something about him that prickled, and not in an altogether bad way. He was rather lean and not tall, maybe an inch or two over my five foot five, which meant our eyes were practically level. And those eyes . . . my goodness. Icy blue with dark brows was a match guaranteed to do major damage, even if the rest of him wasn't all that impressive.

I smiled brightly. "Thanks so much. But what can I do? I'll slice the bread, or—"

He held up a hand. "No. You are the guest. Please, I'll be right in." He nodded toward the front of the apartment.

"Sure," I said. I left the kitchen, stepped over Jules, and went to the twin living rooms, where I made a beeline for the dining table and sat in one of the acrylic chairs.

A few minutes later, he carried a tray to the table, set it down, and sat across from me.

"I've lived in the States long enough to make fairly good coffee, American style. I prefer café crème, but realize it is an acquired taste. But I refuse to eat an American breakfast, so you'll have to settle for something from the boulangerie. There's also a melon, if you like." His accent was slight, and he had one of those deep voices that sounded like he was speaking from the bottom of a well.

The something from the boulangerie was a croissant, and the melon was pale green and thinly sliced. I stirred lots of cream and sugar into my coffee and took a bite of the croissant. It was unlike anything I'd ever eaten before.

"Oh, my," I breathed.

He grinned. His lips were very red, and his small teeth gleamed. "I know. Why anyone would want a bowl of Grape-Nuts instead of this is beyond my comprehension."

Or, I thought, *huevos rancheros.* I concentrated on not stuffing the entire croissant into my mouth and instead took small bites. My hands were twitching, but I managed.

"So, tell me: Who are you again?" he asked.

A reasonable question. "Maggie Bliss. I'm a writer, and Lee is my agent. And friend. I'm experiencing, ah, well, writer's block and am on a bit of a deadline, so Lee suggested I come here to Paris. To find my muse."

"And what, exactly, is the muse? A person? Place?"

He looked completely sincere. What was my muse, exactly?

"Well . . ." I had to think. I'd always tried to avoid explaining my process. Readers were always asking me how I came up with my stories, and my pat answer was that I dreamed them. Not true, but much simpler than trying to explain what it was to actually write something from absolutely nothing.

My fellow writers and I had discussed the subject for years. We hadn't come up with any easy answers either.

"It's . . ."

He raised an eyebrow.

"It's like being in a dark room." I said. "And all you can see are shadows and vague shapes, and then you realize where the window is, and you draw open the drapes and light floods the space, and you can see everything: the four walls, all the furniture, where everything is and how it works together. Even the tiniest details, like the dust motes floating in the air. It's a moment of clarity. And joy. Yes, joy, because now you see exactly where you are, and you know where to go next."

"And that is your muse?"

I shook my head. "No. The muse is the spark that leads you to the window."

"Ah. And you are here to find this . . . spark?" He nodded thoughtfully. "I am a businessman. I know nothing of that sort of inspiration. But for others, well, Paris is certainly good for that." He sipped coffee. "What types of books do you write?"

The types of books where a woman sees a total stranger in a bathtub and they end up having incredibly hot sex 163 pages later.

"Romance novels. Under my real name, and under a few noms de plume. Margaret Baylord. Peggy Brite."

He tilted his head, frowned, then grinned. "My mother reads your books," he said, getting up and going to one of the bookshelves. He spent a few moments looking, then pulled a book from the shelf. "Yes, here you are. There are several, actually, but I believe this was her favorite."

He handed me *The Laird and the Lady,* one of the few historicals I'd written as Margaret Baylord. It was an older book, very old-school, and was obviously the French-language edition. I looked at the dark-haired, bare-chested hero in his tattered kilt kneeling beside the red-haired beauty who had fainted in his arms at just the right angle to expose most, but not all, of her ample bosom.

I smiled happily. "Yeah, I liked that one too. I got to take my daughter to the Scottish highlands, and we toured all the castles we could find. It was a great summer. And I got to write the whole vacation off as a research trip."

"Excellent business sense. And will this trip also be written off?"

I nodded. "You bet. But not as research. The book I'm working on takes place in a totally made-up country, so any research is strictly in my head."

He used his knife and fork to take a small piece of melon from the platter to his plate and then to his mouth. I had been thinking about picking up the whole slice with my fingers and just biting off a chunk. Good thing I waited out of politeness.

"How long have you been writing?" he asked.

"Twenty-four years. I started just before my husband and I split up."

"Ah. That's an unusual time to begin writing about true love."

"I still loved him. We just couldn't stand to be in the same room with each other. And that's a very popular romantic trope, enemies to lovers. I turned it around a bit and made it all work."

He picked up another piece of melon and ate it, nodding.

"Good for you." There was something about the way the melon disappeared into his mouth that made me want to write something. Maybe a paragraph describing the pale green flesh against his very red and lightly roughened lips. . . .

I cleared my throat. "So why are you here, exactly?"

"Well, I am on my way to Marseille for a bit of personal business, and then I will be in Paris the whole of next week, for a conference. After that I have a few weeks off. I told my mother that I would be able to stop by and spend the time with her. But she has, apparently, gone elsewhere."

"Her sister's birthday," I explained. "Her seventy-fifth?"

Max sighed. "My aunt's birthday is in September, and my mother hasn't spoken to her in years. She just needed an excuse to leave the apartment."

I stared at him. "Oh . . . don't you get along with her?"

His eyes began to twinkle. "We get along very well. But she knew you would be here, you see. She still has not reconciled herself to her bachelor son and is on a never-ending quest to find me a wife. She probably thought that you and I, alone in the apartment, would find each other irresistible. She's quite devious that way."

I almost spat out my coffee. "But . . ." Really, Solange? "She knew nothing about me except that I was a writer. How could she think we'd be compatible?"

He grinned. "She probably didn't think that far ahead. She just saw an attractive woman within twenty years of my age and assumed we'd be perfect for each other."

I remembered her comment about my being not as old as

she had thought, and how I was close to her son's age. "How are we going to tell her that her little plan didn't work?"

He placed both of his hands, palms inward, against his chest, and a look of dismay crossed his face. "What? Oh, Maggie, I am crushed. But I understand that you don't find me irresistible."

Not irresistible? Maybe to some. But in my head I was now plotting out a rather delicate scene in which a blue-eyed rogue was slowly peeling off the clothes of a slightly more-than-middle-aged writer. . . .

"Some would find you charming," I said.

"Possibly. I usually rely on my wit. Even now I'm hoping that my charm and sophistication will melt the ice around your cold and disappointed heart."

I laughed out loud at that one. "My heart isn't cold or disappointed. Well, maybe a little disappointed. I did just tell my live-in partner to clear all his things out before I got back to the States, but that felt like a relief more than anything else. And I'm actually going to be seeing my ex-husband today. He's visiting my daughter, and we're all having drinks. See? Civilized and not cold at all."

He laughed in obvious delight, throwing back his head, his deep voice echoing to the high ceiling. "Marvelous! Yes, very civilized. How long has it been since you've seen him, this ex-husband of yours?"

"Three years."

"Ah." He looked at me, very serious. "You are seeing your ex-husband for the first time in three years, and you are in Paris. You need to dazzle him."

I snorted. "At my age, to achieve dazzledom would take a minor miracle."

He narrowed his eyes and shook his head. "Not at all. Just a haircut. And some highlights. And perhaps a new dress, cut low in the front to show off your admirable cleavage, tight at the waist, then flaring out just to the knee. I could not help but notice your lovely ankles."

I probably should have been blushing, or getting indignant, or at least pretending I was insulted. Instead I was still fixated on his mouth and that melon. The scene was unspooling in my head: the juices of the melon trickling down his chin, the heroine leaning over and delicately licking . . .

Wait, what? "You think I have lovely ankles?"

"Very."

Okay, Mr. Smarty-Pants sexy French guy. "Oh. Well, all right then. And where could I possibly get all *that* before three o'clock?"

He waved a hand. "I will make a few calls."

I sat back. "How do you even know whom to call?"

"I have been married three times, so believe me when I tell you I know." He picked up my hand, stared at my stubby nails, and sighed. "And look at this, are you a washerwoman? My mother has nicer hands than this, and she practically *is* a washerwoman. We can get a manicure at the same salon that does your hair."

I jerked my hand away, feeling a bit of a burn now. "I type all day, every day." That was not true for this exact moment in time, but still. "Manicures are a waste of time. I need my nails short."

He lifted his eyebrows. "Short does not mean ugly."

"So. Manicure, haircut, new dress . . . I'm supposed to be writing, not primping to impress my ex-husband."

"But you are also seeking your muse, yes? And meeting your ex-husband again for the first time in years and seeing the look in his eyes that says, ah, this lovely woman, why did I let her go? That would inspire you."

I knew exactly how I'd write that scene. I'd enter the museum and stop (coincidentally) in front of a magnificent piece of sculpture that also happened to be under a skylight (allowing the sunlight to put me in a halolike glow) and look around for Alan. Ignoring the admiring looks of all the other men, I'd catch his eye and lift my hand in a tentative wave. He'd freeze, then take a hesitant step toward me. His face would soften, and he'd smile the same smile that had stolen my heart all those years ago, walking toward me slowly, finally reaching me and enclosing me in the warm and still-loving circle of his arms.

"Max," I said, pushing away from the table, "you've got a deal."

Chapter 4

*A makeover, an ex-husband,
and a great passion revealed*

It seemed that every woman in Paris came out onto the sidewalk to say hello to Max. Some gave him the French kiss-kiss, some just stepped out of their doorways to smile and say hello, a few hugged him, slipping their arms around his waist and whispering into his ear. He was smiling and courteous to them all, the young girls and the old crones. He called them all by name. I felt like I was walking with a French Pied Piper, because I was certain he had to just crook his finger and they all would have followed him anywhere.

The salon was behind two tall, bronze doors, and we got there just as it opened. Max greeted the proprietress with a kiss on both cheeks and then introduced me.

"Nathalie, this is Maggie Bliss, the writer."

Nathalie's eyes flew open. "The writer? You mean, Bella and Lance?"

I had never, in over twenty years, gotten used to the feeling that came over me when someone I randomly met had read my books. I was gobsmacked and giddy every time.

I didn't fight my grin. "Yes, that's me."

Nathalie turned, raised her voice considerably, and let off something of a rant to everyone in the shop, employees and clients alike. It was in French, of course, and all I recognized were the words "Delania" and "Maggie Bliss." Some of the employees smiled and nodded at me.

Obviously Nathalie was a fan.

She took both my hands in hers. "They live happily ever after, don't they?" she asked in careful English.

I nodded solemnly. "Oh yes. They certainly do."

She turned back to her audience, made another pronouncement that was met with sighs and a smattering of applause, then turned her attention to me.

I was whisked into a back room and given a short, pink cotton smock to wear over my clothes, making me, finally, as well-dressed as all the other women in the shop.

Nathalie took care of me personally. She washed my hair and applied the color. She gave me a manicure, washed out the color, and began to cut. She alternated between asking me questions about Bella and Lance and switching to French for lively conversation with Max, who laughed a great deal. She was obviously flirting with him. I didn't need to understand French to interpret her body language and his obvious enjoyment of her attention.

I knew she'd cut my hair short. She refused to let me face

the mirror, but I felt the scissors along my neck and knew that at least six inches had been chopped off. It might not have mattered to me except for the fact that those six inches were usually tied back or twisted up on top of my head. I did not look at the hair as it fell to the floor but instead spent a lot of time looking at my nails, still very short, but shiny and surprisingly pretty in pale gray. Even *nails* were gray in France? Who knew?

When she finally turned me around, with quite a flourish, I couldn't speak. My jaw dropped open. For several seconds, it seemed the entire salon was holding its breath. Finally, when my lack of response became embarrassingly long, Max cleared his throat.

"I think that your ex-husband will be quite swept away. Are you pleased?"

The dam burst and I began to cry. "I look *smoking*!" I sobbed. "Oh my God, I look *hot*!"

Max translated, and the entire salon began to laugh and applaud.

The brownish-gray hair was gone. Instead, my hair was a rich caramel color, streaked with dark honey. And the cut . . . a simple chin-length bob, but all the unruly waves I'd spent a lifetime trying to tame were let free, and soft curls fell around my face, distracting the eye from the faint wrinkles and more obvious laugh lines that made an appearance, quite unexpectedly, on my last birthday.

I looked beautiful. Okay, not beautiful, but the woman who stared back at me was not the discouraged writer who had come to Paris with writer's block and beige hair. No. This new woman would write Bella and Lance in and out of as many bedrooms as the war-torn country of Delania could throw them into, get them to a happy ending, and look damn good doing it.

I jumped up and threw my arms around Nathalie, who managed not to recoil in horror. "Thank you, thank you so much," I told her. Then I threw my arms around Max, who chuckled and patted me on the back. I pulled away from him, took his face between both of my hands and gave him a big, sloppy kiss right on those lips. His eyebrows shot up in shock, but I didn't care.

"Thank you, Max," I blurted. I turned to look for someone, anyone else, to kiss, but strangely enough, everyone else in the shop had his or her back to me. Oh well.

I paid an exorbitant price and, ignoring Lee's advice, handed Nathalie a handful of euros. "Thank you again."

She finally smiled. "I hope," she said in careful and heavily accented English, "that your ex-husband proposes to you again."

I almost wanted to hug her again.

We stepped out into the street, and I was hungry. "Can we stop for something? Before we go back?" I asked. "My treat."

He shook his head. "Not yet. There was a quite nice place I wanted to take you, one of my favorites, but Zoë's shop is right here. Very quickly, yes? A dress?"

I forgot about the dress, but we'd been crossing the street, and sure enough, a dress shop was right in front of us, with an adorable navy-blue dress in the window. It was totally wrong for me, one of those simple, straight sheath dresses that only look good on women who are six feet tall in bare feet, but what could I say?

We walked in, and Zoë practically danced across the floor. She was probably close to Solange's age, dressed in a very chic black dress, her hair dyed a shade of red that was never, by any stretch of the imagination, found in nature. She and Max chattered back and forth for a few minutes while I looked through the racks. The clothes were beautifully and very simply made. They were also not nearly as expensive as I thought they'd be.

"So, Maggie," Zoë said. "Max said you need a dress to seduce your ex-husband?" Her English was perfect.

I shook my head. "Maybe not quite that far. But here's the thing: I'm short waisted with big boobs and no butt. My best bet was always something with an empire waist, even though I'd look slightly pregnant. I think Max has some pretty unreasonable expectations."

"Nonsense," she said. She snapped her fingers and a slim younger woman slipped out from behind the counter. Zoë pointed to the back, where she drew open a curtain to reveal a large dressing room with mirrors on all three walls.

"Take off your things," Zoë said. I sighed and followed her into the dressing room, where the clerk pulled the curtain closed behind us. I tugged off my sweater, carefully folding it and placing it on the single stool, then stepped out of my pants. I looked at Zoë, not the mirror, because I didn't want to ruin the good feeling I'd gotten from my new haircut.

Zoë looked at me for a few seconds, then spoke in rapid-fire French to her clerk, who bowed out of the dressing room.

"You need new foundation garments. Breasts like that need more than mere underwire. We will get those next door. And your legs are glorious." She shook her head. "But you are right. You have no butt. That will be a challenge. Wait here."

I picked up my sweater as she left, hugging it to my chest for warmth and comfort. It was the closest thing to an emotional support animal I had at the moment. I sat down on the stool, still refusing to turn around. I got out my phone and sent a quick text to Cheri and Alison. They probably weren't awake yet, but they would get a good morning chuckle.

> M: Getting a makeover. I now have gray nails and bouncy hair. More to follow.

Zoë came back in, followed by her clerk, who positioned a rack hung with a handful of dresses before leaving. Zoë handed me a bra that appeared to be engineered rather than sewn, and something else that appeared to be the French version of Spanx. "Start with these. Then try on the blue and come out where we can see you," she ordered, then left.

The bra was a struggle, and I'd rather not discuss the Spanx at all. But the dress slid over my head and down my hips without getting hung up on anything, so I dared a look in the mirror.

Oh my.

My boobs were at least three inches higher than they'd been before, and I could discern a faint waistline. My butt was still flat as a washboard, but . . .

I went out into the shop on happy feet.

Zoë smiled. "*Très bon.* How do you feel?"

"I can't breathe very well, and I'm afraid if I bend over my boobs will fall out of the cups, but I feel great."

Max walked around me, eyes narrowed. "Yes, this looks very nice, but try the green. I think that would suit her coloring, yes?"

Zoë nodded. "Yes." She waved both of her hands in the direction of the dressing room. "The green."

The green fit a bit too snugly for me, and as for cleavage . . .

"That's perfect," Max declared.

"No, it's too tight. And short. And low cut."

"Exactly," Max said.

"I'll put this in the maybe pile," I said. The simple black sheath got three thumbs down. The gray looked amazing with the addition of a simple belt. The pale pink was a bust.

At that point, I was feeling delirious with hunger and happiness. I had pretty clothes, but if I didn't eat soon, things would get ugly. As we left the store, I tried to think about how I could write off as a business expense the blue and gray dresses.

"You will regret not buying the green," Max said.

"Maybe. If I don't eat soon, I won't be responsible for my actions," I said.

Max laughed. "It's only twelve thirty."

"My stomach can't tell time," I told him.

He turned the corner. "Can you make it to the end of the street?"

"I'll try. And thank you. I feel like Eliza Doolittle."

He laughed. "Oh, really? Well, that's lovely for you, but I

always felt that Henry Higgins was a bit of a twit and not good enough for her."

"He wasn't. But Max, I'd be happy to find your slippers any day." That just slipped out. Honestly. I grimaced a little when I realized how it sounded. "I mean—"

"No need. I doubt we'll ever be in that particular situation. But thank you, I think." He looked sideways at me, smiling. "You are going to knock his socks off. Is that still a saying?"

I grinned back. "It is in my book."

The Musée d'Orsay sits along the Seine. I walked through the Jardins du Trocadéro and past the Eiffel Tower to get there, wearing my new gray dress and kitten heels, with the navy blazer I'd bought the day before tossed over my shoulders like a cape. My new curls blew gently in the cool spring breeze. It was just two o'clock when I arrived, and as I wasn't meeting Nicole until three, I began to wander. After the first fifteen minutes, I knew I'd be back. I sat, quite happily, in a room with Degas until Nicole texted me that they were waiting for me under the big clock. I sighed, took one last look at all those dreamy balle-rinas, and went off to meet them.

I saw them as I started down the stairs. Nicole looked the same: tall, thin hands moving as she spoke, her dark hair straight and hanging almost to her waist. She was talking to her father, and the sight of them, heads together, Alan lean-ing down to hear her, caused my throat to close up and tears to prick behind my eyelids. They were so alike, with the same wide brow and strong jawline. We had made a beautiful child, Alan and I. She would always be my best work.

Alan looked thinner than when I'd seen him last, the angles of his face more prominent. Although his hair was grayer, it was also longer, falling across his forehead and down over the collar of his shirt, so he appeared more youthful. He was dressed in a chambray shirt and khakis and seemed relaxed, less the stern academic and more the doting dad. His smile was the same, bright and infectious, and Nicole laughed at whatever he said in response to her.

I swallowed hard as I went down the stairs. Nicole turned, caught sight of me, and her face lit up.

"Mom, you look great," she said, hugging me. She pushed me away, her eyes taking in the hair, the new dress, the carefully applied lipstick. "You look perfect."

Alan's eyes popped open and stayed that way. I reached up to give him a cool kiss on the cheek.

"I can't believe you're here, Alan," I said. "Aren't you the man who insisted that everything worth seeing was right in the good old USA?"

He grinned. "I'm living proof you can teach a very old dog new tricks."

"This place is amazing," I told them. "Have you two had enough alone time? Because I can easily wander off and return in, say, three days."

Nicole shook her head. "Dad and I are good. But we aren't leaving. Come on and let's get a little culture."

So we walked, past statues that seemed to glow in the filtered sunlight, past paintings I'd only seen in books but that in real life seemed to breathe from the canvas. Alan analyzed every painting, and he was quite knowledgeable in pointing out technique, lighting, and perspective. Nicole, the historian, knew more obscure facts about art than I realized. I just listened to them both, nodded, and saw every figure in every painting as a story aching to be told. We were a broken family joined together by beauty and wonder, almost as though that was all we had ever needed to be together.

But, eventually, there was hunger. Alan finally slumped against a wall and announced that if he didn't eat soon, he would probably perish, right there in front of Monet and everyone.

Nicole knew of the perfect place only a few blocks away, so we walked some more as the sun began to set over the Seine, my daughter acting as tour guide as Alan and I walked on either side of her, listening.

She turned us down a quiet side street and then opened a tall, narrow, turquoise door. "We're here," Nicole said.

The restaurant was perfect. A dozen tables draped in starched white cloths, tiny candles burning, wineglasses gleaming. We took seats by the window, Nicole and I sitting together, Alan across from us.

"This place is charming," Alan said.

A waiter appeared, hovering a moment before speaking rapidly in French. Nicole answered him, and they engaged in quite the lively conversation there for a few minutes. Finally the waiter bowed and backed away.

"I take it you ordered for us?" I said.

She nodded. "Since Dad here said he was treating, I just asked for wine and a few snack-type things. It's too early for dinner, especially here in Paris, but we can chat and eat a bit." She made it sound like chatting and eating a bit were things she did all the time. I knew for a fact that Nicole thought small talk was completely useless. She also did not think eating was some-thing you did for enjoyment but rather out of necessity. I often wondered how I gave birth to someone with such a completely different worldview from mine.

Alan raised his eyebrow and glanced at me. He knew her as well as I did, and I'm sure he was thinking the same things. "Nothing too extravagant, I hope?" he said in a joking voice. "My budget is rather limited these days."

I unfurled my napkin. "What's this?"

"I've retired," Alan said. "It was time. It was beyond time. The world was changing too fast for someone like me. I still like writing letters."

"With his quill and ink," Nicole added.

"But that's marvelous, Alan," I said. "Good for you. And what do you plan on doing? Going forward, I mean. I can't imagine you sitting around collecting stamps or coins. What about painting? I know that you always loved it." He not only loved it, he was very talented. Right after we were married he showed me his art, and I could see a real gift there. He often drew me: quick sketches, often nudes, drawn with pure, simple lines. I had given him a set of watercolors our first Christmas together.

He nodded. "Yes, I'm thinking about taking it up more

seriously. It's become more than a hobby in the past few years. In fact, I had a show in the art department gallery last fall, and I was not laughed out of the staff room. I think this may be what I want to do going forward. I want to take a few classes. I was going—"

The waiter interrupted with three small wineglasses on a tray and a plate of bubbling shrimp swimming in garlicky-smelling butter and surrounded by slices of toasted bread.

The wine was not too dry and quite lovely. I took a shrimp, swirled it around in the butter a few times just for luck, then placed it on a piece of toast.

Perfection.

"You were going . . . ?" I coaxed Alan.

"Yes, I was going to move to Vermont. That was the original plan because Heather had family there, and we were going to, well, whatever. That's off the table now. So I may head south."

"And who is Heather?" I asked.

"She was a visiting professor," Alan said, wrestling with his own shrimp. "Sixteenth-century French poetry. There had been a round of parties last fall when I announced my retirement. I knew her—that is, I'd seen her around—but at the party we started talking and we sorta clicked."

I don't know what shocked me more—the fact that Alan had *clicked* with a woman or that he actually went to a party. Alan had been the head of the mathematics department at Lehigh University for years, and I knew he was well liked, so it was reasonable to assume there would have been parties in his honor. But the fact that he went to one . . .

I narrowed my eyes and turned to Nicole.

"Since when has your father gone to parties?"

She shrugged. "He's changed. He's a lot more social. I think he got tired of being the socially awkward math geek. It was adorable when he was younger, but . . . at his age it's just creepy."

Alan cleared his throat. "I'm right here."

She smiled sweetly. "I know." She looked sideways at me. "Obviously you've changed as well. A dress? Since when have you become a fashionista? And are those actual highlights in your hair?"

I shrugged. "Max's idea."

She arched her eyebrow. "Max?"

"He's the son of Lee's housekeeper, and he's staying at the flat because he's attending a conference here. He's a banker. But he has excellent taste in clothes."

The waiter drifted by and set down a plate of three different cheeses and what looked to be pâté. More toast. A few olives. I sighed happily.

"Besides, we were discussing your father's love life, not mine. What happened?"

"She was totally unsuitable," Nicole said smoothly, spreading a thin layer of pâté on a toast triangle. "Brilliant, or so everyone said. And beautiful. In her forties, I would say. But her temperament was too volatile. She was also very ambitious. I couldn't imagine her settling down to be an artist's wife."

"Once again," Alan said mildly, "I'm right here."

I nodded. The bit of cheese I'd taken was mild and sweet

and tasted the way fresh-mown grass smelled. "Yes, you certainly are. I'm sorry, Alan. Why don't *you* tell me what happened?"

He shrugged. "She was very attractive, with a brilliant and original mind. But she was younger, you see, and at the top of her career. For her to give it all up to sit around and watch me paint was, well, unimaginable to her. And after all, we'd only known each other a few months. We had made plans in, well, let's say the heat of passion. But they really didn't hold up in the cold light of day."

Nicole turned to me. "See? Told you." She dribbled a bit of the garlic butter from the shrimp onto the slice of cheese she'd put on her toast. It looked like a marvelous idea, the warm butter softening the cheese, soaking into the bread . . .

"Let me try that," I murmured.

"But we can thank her for Dad being here. If she hadn't planned the trip, he'd be celebrating his retirement in Pittsburgh," Nicole said.

I washed down the cheese with a sip of wine. "This trip was her idea?"

He nodded. "She couldn't believe I'd never been to France and convinced me it would be a perfect vacation for the two of us, coming here, seeing Nic, and having her show me the sights. And all the art. My last official day was April tenth. She arranged everything. Then she changed her mind."

"I'm sorry," I said.

He nodded. "Yes, me too. But she was right about Paris. It's beautiful, and seeing Nic has been great, and now you're here, which is a bonus. I was thinking that maybe I'll move here, get a small garret apartment, set up my easel out in the street." He grinned. "Can you see me as a starving artist? At my age? But Paris is quite inspiring."

I speared another shrimp. "You're right about that. I'm a bit stuck on a book, and Lee suggested I could find my muse here in Paris. I think he's right. If this place can't kick-start my imagination, I might as well stop writing altogether."

"What about Greg?" Nicole asked. "He's your ultimate alpha male. Doesn't he kick-start your imagination?"

She had a very legitimate point. "I told Greg to move out," I said.

Alan almost choked on his wine as the waiter presented us with a dish containing tiny mushrooms marinated in a sauce containing garlic, balsamic vinegar, and possibly thyme. Also, a small bowl of radishes, tiny and the most beautiful color of pinkish red I'd ever seen. I snagged one and popped it into my mouth, where it practically exploded.

"Oh," I breathed. I looked at Alan and Nicole who were both staring at me. "What?"

"You might have mentioned it earlier," Alan murmured. "You and Greg splitting up. You know, taking the heat off me for a bit." He raised an eyebrow. "This sounds very final."

I sighed. "Greg and I had reached an impasse. He thought my work was insignificant, unimportant, and unworthy of discussion. I didn't."

"It's about time. He was a horrible man," Nicole said.

"No, he wasn't," I argued. "He was interesting and funny and very smart. He was just . . ."

"Conceited as hell? Totally full of himself? Thought that his shit—"

"Stop." I held up a hand. "Stop. He's gone. End of discussion. Now it's *your* turn."

She actually turned a bright pink. "I don't know what you mean."

Alan held up his wineglass, signaling for more. "Well, I've shown you mine, and your mother showed you hers, so tell us all about Louis."

She ate another piece of cheese, then another shrimp, in no hurry at all. Then she glanced at Alan and me and sighed. "I guess you're not going to let this go, are you?"

I shook my head. "Absolutely not."

She sniffed and refused to meet my eye. "Just a student. We met last spring, right after I got here."

I sat back and tried to keep my face, voice, eyes . . . well, pretty much everything under control. "Oh?"

"He's older."

Please God, I thought, not *too* much older. Knowing Nicole, he could be seventy-five, and she wouldn't see any problems at all. "So, a graduate student?"

"Yes. And he's very political."

Well, he has to be, I thought. He's probably a communist, at least a socialist, possibly an anarchist. . . .

"And an atheist."

I sighed.

Alan shifted in his chair. "Can we meet him?"

"He's in Rennes."

"Why didn't he come to Paris with you?" I asked.

She shrugged. "He is very understanding of my need for personal space." He'd have to be. "I told him I wanted to spend some alone time with Daddy, and he understood that. He is planning to come out on Saturday, for the weekend, and then we'll go back to Rennes together."

"So, we *will* get to meet him?" I asked.

"Yes. And he wants to meet you."

"Oh?" Dare I say it? "So, this is rather serious then?"

"We're living together," she said as though it were not an important thing at all.

"Since when?" See, I was calm, not reading too much into what she was saying.

"Last fall."

"*What?* You've been living with a man for over six months and you never even *mentioned* it to me? What is *wrong* with you?" Control, as it were, was lost.

"Mom, this really has nothing to do with you," she said, looking at me steadily.

I glared at Alan. "Did you know about this?"

He was looking at Nicole with a mixture of admiration and disappointment. When Alan's father died, Nicole, his only grandchild, received a very nice amount to be held in trust. Alan was the administrator of that trust until her thirtieth birthday and had been doling out a reasonable allowance when she didn't have a steady income, as well as dutifully paying rent on all her various apartments, including the one in France. "She did mention a roommate, but . . . Nic, really? You couldn't trust us with this rather important piece of information?"

She looked completely guiltless. "I'm trusting you now."

I realized that in her mind, it made perfect sense, but her mind had always been a strange and quite distant land I never felt quite comfortable in. Or near. Or even in shouting distance of.

I drained my wineglass. "So how serious is all this, exactly?"

Her face softened and there was a quiet smile on her lips. "I think he is my person," she said.

Our plates were all empty and the nearby tables were starting to fill up with more serious eaters. I looked at my daughter, lovely and composed. She was the most extraordinary human being I'd ever known, and for her to have found her *person* . . .

"Oh, Nic, I'm so happy for you," I said softly.

My mind was going in too many directions at once—she was still so young, he was older, she just met him a year ago, she was alone in a foreign country . . .

But then, I was even younger when I met Alan, and we had known each even less time before we married. We had not ended well, but when we were together, my love for him was fierce and very real. And although Nicole might have been alone in a strange place, she was self-assured and self-sufficient, and loneliness was not something she would even recognize.

I looked over at Alan and knew he was thinking the same thing. The reasons our marriage fell apart were many and valid. But so were the reasons we had come together in the first place.

"I can't wait to meet him," I said.

Alan leaned over and kissed Nicole's cheek. "Me too. I'm very happy for you both."

She beamed. "And he's really cute."

Ah. Perfect.

I walked back to the flat in the warm evening. I had to keep looking at my phone, following the red line of the GPS, but it was a fairly direct path. I stopped to lean against a stone balustrade and stare up at the Eiffel Tower, silhouetted against the darkening sky. It was beautiful. The sky was beautiful. The whole damn city was beautiful.

I walked up the Rue Boissière toward Victor Hugo, and as I turned into the circle I saw a familiar face at a café table.

"Max?"

He'd been staring off at something in the crowd, a glass of wine in front of him. He looked up, and that wide mouth and too-red lips broke into a smile.

"Maggie, how was your afternoon? And evening, it seems. Please, sit."

I sank into the chair across from him and eased out of my shoes just a bit, giving my toes room to wiggle. The street was full of people sitting at the cafés that lined the cobbled street. Everyone was talking quietly but with interest and intent, waving their glasses of wine about, bursts of laughter coming from every corner and doorway. I felt very . . . Parisian. Especially sitting with Max, his body lean and relaxed, his dark, collarless shirt unbuttoned enough for a dusting of gray chest hair to peek out, his cuffs rolled up, showing muscled forearms. . . .

A waiter appeared and I thought about another glass of wine, then ordered an espresso instead. I usually didn't do caffeine this late, but I had a feeling I was going to be up late tonight anyway. All the way back from the museum, a scene was playing out in my head between Bella and Lance involving two exhausted, filthy people who'd been living rough and on the run but finally found a bathtub. . . .

"I fed Jules, by the way," Max said.

Oh my, I'd completely forgotten all about that poor dog. "Max, I'm so sorry. Don't tell your mother that I completely forgot about him, please? It was the one thing she asked. . . ."

He waved a hand. "It is nothing. Besides, Jules could live off his extra weight for a month."

I felt a giggle. "That's probably true. He's . . . corpulent."

Max nodded. "Excellent word. Yes, he is. And flatulent. I sometimes cannot bear to be in the same room with him."

The giggle burst out, full strength. "And your mother is so elegant and refined. To have this stinky little thing waddling after her . . ."

Max smiled. "She might look elegant and refined, but my mother is a warrior. She became pregnant with me when she was just sixteen. She went to Lee's aunt, Helene, explained that she had no intention of marrying, and offered to go to Paris as a housekeeper. She was quite unusual, Helene. She admired my mother's pluck and they got along very well. Helene was very demanding. She kept my mother on her toes." He sipped his wine. "I had a very unique childhood."

"I can imagine. Is that why you know every shopkeeper, including hair stylists, on such an, ah, intimate basis?"

He raised his eyebrows. "Why else would you think?"

I shrugged. "I don't know. You slept with them?"

He looked thoughtful. "Not all of them. Zoë, well, she was my first. I was young, and she was very patient with me. She and Mother are still very good friends, although I'm quite sure Zoë never said a word about us."

Luckily I'd already swallowed my sip of espresso or I would have coughed, spraying it all over his nice, clean shirt. "How old were you?"

He narrowed his eyes, thinking. "Seventeen? No, eighteen. I do think I was barely legal. Helene made me come with her to carry home the dresses she bought. I was short and quite ugly back then. I had not grown into my nose or my chin, and I'm sure Zoë thought that, left to my own devices, I would never get laid." He smiled wistfully. "She was quite a teacher."

"I have to put this in a book," I blurted.

He turned to me, surprised. "What, you have never written something like that before?"

I shrugged. "I'm still old-school, I guess. Usually my heroines are the ones to get . . . educated."

He shook his head. "Maggie, shake out those cobwebs. There is nothing more romantic, or erotic, than an older, experienced woman." He leaned toward me, his eyes dancing. "Young virgins are overrated. Give me a woman who's lived a good life anytime."

Our eyes were locked, and I had a very odd feeling right in the middle of my chest, a knot that was slowly unraveling.

"Oh?" My voice came out as a croak, and I quickly drank the rest of my espresso.

"You haven't mentioned your daughter. Or your ex-husband. How was your day?"

"The museum was incredible. I'm going back tomorrow. My daughter is fine. Well, she's always fine. She's the most self-sufficient person I know. She's also, apparently, in love, which is something I'm struggling with. I mean, I always hoped she'd find her happily ever after. It's kind of my whole life. It's just . . . well, I'm happy for her."

"Then I'm happy for her too," he said. "Everyone should be in love. And your ex-husband?"

"I got to hear the sad tale of his beautiful girlfriend who left him in the lurch after planning a trip to Paris that he didn't want to go on in the first place. It's interesting, though: He always painted a bit, and he's taking it more seriously. When we were married he dabbled, mostly sketches and a bit of watercolor, but he always had an eye, you know? It was good to see him. And I had the most delicious plate of cheese I've ever eaten. The shrimp was also good. And there were these tiny radishes that were indescribable."

He grinned. "You will have many meals like that." He threw some coins on the table. "I'll walk you back."

I nodded, and we went back to the flat in silence. Once inside, he bent to pat Jules. "I'll walk him, if you like."

"Would you? I actually feel like doing a bit of work."

"Certainly. After all, that's why you are here, yes?"

I changed quickly, hung up my new dress, smoothed out the wrinkles, and slipped into my familiar sweatpants and T-shirt. I instinctively reached to pull my hair up and back, but it was too short. I took another look in the mirror at my new curls, then made my way to my laptop.

I sat, eyes closed, taking a few deep breaths.

Bella and Lance. *It was morning, and when Bella opened her eyes* . . .

I opened mine and began to type.

Sometimes if you're a writer and you're very lucky, you find yourself *in the zone*. Bella and Lance had just crossed a mined expanse of desert. Fear of sudden and painful death heightened sexual tension. Sounds crazy, but . . . I wrote for three straight hours before I finally admitted I was too tired to type one more word. All the lights in the apartment were turned off except the single light in the bathroom. Jules was sleeping down the hall. Max must have come back in, but I never saw or heard him.

I crawled into bed, still dressed in my writing clothes, smiling.

Maybe it was Paris.

Maybe it was seeing Alan again, imagining him in a sunlit attic, sleeves rolled up, squinting at his easel.

Maybe it was the thought of my beautiful daughter in love.

Whatever the reason, I was back.

Chapter 5

In which a diabolical plan is exposed,
and I write a waterfall scene of epic
proportions

I woke up after four hours' sleep. Lance had left Bella in a Doctors Without Borders hospital, where the handsome and dashing surgeon Henri Dumond was trying to convince her to leave Delania with him on the next transport. She was stalling, claiming to be worried about her coworker, but actually frantic about the safety of Lance, who had vanished back into the desert in search of a cache of medical supplies. Things were getting tense. Thankfully, Lance turned up at the last minute, and they were off again.

I hit SAVE, brushed my teeth, drank two glasses of water, then went back to bed. There were texts from Cheri and Alison. I deleted the ones from Greg.

C: Since when do you have bouncy hair? Send pics

A: Why gray nails? What's wrong with pink? Don't
the French like pink?
C: Gray is chic. Go with the gray

I texted back.

M: Too tired for pics and gray is prettier than it sounds.

I woke again just after eight the next morning, washed
my face, changed into one of my new skirts and a cashmere
sweater, fussed with my hair a bit, and slid my feet into my
flats before grabbing Jules's leash. I carried him down the stairs
and outside, where I was not stared at in utter disbelief by the
well-dressed and impeccably groomed passersby. After he'd
finished his business, I brought him back up to the flat, grabbed
my tote bag off the tiny kitchen counter, and went back to the
Monoprix, where I greeted every single employee, bought eggs
and more bread as well as strawberries and parsley, and bagged
my own groceries with a smile.

When I got back to the flat, I heard the shower running.
My plan was to make Max breakfast, but since he was in the
shower . . .

I went back to my laptop and started writing again.

When you're on the run in a made-up third-world country,
you have to take advantage of any and all running water you
can find. Bella and Lance had just come across a small waterfall
in the middle of nowhere, and since they were both hot and
sweaty . . .

"Oh my goodness."

Max's voice behind me jolted me back to Paris. He was standing over my shoulder and had obviously read every word I'd just written. I shut the laptop and stood up, turning around quickly. He was right behind me, our noses inches apart.

"Can I assume," he said, his eyes dancing, "that you have, indeed, found your muse?"

His face was extraordinary, with wrinkles around his eyes and mouth, his nose long and narrow. But there was so much charm beneath those dark and bushy brows, as well as humor and intelligence.

"Max, standing over a person's shoulder while they're writing is considered very bad form."

"I called your name twice. I finally had to come over to see if you were still breathing."

We were still standing very close together. To be fair, I couldn't step back without climbing onto the desk behind me. If I had stepped forward, I would have been able to climb right onto him, my legs around his hips . . .

I cleared my throat. "Well, yeah, I guess that can happen. When I'm writing like this I get sort of self-absorbed."

He finally stepped back. "So, that is good?"

I nodded. "Yes. Very good." I moved sideways away from him and headed for the kitchen. "I bought eggs and things for breakfast." I looked around. There were two plates on the counter, a beautifully made omelet and a slice of toast on each.

"I saw the eggs and, well . . ." Max shrugged. "I hope you don't mind."

I picked up my plate and mug of coffee. "Are you kidding? You're spoiling me, Max. Thank you."

We ate again by the tall windows, which were cracked open enough to let in the noise of the street and a warm, damp breeze.

"So today will be a good writing day, then?" Max asked.

"I've already written enough to reward myself. Alan is meeting someone, a colleague also here on vacation, something else that Heather arranged, so Nic and I decided to go back to the Musée d'Orsay," I said. "This time I'm going to see every single thing in that museum."

Max shook his head. "No. That is impossible. If you see every single thing, you will not appreciate any of it. What did you see yesterday?"

"We just walked the first floor."

"When you get there, keep your head down and go to the top floor. Stay there. That will be a whole day, believe me. You can go back in a day or two if you want to see something else, of course. But you may just go back to the top floor again." He shrugged. "Renoir is there."

The omelet was light and perfectly cooked, fluffy egg sprinkled with chopped parsley. Simple and delicious. "That sounds like the way to go. But I can't spend my entire time in Paris at the Musée d'Orsay."

"True. Not when there are dozens of museums, not to mention all the gardens. And you must go to Versailles, especially in the spring."

I sat back, laughing. "Max, I have to work. And I can't stay here indefinitely."

He shrugged. "Why not? You can write here just as well as in—where are you from again?"

I fiddled with my fork. "New Jersey."

"Yes. New Jersey. My mother would love the company. She truly enjoys cooking and doing for others."

I heard a familiar ding from my phone and crossed the room to grab it. A text from Nicole. She was turning the corner from Victor Hugo.

"That's Nic, and as usual, I'm not ready. Would you mind if she came up and waited a bit?"

"Of course not," he said. "I would love to meet her."

I left the apartment, ran down the steps, and opened the outside door just as her finger was poised over the buzzer.

"Hello! Perfect. Come on up. Max is here, I can't wait for you to meet him."

She was dressed in leggings and her Dr. Martens boots, a T-shirt, a faded gray hoodie, and a small cross-body bag. I knew it never occurred to her that Parisians would see her walk by and shake their heads. It wasn't that she didn't care, although I'm sure she didn't. She was just so sure of her own self-worth that it would never occur to her that what she was wearing—or doing or saying—wasn't the absolute perfect thing for her true self.

I stopped to press the elevator button, but she practically ran up the steps, with me puffing behind her.

She entered the apartment. "Nice," she muttered, walking forward.

Max rose and held out his hand. "Nicole? A pleasure. I am Max. Are you enjoying Paris?"

She grinned. "Oh yes." She then plunged into rapid and animated French. Max's eyes opened wide with obvious delight, and they were off, their faces open and expressive, hands flying. I had no idea what they could be saying to each other, but boy, were they having a good time.

I went into the kitchen, made another pot of coffee, hoping I didn't screw it up too much, then brought a tray back out, setting it on the long dining table.

"Nic, honey, coffee?"

She walked over and proceeded to fix herself a cup without breaking the conversation at all.

"Max?" I asked.

He nodded, came over, and poured himself another cup. I sat and watched them for about another five minutes. They were still standing, each sipping their coffee, having one heck of a conversation. What on earth could they be talking about?

"Ah, guys?" I called at last. They both turned to look at me.

"Ah, Maggie," Max said. "We did not mean to shut you out. But Nicole here is staying in Rennes, one of my favorite cities, and it is always such a treat to revisit such places."

Nicole sat next to me at the table. "Sorry, but we were comparing places to eat. And drink. He knows exactly where in Old Rennes I'm staying. By the way, good coffee."

I beamed. "Thanks."

She sat back with a rather satisfied smirk. "You really surprised Daddy, by the way. He couldn't stop talking about how much younger and prettier you look."

I drew back. "Younger and prettier than *what*? This is what forty-plus looks like. Well, except for the hair. I mean, *that's* an upgrade. What is he even comparing me *to*? He hasn't seen me since your graduation, when I actually *was* younger."

Nicole sighed. "Facebook. You and Dad are friends, right? You posted that picture at Christmas. You were at a party, I guess?"

"Oh, right." The annual Christmas party for Greg's department at Drew University. "What about it?"

She made a face. "Mom, you were head to toe in black, your hair looked positively bland in some sort of topknot with, what were those, chopsticks? You looked like you were auditioning for a role in *American Horror Story*."

Max made a discreet noise, somewhere between a snort and a cough.

Nicole looked at him, a smile playing around her lips. "This new look is your doing, I understand?"

Max shrugged, looking very French. "Your mother is in Paris to find her muse. One cannot do that without looking one's best."

"Hmm. Yeah, well, whatever." She turned back to me. "You wanted to go back to the museum?"

"Yes. Absolutely. I got a lot of work done last night, so I deserve a break. Max, come with?"

Max looked surprised. "You don't want to spend the time alone with your daughter?"

"Actually, she does," Nicole answered. "But as much as we love each other, we usually don't find common ground. We'd be perfectly comfortable looking at the art, but lunch would be

a long, drawn-out silence. Please come. You'd be making it easier on us both."

I nodded. "Please."

He smiled. "My pleasure."

After hours at the museum, my stomach started making noises
loud enough for other museum guests to hear. When I admitted defeat, both Nicole and Max agreed it was time for lunch.

"I know how you get when you're hungry," Nicole said.
"Seriously, can you wait ten minutes?"

I nodded. "As long as we keep moving, I'll manage. If we
stop anywhere and there's food, I probably won't leave."

We walked along the river, crossed one of the many
bridges, and finally settled into tiny chairs around a weathered table somewhere in Le Marais. I ordered something with
chicken, Max ordered something with fish, and Nicole, typi-
cally, a salad.

"I can't believe," I said, "you live in one of the great food
countries in the world, and you eat salad."

"The salads here," she replied, "are unlike anything green
and crispy you've eaten anywhere else."

"This is true," Max said. "A salad in the States would not
even be called a salad here. Just wait. You'll be dreaming about
baby lettuce leaves before you go back."

Nicole grinned. "Hear that? Leave me alone and drink your
wine."

I sat back and did as I was told. I was wearing one of my cashmere sweaters against the cool spring breeze, and the sun was just perfect on my face.

Max stretched out his legs in front of him. "So, Nicole, I am curious. How do you like living in France?"

She paused for a moment before speaking. "I think I will stay here," she said at last. "I think this is a place where I could be happy. The people, the culture, the food . . . it's a very different experience, and I find that I am much more relaxed here than I ever was back home."

I stared at her, a lump forming in my throat. "Really?" I croaked. "You want to stay here? Like, forever?"

She shook her head. "Mom, nothing is forever. But for the immediate future, yes."

Max tilted his head. "But what of your parents? You'll miss them, yes? And won't you worry about them? After all, we all get older, and it is much harder to do that alone."

She shrugged. "They won't be alone," she said.

The waiter arrived with our food, which is why I didn't immediately ask her what in the hell she was talking about. But after our plates were all arranged—looking quite beautiful—I picked up my fork and pointed it at her.

"Nic, would you mind explaining that particular train of thought?"

She speared a few lettuce leaves, chewed, and swallowed. "I'm thinking about you and Daddy. I imagine this Paris trip will bring you back together, and I won't have to worry about either of you being alone because you'll be together again."

I dropped my fork and stared. I think my mouth dropped open. What . . . ? "What on earth are you talking about?"

"Why so surprised?" she asked. "Is the idea of you and Daddy getting together again after all these years so far-fetched? After all, I think you write books about that sort of thing happening all the time, right?"

Max had his head down, his shoulders shaking with laughter. "What brilliant reasoning," he said at last.

She beamed. "Thank you. I've been thinking about it for a while now, and after seeing how they got along yesterday, why not? They're both single again, and at a time in their lives when changes are coming up fast. It makes sense."

"But this is real life, Nicole, not one of your mother's books," Max countered. "In real life, ex-husbands and wives *stay* exes."

"In real life," she said easily, "exes barely speak to each other. These two have been friends for years. Besides, who else are they going to end up with? Every single relationship each has had over the years has ended. Rather badly in most cases. I mean, Greg . . . what a disaster he was, from the very beginning."

I drew myself up straighter. "Nicole, I don't think you're in a position to comment on my relationship with Greg."

"Why not? I was in college for the first part of it, sure, but then I was living ten minutes away and pretty much saw the whole thing." She leaned forward. "Mom, your problem is that you always try to date your heroes. Your early books? Every single one of them had a Dad type: sensitive and thoughtful, the bookish nerdy guy who suddenly sweeps the heroine off her feet. Then you started writing more macho types and started dating them too, the ultimate being Greg. I mean, I got it. He *was* Mom's perfect hero. But such an asshole."

She looked smug as she sat back. "And this whole thing with Daddy and Heather? Obviously he was trying to recapture a bit of his passionate youth. I get that too. But the truth is"—she fixed her eyes on me—"you and Daddy were each other's first great love. That will never go away. And I don't think anything else will come close."

I didn't know how to respond. I sat back, staring at my chicken, so stunned it didn't even register how amazing it smelled. I glanced up at Max. Those blue eyes were dancing, laughter very close to the surface.

"It would appear," he said, "that Nicole here loves you and her father and only wants to see you both happy."

"Exactly," she said. "Max, I really appreciate your understanding."

"But perhaps," he went on, "your mother has, say, another plan?"

She narrowed her eyes. "Like what?"

I cut off a piece of chicken and put it in my mouth, thinking fast as I chewed. "For some time now I've been seriously thinking about hiring a full-time assistant. I'll just find some handsome young man, possibly someone out of the Iowa Writers' Workshop MFA program, offer him a position, and then I'm set. He'll fall madly in love with me, we'll cowrite something amazing, move to Belize . . ."

The waiter appeared with more wine, and it was almost enough to take my mind off the sudden vision of being massaged on a sun-drenched beach by someone in a Speedo and horn-rimmed glasses.

Nicole made a noise that may or may not have been a snort. "God, Mom, really?"

"It could happen," I said. I glanced at Max, who seemed to be smothering laughter again. "Maybe I'll write my next book along those lines, just to prove my point."

Nicole made a face. "Really?"

"And besides," I went on, "your father may have something to say about all this."

She nodded. "He probably does. But last night, back at the flat, all he could talk about was how good you looked and how much he'd missed you."

I cut some more chicken.

Alan?

Sure, I'd imagined Alan and me growing old together. In fact, every time I wrote a scene about two characters coming together again after any kind of separation, the faces in my head were always mine and his. But Max was right: This was not one of my books. This was Paris where, I imagined, any relationship would be bathed in a far-too-romantic glow. It would be easy for us to fall in love again while walking hand in hand under the shadow of the Eiffel Tower. But what about in the real world?

"Nicole," I said, "as much as I admire all the thought you've given to my years of dating, you're totally off base. And as for your father and me? I think it would be best for all of us to just put that idea somewhere else. Like, in a suitcase, weighed down with rocks, and thrown into the Seine. Your father and I have been leading very separate lives for a very long time, and we've both been happy. Let's just leave it at that, okay?"

She sighed. "Whatever. But at least keep an open mind?"

I shrugged, then finally stuck my fork into the tiny mound of greens that had been nestled against my chicken. And . . .

Oh.

Oh my goodness. It was unlike any salad I had ever tasted before in my entire life and made me think that maybe Nicole had the right idea after all.

About salads. *Just* about salads.

Nicole walked back to the apartment with us. It was a long, meandering kind of walk, full of pointing and smiling, happy laughter and comfortable silences. Max and Nic had apparently firmly cemented their friendship sometime after our late lunch, and they exchanged quick comments in French that left them smiling and me marveling at Max's charm and my daughter's obvious appreciation of it.

Back at the apartment, Nic and I went out again, this time with Jules, and I showed her a bit of the neighborhood.

"Very elegant," she said, somehow making the word sound vaguely distasteful.

"There's nothing wrong with elegant," I said, watching Jules lift his leg against the side of a building that looked to date back to the 1700s, all gray limestone and tall, narrow windows.

"True," she said.

"I love the history here," I said. "Why is it in America we feel the need to tear down buildings and build everything *new*?"

"Because that is what we are. A new country. Let's face it, France was the center of art and literature when New York was a cluster of log cabins and dairy farms."

I sighed. "It is remarkable here. I guess I can see why you'd want to live here."

"Wait until you see Rennes. It's hundreds of years old, and the streets are narrow and beautiful, and the buildings are just amazing."

I laughed. "Maybe I can make it out there to visit you. Max says I can stay here and write as long as I'd like, and since there's not much for me to get back to in the States until my book launch . . ."

She glanced at me. "It's really over between you and Greg?"

"Oh yes, although he's sent me several texts asking if I've changed my mind. I imagine he's having a bit of a hard time finding a place to live. He has very high standards for someone who's living on a part-time academic salary and negligible royalties."

"But he was paying some of your expenses, wasn't he? Will you be okay without him?"

I smiled. "As soon as I hand in the first draft, I get more of my advance. And then there's the option, which will be real money. Another reason to finish this book on time."

We returned to the apartment with fresh-baked bread, a piece of fish that Nic said she'd cook for dinner, and—need I say it—more wine.

Max came into the hallway with a sleek leather duffel bag in his hand. "That looks promising," he said.

She grinned. "I can't wait to cook in a kitchen with more than twelve inches of workspace," she said. "My entire flat could fit into this living room."

Max watched her go into the kitchen, then turned to me. "She's remarkable," he said. "I wish I could spend more time with her. And you, Maggie. But I'm off. I'll be back Sunday afternoon. If my mother returns before then, you will tell her, yes?"

"Naturally," I said. What personal business could he have in Marseille? I imagined him in a huge four-poster bed in a cramped attic flat with a redhead, in her thirties, with very red lips and a deep, smoke-and-whiskey voice, wearing a long kimono of black and red roses. They would probably stay in bed the whole time, eating peeled oranges and reading erotic French poetry to each other.

Hmmm . . . would Bella and Lance ever . . . yeah, they would.

He leaned forward to speak softly right into my ear. "If my mother starts asking questions, tell her we made love all over her dining room table. That will satisfy her enough to keep her from asking questions until I return."

I couldn't help it—I pulled away from him and stared at the dining room table. "Wouldn't the couch be more comfortable?" I blurted, imaging my back against the hard wood surface of the table. The couch, on the other hand . . .

"She just had the couch recovered," he said with a grin. He reached for his bag and slipped out the door, leaving me standing alone in the hall feeling the heat rise in my cheeks. If not the couch, then what about the faded oriental rug, in front of the fireplace, with a few soft pillows. . . .

"Mom?"

I jumped.

"Ah, you okay?"

I nodded. "Just writing stuff. In my head. You know."

"Yes, I do. Well, that's good, right? Isn't that why you're here in the first place?"

I nodded again. For some reason, my throat felt so dry I knew that if I tried to talk, my voice would crack.

"If you want to do some writing, I'll be perfectly happy sitting here. I can find something to read. We won't be eating for a while. . . ."

"Good idea," I said, clearing my throat. "A great idea. You won't mind?"

She shook her head. "Not at all. Like I said, I'll find something to read."

I smiled. "You'll find copies of my books on those shelves. The French versions."

Her face lit up. "Really? Now that might be fun."

I put on my writing clothes, silenced my phone, and set the alarm on my laptop. My mind had been racing. Bella and Lance had left an adorable five-year-old boy named Twan in a ravaged village halfway through book two, and I felt, very strongly, that they needed to go back and find said little boy. Once they found Twan they could bring him back to the United States with them and adopt him. Since neither they, nor I at this point, knew if the almost-fatal virus that Lance survived in book two had left him sterile or not, Twan could be their only chance at the family they both wanted.

It took me five minutes to remember that throughout book two, my autocorrect kept changing Twan to Twin. Sometimes I really hated technology.

When the timer went off, I'd written an entire chapter. I didn't want to leave the chair, but I could hear the click of Jules's nails on the floor, and I knew I needed to get up and stretch. Nicole was reading on the couch, and it was, indeed, one of my books. *When Love Is Lost,* the very first of the Delania Trilogy.

"Well?" I asked.

She laid the book down. "You met Greg right before you started writing this, didn't you?"

"Is it that obvious?"

She shook her head. "At least Lance has a certain empathy. And a sense of humor. And is taller. Good writing?"

"Very good. I'll change, take Jules for a walk, and then maybe you could start dinner?"

She nodded, and I went to change. Jules and I returned to find the fish gently poaching in white wine and fresh herbs, so he ate while Nicole and I sipped wine.

"Dad wants to see Versailles tomorrow," she said. "He called while you were out."

"I would love to see Versailles," I said. "And if I write enough tonight, I'll allow myself another day of being a tourist."

"Daddy and I can meet you here and take the Métro together. It will be easier than coming in from two different directions."

"Good. Because I don't think I feel quite comfortable finding things on my own."

"You found the museum just fine."

"Yes, but you were right about all those signs."

We ate quietly, finished up with cheese and more wine, then Nicole left. I cleaned up and poured more wine but left it untouched, as I had a sudden thought.

I wrote. I took Jules for his evening walk, then wrote some more. Finally, I crawled into bed and dreamed about Lance drinking from a canteen as water spilled from his mouth down his naked chest. Then Lance morphed into Max, laughing and spilling wine and staining his white shirt a dark, deep red.

I got a text from Lee.

    L: How is Max?

I'd been up for an hour, walked Jules, gotten my café crème and croissant, and was reading what I'd written the day before.

    M: Max was wonderful. Got me a haircut and new dresses. Writing like crazy. Going to Versailles.
    L: How can you continue to write like crazy at Versailles? And since when do you wear dresses? Be home this evening Can't wait to read what you wrote Solange wants to know if Max is with you?
    M: Tell her Max is in Marseille until Sunday

I sipped my coffee and nibbled on the corner of my croissant.

> L: Solange just unleashed a string of profanity that would make a longshoreman blush. I will never understand her

I understood her just fine. Max wasn't supposed to be in Marseille. He was supposed to be in Paris, falling in love with me so that Solange could die happy, knowing her son would be properly taken care of by that most valuable of objects: a wife. Even though, to me, anyway, Max was more than capable of taking care of himself.

I took a selfie of my new hair to send to Cheri and Alison. I wanted to also hold up my pretty nails next to my new hair but wasn't coordinated enough to hold the phone with just one hand. I took a separate shot of my hand against the window, the view of the street below.

> M: My new work view. It's doing the job! Writing like crazy.

I'd already risen early enough to rewrite a portion of what I'd finished the night before and start a new chapter, so when Nicole texted that she and Alan were waiting down on the street, I felt no twinge of guilt. I made sure Jules had plenty of water and went down to meet them.

Nic was dressed in leggings, Dr. Martens boots that laced up to her knees, a bright orange thermal T-shirt, three scarves around her neck, and a short denim jacket.

I sighed. "Why don't the French look at you with disdain because of what you're wearing?" I asked her. "The first day I went on the street not looking like a magazine cover, I was practically pelted with tomatoes and soggy lettuce."

She frowned. "Why would I care what people think about what I wear?"

And there you have it.

Alan slipped his arm over her shoulder as we walked to the Métro. Nicole had never been very comfortable with being touched. She was not a hugger and made sure that her hand-shakes were firm but very brief. Alan had always been the exception. And Louis?

"Is Louis still coming tomorrow?" I asked her.

"He should be here by early evening."

"And he'll be staying with you and Dad?"

She looked around her father to give me a look. "Yes. Did you think he was getting a hotel?"

"Well, no, I guess," I said. "It's just, well, let's face it, Nic, the idea of you, well . . ."

"Being an independent sexual adult?"

I saw Alan tighten his grip around her shoulders for just a moment. "Honey," he said, "the last time you talked about a boy you were fifteen, and you said he smelled gross. Please try to cut us a little slack here, okay?"

We descended into the Métro station and glided off to Versailles without, mercifully, mentioning independent sexual adults again.

Versailles is not just the palace, it's a whole town, ancient and charming—of course—with baskets of spring flowers everywhere. We followed the crowd through the cobbled streets to the palace that Louis, the Sun King, had built for himself and his court.

I stopped at least four times to just stare as we walked through the gate. The bricked courtyard seemed to stretch for miles leading up to the palace itself, pale and shining, its roofline sparkling gold in the sun. There were swarms of people and a very long line.

Nicole looked around. "I'm not waiting in line. And I'm not paying to see the palace. The gardens are free, and I'm much more interested in them. You two go through, and I'll meet you out by the first fountain. Text me when you're done."

"I'll pay for your ticket," Alan offered.

She shook her head. "No, thanks. Really. See you later."

Very smooth, Nicole. Very smooth.

Alan and I dutifully got in line and began to wait. There was a couple behind us, American, younger, and the woman did not stop talking for the entire inch-by-inch progression across the cobbled yard. Alan and I exchanged occasional glances as she complained about their hotel: the rough sheets, the funny smell in the closet, the tiny bathroom, the water pressure, the water temperature . . . it took everything I had not to turn around and scream, just *move!*

And then . . .

"Honey, look, those people just cut in line."

I had seen them: two women who casually walked up, past us, past the next dozen or so people in line, and then just sort of stopped.

"Dave," she said louder. "Did you *see?*"

Stupid question. He saw. Unless he was blind, of course. But having glanced back at them a few times, I knew that wasn't the case.

"They cut in front of us," she said, even louder. "Those two women there."

The two women there were having a lively conversation, and if they heard the woman behind me, they gave no sign. I glanced up at Alan. "Lee told me this happens all the time," I said in a low voice.

He bent down to speak in my ear. "Nic said the same thing to me. I look really American, don't I?"

He was dressed in navy trousers, a pale pink button-down shirt, and scuffed loafers. He might as well have been wearing a Yankees baseball cap. I nodded. He moved around to my other side, farther away from the couple.

"Do you think people will think I'm with *them*?" he whispered.

I looped my arm through his and pulled him tight to my side. "They'll think you're with me, the chic Frenchwoman with fabulous hair and great ankles," I whispered.

"Thank God," he muttered.

"Did you all *see*?" the woman continued.

Obviously. We were all *there*.

"Doesn't anyone else care?"

Obviously *not*. Can you hear anyone else complaining?

"What is wrong with you people?" she said, her voice now in the range that could easily shatter glass.

I kept my head down and tried to keep from laughing.

"Dave, go tell them to go back to the end of the line."

My head shot up. This I had to see. And I wasn't the only one. All eyes went from looking at the grandeur of Versailles to watching to see what this poor, henpecked American man was going to do next.

He mumbled something in her ear. I wasn't close enough to hear, but could see he was beet red.

His wife—girlfriend? Best friend? Casual travel buddy? Person to whom he was somehow manacled as a form of punishment on a par with the Third Circle of Hell?—clearly wasn't happy about whatever he said, because she turned to him with a look of disgust. And then her eyes widened. She had become aware of Alan.

"Hey, are you American?"

Alan, to his credit, looked around, obviously trying to find who, exactly, she was speaking to.

"No, you." She reached out and tugged on his jacket. "Are you American?"

I closed my eyes. What next? Oh, Alan, what on earth were you going to say to this woman?

Whatever it was, he said it in Hungarian. Not that I recognized it as Hungarian, but I did know that Hungarian was the only foreign language Alan spoke. For some obscure reason, he had studied it for years and always prided himself on speaking without, he insisted, an obvious accent.

The woman looked taken aback. Obviously this was not what she was expecting. She shifted her steady and very hostile gaze to me, but I just shrugged, trying to look as non-American as possible.

The line moved, eyes went back to the front, and I spent the next five minutes with my shoulders shaking in silent hysterical laughter. Alan, to his credit, stood directly behind me, his hands resting on my shoulders, shielding me completely from the woman who had, at last, stopped talking.

We eventually reached the front of the line, showed our tickets, and went in. I immediately pulled Alan to one side and watched the American couple walk past us. I finally exploded into audible giggles.

"The Ugly American?" Alan suggested.

I had no words. I didn't need any. Alan bent his head down to mine, our foreheads touching as we laughed out loud together. Then we broke apart and turned, finally, into the Palace of Versailles. His arm slid across my shoulders and I leaned into him, slipping into a feeling as warm and comforting as a favorite old sweater.

Chapter 6

A discussion of love, regrets,
vineyards ... and I find my muse

Whoever said it was good to be king wasn't fooling around.

It took us almost two hours to walk through the palace, and it was magnificent. The gold, the opulence, the attention to detail, all built while peasants froze to death, women on the streets of Paris sold themselves for food, and children died from drinking filthy water.

I would have been happy just to ooh and ahh, but Nicole got her social conscience from her father, and Alan's constant flow of Depressing History 101 followed me though the palace and into the restaurant, where we purchased incredibly overpriced sandwiches and bottles of water for lunch with Nicole.

"Can you stop now?" I pleaded. "Yes, life here was terrible for everyone who wasn't rich. The nobles were awful people. They were immoral and had no empathy. I get it. But we're going into the gardens now. Can't I just look at all the pretty flowers and think happy thoughts?"

We were looking down toward the gardens, and it was a little overwhelming. The place was beautiful, but huge. There were vast patches of green and miles of pathways. I fixed my eye on the most obvious marker, the large fountain, and texted Nicole that we were ready to meet her.

The steps leading down to the fountain were wide and stretched for what seemed like acres in front of us. Sitting on them seemed almost sacrilegious, but if it was good enough for the French, then it was good enough for me. I sat on the cool stone and watched the ebb and flow of people down and away into the gardens, perfectly happy.

"What," Alan asked, "is different about her?"

"Nicole?" I thought. Yes, she was different. She seemed . . . softer. Less angry. Less determined to find fault. She had always been a different kind of child, rebellious in an odd sort of way. She despised organized religion, big government, and capitalism. She spoke out, eloquently, and was not afraid to act out as well. Before leaving for France, she'd been arrested three separate times, protesting against local ordinances that she felt were unfair to the homeless population. She was right, and one of those ordinances had been overturned.

But now . . . maybe there was less to be angry about in France, where every citizen was entitled to free health care, free education, and a living wage?

"She's more relaxed," I finally said.

Alan made a face. "It's more than that."

"She's happy," I said, surprising myself. Yes, that was it. She was happier than I'd ever seen her.

"That would suggest," Alan said dryly, "that she's been *un-happy* for most of her life."

"Well, let's face it, she didn't smile until she was two."

"Ah yes. The first pony ride."

"Or maybe," I said, "she's in love." I glanced at him. "Love changes people."

"Yes, I know," Alan said. "And maybe that's it. But that means that everything could be taken from her at a moment's notice. I'd like to think that there's more to it than just Louis. That maybe she'd be happy here without him."

We sat again in silence—the lovely, companionable kind of silence that happens between two people who are comfortable enough with each other to simply sit together and *be*—until Nicole tapped me on the shoulder. The three of us walked down the paths and through the groves before stopping in the Colonnade Grove to eat our lunch. Nicole, who had been perfectly happy regaling us with all her tales of the Sun King and his court, suddenly changed tracks.

"You know, Mom, Daddy has been thinking about Vermont. You know, for his retirement."

I looked at her, then at Alan. "And . . . ?"

She shrugged. "Just curious. How do you feel about Vermont?"

"I would never," I said slowly and very deliberately, "move someplace where the winters are *colder* than New Jersey. If anything, I'd go south."

Alan looked thoughtful. "You're right about those winters. I was almost thinking south too."

"Not Florida," I said.

He shook his head. "No, absolutely not Florida."

"But there's got to be an ocean. You know there's got to be an ocean there somewhere," I said.

"You liked Savannah," Nicole said. "We went there for the book festival, remember?"

"Yes, I do remember. Savannah was a great city. Small, but beautiful. A fun food town, lots of history, and all those lovely old houses." I sighed. "And Tybee Island is right there. Maybe Savannah, when the time comes."

"And Daddy, it's got a very active art scene. I bet you could find all sorts of classes to take."

Alan folded up the remains of his lunch and stuffed it all back into the paper bag it had been wrapped in. He turned to her, very calm. "Nic, why do you think your mother and I would be living in the same city?"

I gave Nicole a look. Obviously she hadn't shared with her father her idea that he and I would still have our happily ever after.

She didn't miss a beat. "Isn't it obvious? The two of you being together? Why, I bet you could pick up right where you left off and be perfectly happy."

Alan, to his credit, did not react at all the way I did. He took a long swallow from his water bottle, all the time nodding his head.

"The place where your mother and I left off," he said at last, "involved a lot of screaming and, I believe, crying. And there was flying cookware, if I remember correctly."

I nodded. "Our very last fight," I said fondly. "Cookware *and* dishware. Many things were broken."

"All over the kitchen floor," Alan agreed. "We could no longer live together, and we had very good reasons for that."

"What reasons?" Nicole asked.

Alan looked at me, and I could see him thinking back. "I wanted to be married to a woman who would be a dean's wife. Your mother wanted to be a writer and had no interest in academics. We had very different ideas about what our life together should look like, and at the time, neither of us would compromise."

"Exactly," I said. "There were very valid reasons for us to divorce."

"Yes, I can see that they were. Very valid," she said. "But you've both outgrown the reasons you split apart. And maybe what's left are the reasons you were together in the first place." She gathered her lunch scraps, smiling brightly. "That's what I'm thinking. I'm getting tired, but if you two want to stay a bit longer, you can probably find your way back just fine."

I shook my head. "No, I have to get back. I worry about Jules."

Alan raised one eyebrow. "Jules?"

"He's the dog," I explained.

"Jules," Nicole said dryly, "strikes me as the kind of dog who could survive the zombie apocalypse without missing a beat."

"True. But I am supposed to be taking care of him. That was the deal."

She stood. "I need the restroom. I'll see you at the entrance."

I watched her walk off, then looked at Alan, who was watching me. "What?" I asked.

"She really thinks that? About us?"

I sighed. "Yes, I think she does. Something about the two of us growing old together. She doesn't seem to understand that we are two very different people now, and what we want and need are also very different."

His eyes softened. "You're right. And we don't always get what—or whom—we want."

He walked off after Nicole toward the Fountain of Apollo, leaving me standing in the warm French sunshine, feeling strangely sad.

I declined Alan's invitation to dinner and went straight back to the apartment. If Jules was suffering from any deprivation, he certainly didn't show it. After his walk, I ate cold leftover fish, bread, and lots of cheese, as well as all the remaining strawberries.

Then I wrote. Bella and Lance had separated, looking for Twan. Henri Dumond, from Doctors Without Borders, had new and pressing reasons for Bella to leave with him. Poor Henri. He was in love with her but didn't stand a chance against Lance. About two hours later, I stood up, did twenty jumping jacks, went to the bathroom, ate more bread, and wrote some more. I finally crawled into bed with my head buzzing.

In the morning I showered so quickly I barely got my hair wet. As I wrote, my phone made noises, but I ignored them. I was finally jolted out of Delania by the sound of Jules barking.

Barking? Who on earth would he be barking at?

It was Solange, who swept into the living room. She was beautifully dressed in sleek black slacks, a pearl-gray silk blouse, and a scarf around her neck. She dropped her black tote bag to the floor and crossed over to me, obvious concern on her face. "You look terrible."

"Oh, Solange, no, I'm alright. I'm working."

Her expression went from concern to . . . what? "Working? Where? Have you been cleaning out someone's attic?"

"These are my writing clothes," I said.

Her brows drew together. "You didn't go out of the flat looking like that, did you?"

I sighed. "Only once. Where's Lee?"

"He had to stay to meet with the lawyer. Problems. I could not wait to get away. Have you eaten?"

I shook my head. "No, but I did buy food."

"Good. I will fix something. Do you need to continue your work?"

Yes, I did. I needed to figure out how to transition from Bella agonizing over a sweating, crying child to a hardened ex-Navy SEAL trying to take out a cadre of bandits while armed with only a handgun and nerves of steel.

I typed and typed some more and finally stopped because I'd written the same scene four different times and was still not happy. I needed to step away and focus on something else for a bit. There was also the enticing smell of sautéed onions and herbs coming from the kitchen. I stood and stretched, and Solange hurried in.

"I am making crêpes," she said. "Would that be all right?"

I had no idea what crêpes would involve, but if it tasted half as good as it smelled, I'd be perfectly happy. I touched my toes and did a few lunges, then closed my eyes and took some deep, cleansing breaths.

When I opened my eyes, the table was set, and Solange was hovering.

I sat and waved her closer. "Sit with me. I need a human voice. What was the problem at the vineyard?"

She sat across from me and folded her hands. "Something about the taxes, I think, and Lee is preparing for the end of the world. The vineyards have been in his family for generations. It will take more than his benign neglect to bring them crashing down, but . . ." She fluttered a hand. "He enjoys the drama."

The crêpe was wrapped around onions, leeks, and potatoes, with fresh thyme and butter. "This is delicious. I hope cooking for me isn't too much trouble."

"Nonsense. First of all, it is my job. And it is good to have someone to look after." She cleared her throat. "I understand Max is here? I didn't see his suitcase in his room."

"His room?"

She shrugged. "It is actually a closet behind the kitchen. It was his room as a child, and he insists on keeping it exactly as it was. But . . . it seems empty?"

I nodded. "Yes, he was here, but he went to Marseille. Personal business, he said."

She registered her disgust with lifted eyebrows and a snort. "One of his ex-wives is in Marseille. I can only imagine what kind of business he has in mind." She sniffed. "But he was here?"

I looked from one end of the smooth dining table to the other and for just a moment thought about taking Max's advice and fabricating a bit of romance. I felt my cheeks grow hot as I pictured my fingers slowly undoing the buttons of his shirt, my hands slipping under the waistband of his jeans. . . .

"Yes, he was here. He's very charming, your son. And such a gentleman."

She narrowed her eyes. "You've had your hair cut," she said slowly. "I imagine Max called on Nathalie?"

I was trying very hard to take small bites of the crêpe, but I still had to pause to chew and swallow. "Yes. She was lovely." I waggled my hand at her. The hand without the fork. "I even got a manicure."

She sat back and folded her arms across her chest. "My son is a gentleman, true, but most often he does things for his own pleasure."

Well, now, that was interesting. Did Max suggest a makeover so that he wouldn't have to look at a decidedly unchic guest? "He and my daughter got along very well," I said.

"Yes, Lee mentioned that you would be seeing your daughter. She is a student, he said?"

I finally pushed the plate away, resisting the urge to lick the remnants off its edge. "Yes, she's on break. She was visiting here with her father."

Solange sat up. "Her father. Your ex-husband?"

I nodded. "Alan."

She pursed her lips. "And you are friendly with this ex-husband?"

"Yes, as a matter of fact."

She sighed. I didn't imagine that went along with whatever matchmaking scheme she had concocted. She stood and took my plate. "I have errands. Should I get something for dinner?"

I shook my head. "No, thank you. I'm meeting Nicole. What about Lee and Martin?"

She shrugged. "They should be here tomorrow."

She turned and left.

I checked the series of texts on my phone.

> A: You look very sexy with that new hair. Is it getting you anywhere with Alan?
>
> C: Forget Alan. Any charming Frenchman hovering?
>
> A: Frenchmen don't hover. You're right gray nails are pretty. How is Nicole?
>
> M: Nic fine. No hovering anybody. IM WORKING

I stood and found myself looking back down at the dining room table.

Charming Frenchmen . . . and then, a fleeting thought about Max . . .

I went back to the laptop and began the fifth version of that oh-so-tricky scene, and the words flowed like warm honey.

I was beginning to wonder if I could write without Max.

I normally wasn't a superstitious person, but when it came to my writing, all bets were off. Most books just happen, but some require something extra—that whole muse thing again. When I started *Time Left for Love,* which won me my very first Romance of the Year award, I had been stuck for weeks until I accidentally wore my favorite sweater inside out and sprinted through almost eight thousand perfect words. I wore that sweater inside out every day until I finished. I ate two Mallomars a day while writing *A Duke Soon Departed*. And I didn't wear shoes for almost three months during *A Day Like No Other*. When I found something that worked, I stuck by it religiously. And it seemed that here in Paris, Max was my something.

Maybe it was Paris itself. Maybe it was the food. Maybe it was the beauty of the place, the gracious buildings, or the flowers in the street. Maybe it was the way the night sky breathed darkness like a lover's kiss. But I had it in my head that it was Max.

It was late afternoon when Nicole texted to tell me that Louis had arrived and asked if we could meet for a dinner. I immediately texted back a yes and said I'd meet her wherever she chose.

I braved the Métro alone. It was a fairly straight shot with only one transfer, and Nic had sent very detailed instructions that should have been insulting to an adult woman with an advanced degree but for me were as comforting as warm milk. I climbed out of the station into Montmartre. I was glad I'd given myself extra time, because everywhere I looked there was something I wanted to look at even longer. I finally forced my eyes forward and made it to the café just a few minutes late.

They were sitting outside at a table: Nicole, Louis, and Alan. Both men stood as I approached, and Alan leaned over to give me a kiss on the cheek. He held the chair as I sat down, and I felt his hand along my back.

I think I was waiting for some response to his touch: a warm rush of blood to my skin, a tingle in my belly.

And it was there. Very faint, but not enough for me to think, yes, maybe. . . .

I looked at my daughter. "Introduce us?"

Her face softened and suddenly got a look I'd never seen before. Not happy, exactly. And not . . . proud. Although, looking at Louis, if he'd been my boyfriend, I'd have stood on the nearest chair and shouted at the crowd, hey, look who's *mine*.

Louis was one of the most beautiful men I'd ever seen. His eyes were large and deep green, his dark hair was thick and straight, his face a master class in perfect proportion. His teeth were white and even, and his smile lit up the entire café.

He took my hand and kissed it. "A real pleasure," he said with barely an accent. "Nicole has told me so much about you." He then sat down, and our eyes were level.

My heart stopped, just for a second. "Oh," I managed. I swallowed hard and looked back at Nicole, who suddenly smiled, her eyes dancing. I cleared my throat. "Nicole says you're a student?"

"Philosophy."

Sigh. Because there are so many job opportunities for philosophers in France. But he was so handsome, the thought didn't stay in my head long enough to make any real impression. Who cared if he'd be unemployed his entire life? That only meant more time to stay at home, where Nicole could spend all day just looking at him.

"We ordered a bit of something, but not dinner," Nic said.

"Yes, well, sorry I'm late. The Métro was on time, and as usual your directions were perfect, but there was just so much to see."

Louis flashed a killer smile. "Lovely women should never apologize for being late," he said. "And your excuse is perfectly valid. This is one of my favorite neighborhoods."

So far every neighborhood I'd seen in Paris was in contention for my favorite. Montmartre had a decidedly boho feel: the buildings were small, colorful, with vines and ivy growing around doorways and flowers spilling from window boxes.

"In fact," Alan said, "I'm dying to go up to Sacré-Cœur."

"But not on the weekend," Nicole said. "Too many tourists. And on Monday, things are closed." She looked at the menu, all innocence. "Louis and I will be back in Rennes by then, so the two of you will have to go it alone."

I met Alan's eyes across the tiny table, and he grinned.

Louis seemed unaware of the game being played out in front of him. "May I recommend the beefsteak? Nicole tells me the meat here is quite unlike anything you can eat in the States."

"I'm pretty sure everything here is unlike what I can eat in the States," I countered. "Beefsteak it is."

The waiter appeared with a plate that held four tiny tartlets: red sliced tomatoes on a thin crust, sprinkled with some sort of cheese, drizzled with oil, and dusted with green bits. I sighed with pure happiness.

"Red wine for me," I told him, and he bowed away. I looked around. "I'll have to navigate my way home alone, and the wine probably won't help my powers of concentration, but I don't care."

Alan leaned back and stretched out his long legs. "That's rather unlike you. Usually you'd care about something like that very much."

I nodded. "You're right. But there's something about Paris that is making me feel a bit . . . reckless. Adventurous. May I say . . . bold?"

Louis reached over, took a tartlet, and held it to his nose, breathing in deeply. "Paris does things like that to people. There's something in the air here that is quite out of the ordinary." He smiled at me and took a bite. "You'll get used to it."

I smiled back. I sure hoped so.

Louis was not just beautiful. He was charming and very smart and had a dry sense of humor. We spent almost two hours sitting at our table, eating and drinking excellent wine. By the end of the meal I was ready to sign adoption papers. If Nicole ever decided she didn't want him anymore, I wanted to be sure that *I* could at least keep him in my life.

The beefsteak, incidentally, was so remarkable I almost wept when I finished the last bite.

Alan was attentive. No, more than attentive; he was trying

very hard to please. Tonight he was as close to the awkward-but-earnest suitor of our courtship as he had been in thirty years.

Could it be that Nicole's crazy idea had taken root?

I could see Nicole watching him. She had noticed it too, and whenever I felt her eyes on me, I knew she was looking for my reaction.

I had none. I glanced over at Alan. I'd been waiting all evening for . . . something. His little exchange with that horrible woman at Versailles had me thinking for a moment that yes, here it was, we were back. And then what he had said later in the Colonnade made me think that he had been thinking about me. And tonight, the subtle flattery, the quiet, knowing looks.

Yes, I had a warm and fuzzy feeling about Alan. And it seemed to be getting stronger. But I didn't want to spend the rest of my life with warm and fuzzy. Could the two of us, in fact, find the something that had drawn us together all those years ago and fan that spark into something more?

This was Paris. If it was going to happen at all, we were in the right place.

I finally stood to say goodbye.

"Will we see you tomorrow?" Nicole asked. "We're playing tourists. We could take one of the boats up and down the Seine."

I smiled. "Oh, that sounds lovely. Lee will be back tomorrow, and I'm sure we will have a lot to discuss." I leaned toward Louis. "A good agent is always your first defense against a crappy book. I trust Lee more than my editor when it comes to sheer honesty. But I will let you know. I'd love to see you both again before you go back to Rennes."

I gave Alan my cheek for a kiss. "How long will you be staying?" I asked him.

He made a face. "Heather booked the Airbnb for two weeks, so I guess I'll be on my own for the rest of my stay."

"Nonsense," Nicole said. "Mom is right here."

"Working," I said. "But, we'll talk tomorrow." I let Louis kiss both my cheeks. "It's been a real pleasure meeting you," I told him. "I can see that Nicole is very happy. You're a very good influence, I think."

"I hope so," he said. "The best of luck to you, Maggie. I hope your book is a huge success and that you decide to find a place in the countryside here to write your next book."

"If I write my next book in France, it will be in this city," I told him. "You're right. The air here is quite out of the ordinary. I'll be back, I'm sure."

I walked back to the Métro and enjoyed the ride back to the flat, thinking about Nicole and Louis, Lance and Bella, and Alan.

And about second chances and how infrequently they actually occur in a person's life.

I woke up early. Was it Sunday already? I sat in the sunlight and sent a group text.

> M: Ladies—met Nics beau and he's perfect. Alan
> being charming and sweet. Writing up a storm
> and loving everything about this city. Can we all

come here together and just walk and talk and
EAT???

I didn't even bother with coffee. I sat at the keyboard and
wrote, my fingers moving so quickly that they almost kept up
with my brain. I was dimly aware of a cup of café crème ap-
pearing at my elbow and I drank it greedily, holding the cup in
one hand while my other hand moved the mouse as I scrolled
and reread what I'd just written.

Poor Henri. Stepped on one of those pesky land mines.
Bella is upset and is in obvious need of emotional healing.
How lucky that Lance found the one un-bombed-out hotel in
all of Delania. . . .

God, this chapter was *so* good.

Toast magically appeared, then more café crème, and when
I finally pushed myself away from the keyboard, my fingers
were stiff, my back ached, and my eyelids felt heavy and gritty.
I sat on the couch, leaning back against the soft cushions, and
brought my feet up for just a second. . . .

"Well?" Lee demanded. "Have you been writing?"

I opened my eyes. The room was bright, and I squinted at
Lee. "What time is it?"

"After noon. Is this what you've been doing with your time?
Sleeping the day away?"

Solange came in and swatted his arm with her hand. She
was dressed quite simply in tan slacks and a white button-down
shirt, her narrow feet in soft-looking flats. "Lee, she was up
at dawn and wrote all morning. Stop being an ogre. She was

working." She looked at me, concerned. "You must be hungry. There's soup."

I nodded gratefully and struggled to sit up. "Did you just get here? How were the vineyards?"

"In a financial mess. I know nothing about wine, tariffs, grapes, France . . . I should have sold the vineyard years ago."

Martin was carrying luggage down the hall but stopped long enough to shake his head and cluck, quite like a disgruntled chicken. "There is nothing wrong with the vineyards, Lee. Stop being so dramatic. How are you, Mags?"

"Writing."

Lee clapped his hands together. "Thank God."

I waved at my laptop. "Go read. Leave me in peace."

Lee took my laptop, sat, and opened it. "Password?"

"My agent is a slave driver."

"Mags . . ."

"Lotus-eater. No caps."

Lee shot me a look, hit a few keys, and started to read.

I looked at my phone. Cheri and Alison had gotten my text.

A: So happy for Nic. Send pic of happy couple. Also more of the city

C: Told you about the food. I should have put money on it. No mention of sexy Frenchmen and I bet they're everywhere What gives?

M: OK yes here are so many sexy Frenchmen around I have enough ammunition for ten books. Is my condo still standing?

C: Yes Lights on at night so I guess Greg still around.
Alan being sweet? Sounds good!
M: Greg better be looking for a new place. Alan is
retiring. Gotta go and write. Kisses
A: Don't just write ITS PARIS

Martin returned, sat beside me, took my hand, and kissed it. "How have you been?" he asked. "I like your hair, by the way. What made you cut it?"

"Max talked me into it," I said. "He also made me get a manicure, new underwear, and dresses. He seemed to think I wasn't quite ready for Paris. Or to see my ex-husband after three years."

Martin looked delighted. "Alan is here?"

"Yes. He retired, and it seems that the woman he'd become involved with planned this trip for the two of them. Then they broke up, so he came over alone."

"How interesting." Martin grinned. "And Nicole?"

"She's in love with a beautiful young man named Louis who is, it goes without saying, brilliant. They've been living together since the fall, something she completely neglected to mention to me or her father. She seems very happy. Oh, and she thinks that Alan and I should reconcile our differences and spend our golden years together."

Solange brought me a tray loaded with bread, a glass of water with a sliver of lemon floating on top, and a bowl of soup that was steaming and brimming with potatoes and carrots. I took a tentative spoonful.

"Mags?" Lee called from his chair. "You're bringing back the annoying child?"

"Lee, you think any character of mine that's a child is annoying," I said. "Twan is adorable. Readers loved him. I have the emails." I took another spoonful, and Solange settled in a corner chair, looking attentive.

I broke off a bit of bread, dipped it in the soup, and tasted. I sighed happily. I looked at Martin. "Solange has been wonderful."

He nodded. "She always is."

Lee yelped. "Sex in a *tree*? Really?"

"Very slow and careful sex in a tree," I corrected him. As I said that, I suddenly thought of Max and how he and I would manage that. Not the tree part, but slow and careful . . .

"The buildup is spectacular," he said, looking at me over the tops of his glasses. "This trip has been a real inspiration, I see."

Martin nudged me again. "This is all very interesting about Alan, but you have just managed to get Greg to move out. This could be a very fragile time for you, Maggie. You should be careful."

"And who is Greg?" Solange asked.

The soup was cooling, and I could manage bigger spoonfuls. "He's just like Lance, but without the humor. And he's shorter."

Solange raised an eyebrow. "There really are men like that? And you were living with him?" She said something in French I was glad I did not understand because Martin rolled his eyes.

"Solange, men like Greg are very charismatic and attractive," he said.

She sniffed. "I'm sure. He was also probably like a bull, you know?" She made a gesture that needed no interpretation. "But men like that, they don't understand women. I don't even think they *like* women. They are perfect in books, yes? Every woman has that fantasy. But in the real world, you are much better off alone."

"She doesn't have to be alone," Martin said. "I mean, well . . ." He gave me a look. "How do you feel about the idea of getting back with Alan? I never met him, but you have always spoken well of him. Fondly."

"The thought had always been in the back of my head. I mean, how perfect would it be to end up back with my first great love? Seeing him here, being with him, it's so . . . familiar. I remember so much of the good times we had together. But I also want that old fire back."

Martin sighed. "Passion can be somewhat overrated," he said.

Solange made another noise, this time of total disgust. "*Non.* You are wrong. Passion is everything. I speak not of the body, although that is marvelous, but that can be deceiving. This Greg person had that kind of passion, but to what end? I am speaking of the fire in the soul. Two people can burn together without ever touching each other. It is the best thing. It is the only thing." She looked at me intently. "Wait for that, Maggie Bliss. Find a man who makes you think of music and wine and long summer nights. Find someone you can feel . . ." She made a fist and held it in the center of her chest. "Here. You should feel him, right here."

"What if I don't find him?" I asked in a whisper. I thought

about Alan and the comfort I felt with him. Would that really be enough?

"Then live alone. But find a way to keep your fire alive, yes? I have, for years. It was that or settle. And I would never settle."

"You're brave," I said.

She shook her head. "No, Maggie. Not brave. But I know myself, and that gives me the courage to live as I do. Courage and bravery are not the same. But you know that already, *non*? I know you, your books, the women you create. They always live happily ever after. But on their terms. Because courage."

Martin reached around my shoulder and hugged me close. "This is a wise woman here, Maggie. Listen. She's right. Don't settle."

"Maggie?" Lee called from the other side of the room.

We all looked over.

He pulled off his glasses. "I have to tell you, this writing . . . did meeting Alan again have anything to do with this?"

"Lee," Martin snapped. "Really?"

Lee spread his hands out, helplessly. "This is *so* good. . . ."

"Lee," Martin said again, his voice louder.

"She came here to find her muse," Lee said. "And this is some of the best work I've read in ages. It's entirely possible that Alan has something to do with this."

"It's also entirely possible that Paris has worked its magic," Solange countered. "It is entirely possible that meeting Max . . ."

Lee sat up sharply. "Solange, don't start. Your son has repeatedly asked you to not interfere with his love life. And Maggie certainly does not need your help."

She shrugged, the picture of innocence. "Don't be absurd. I would not interfere in Max's life," she said. "And Maggie is perfectly capable of looking after her own interests. But they were here, together . . . who knows?"

"Well, I'm going to see Alan this afternoon," I said. "We're taking a boat ride on the Seine with Nic and her boyfriend—that is, if you think I've earned a break?"

"Of course you have," Solange said. "Lee, tell her. And then bring them back here. I would love to meet your daughter. And her beautiful young man. Lee will cook."

"Lee? But Solange—"

She waved a hand. "You did not know this about him? He is a genius, but lazy. When he is here he leaves everything to me, but I will put him to work."

I looked over at Lee. "Really?"

He tried to look modest. "My coq au vin will make you cry."

Solange stood and began gathering plates. "You must bring them. Max will be back and we can have a great feast, yes?"

Martin chuckled. "It will do him good, Mags, to do a bit of actual work."

Solange nodded. "Yes. So we are agreed?"

I took a breath. "I'll ask Nicole. She's sometimes not so good with strangers."

Solange looked at me for a moment, then nodded. "I understand. But Alan?"

I nodded. "Yes. Thank you."

"*Finally* I'll get to meet Alan?" Lee said. "Excellent. I want to see what your inspiration looks like."

I shook my head. "I don't think it looks like Alan. Comfortable and familiar don't inspire having sex in a tree. It may very *well* have been Max."

I really hadn't meant to say that. And I certainly didn't mean it the way it sounded. I glanced around. Solange looked rather smug. Lee and Martin slightly stunned.

"Oh?" Lee said slowly.

I flipped at my hair. "He got me to cut my hair. And highlights. Not to mention the clothes . . . he was Higgins to my Eliza Doolittle. That's inspiring, right?"

They all nodded. Solange murmured something in French and Lee threw her a dirty look. No one looked at me.

But I was suddenly struck.

Max. It *was* Max. All the ideas bouncing around my head, the excitement, the energy at the keyboard.

It was Max.

I had found my muse in Paris after all, and he had the bluest eyes I'd ever seen.

Chapter 7

Wherein a dangerous rescue is made

Riding in a boat up and down the Seine was indeed something for tourists. The boat was full of them, speaking a variety of languages, taking endless pictures and videos, and trying to entertain bored toddlers. It was wonderful. We sat on the top level, drinking wine and basking in the spring sunlight. Louis was our guide, and he was funny and very knowledgeable.

We didn't get off at any of the stops, just sat and looked as Paris glided by, a slow and graceful passing of beautiful buildings that wore their centuries with pride.

And then we walked, beneath the Eiffel Tower, around the Champ de Mars, then back over the river toward my neighborhood. I had invited them all to dinner. Alan had said yes right away, but Nicole took her time and Louis let her. It was not until we were passing the Trocadéro that she agreed, yes, dinner with Max and Solange sounded perfect, and she'd love to finally meet Lee and Martin.

We were quite the party, arriving laden with wine and a few rustic fruit tarts for dessert. I could smell the cooking from the flat as we turned up the stairs and almost ran the rest of the way up.

Max had come back from Marseille and was looking rather tired, but he greeted Nicole like an old friend and slipped into the role of host even though, technically speaking, it was Lee's flat. Lee and Martin were charming and put Nicole at ease. The coq au vin brought tears to my eyes. Lee fluttered and smiled, brushing away the compliments until he finally just sat back and shrugged as we applauded at the end of the meal.

Louis lifted his wineglass. "To Maggie, for having a wonderful daughter and friends in Paris who can cook."

Alan cleared his throat. "I'd like to take part of the credit, please. At least for the wonderful-daughter part."

Louis nodded his head. "Yes, sir."

"You can also claim the friends who can cook," Lee said. "After all, I feel I know you like a brother for all Maggie has spoken of you through the years."

Alan caught my eye and gave a hint of a smile. "Maggie," he said, "has a way of collecting people. I think it's so she has plenty of characters for her books."

Max raised an eyebrow. "Ah, so there is a chance that perhaps I can be immortalized in popular fiction? Can I be one of your dashing heroes?"

Solange made a noise and waved her hand. "I'm sorry, but I believe you are a bit old to be a romantic hero. At least in any of Maggie's *books*." She shot me a look.

"*Maman,* you cut me to the quick," Max said, eyes twinkling. "Surely, there's room in one of those books for a dashing older gentleman who can ignite a bit of passion, *non?*"

Alan smacked his palm against the tabletop. "I'm with Max on this one. We older men don't get nearly enough credit, do we, Max? Lee and Martin, you can chime in here too."

Lee wore his most diplomatic expression. "I will say that men of a certain age have much more, shall we say, patience?"

"Exactly," Alan said. "We aren't in a hurry. We're willing to devote more time to the . . . how can I put this . . . pregame?" He shot me a look and I remembered the pregame of our marriage. *Hours* of pregame that would leave me panting and breathless.

"Pregame?" Lee laughed. "Yes, that's exactly right. We're very good at the pregame."

Martin broke off a bit of baguette and waved it in the air. "That's because men of a certain age need to fill in the extra time it takes to get things, ah, actually *moving*."

Nicole snorted. "Please, no more. I really don't want to hear this."

Max leaned toward her. "Nicole, if I were you, I'd pay attention. Don't you want to know that whatever you and Louis have right now, when you are both young and eager, will evolve into something just as satisfying?"

Nic's eyes were squeezed shut and she shook her head, rather vigorously. "No, I don't want to know any such thing."

Louis, on the other hand, was grinning. "I, for one, am very grateful for this entire conversation. Perhaps because this is something men think of more than women? Women never lose their drive, *non*? Age does not change their biology."

"Yes, it does," Solange and I said together. We looked at each other, then burst into giggles.

"I think Nicole is right," Solange managed as she stood up. "This is not suitable dinner conversation." She began to gather plates, and Nic sprang up to help her.

Solange pushed her firmly back into the chair. "You are a guest. I have three men right here to help me. Sit and finish your dessert."

Max, Lee, and Martin all rose and gathered dishes and silverware, and from the laughter coming from the kitchen, I guessed that the conversation had continued.

Nicole poked her finger at the last of the crumbs on her plate. "What do you think, Mom? Aside from the biology part, I mean. Do you think a person becomes too old for love?"

I glanced at Alan, who was watching me, a serious expression in his eyes. "No, I don't think you're *ever* too old," I said. "But I do think that *how* you love changes. The things you look for when you're young are not the same ones you want when you're older. Not in your life, or in the person you want to share it with."

"And what," Alan asked quietly, "are you looking for in your life now, Maggie?"

To be swept off my feet, I thought.

No.

To be appreciated and admired for who I was and what I did.

No.

To feel safe. To be reckless. To be cared for. To go on an adventure.

"I have no idea," I said softly, and as I turned my head, there was Max, standing quietly, a faint smile on his lips.

Every Delania book has a big action sequence. After all, when you're in a war-torn country trying to do good things, action happens. In the past, it took an entire chapter to get Bella and Lance out of whatever situation I'd written them into. It would take me at least a week to plan out and execute the chapter, and by the end I'd have cleared off my dining room table and lined up various objects, moving them around, seeing if what I had in my head could possibly work in a real world, much the same way Churchill did in his war room while planning out D-Day.

Right now, Bella and Lance were in trouble. They had left Twan in the tiny village of Sheon in the care of a local woman while they tried to buy the papers needed to get the child out of Delania. There was a man who, for the right price, could get anything. While they were gone, Sheon had been raided, and when they returned, buildings were burning, and the high, shrill keening of the women filled the damp, fetid air. They learned that Twan was alive but was being held in the local school, along with other women and children. The papers were only good for seventy-two hours, and they needed to get Twan out and away as soon as possible. But how? There were only the two of them, and the village was swarming with rebels. . . .

I had risen before the sun and written so long into the morning that when I finally stood to shake out my hands and stretch my legs, the dining table was occupied and the remains of what looked to be a delicious breakfast lay scattered across empty plates.

"I wanted to shake you," Solange said, immediately standing as I came over, "but Lee is an unforgivable beast and insisted I leave you alone. I will get coffee. Fruit? Bread? What . . . ?"

"That sounds perfect," I said. "And Lee was right. If I wrote around you all eating for this long, merely shaking me would have done no good."

I sat next to Martin and leaned my head against his shoulder. "Would you feed me a strawberry?"

He plucked one from the bowl and brought it to my mouth. It tasted like the promise of summer.

"Good morning?" Max asked.

I shook my head. "Not really. I've written myself into a corner and I don't know how to get out. How's yours going?"

"Well, I have decided to pass on the opening of this conference, so I'm already counting the day as a win." He shrugged. "Too much shaking of hands and boring introductions to people I already know."

Solange came up behind him, a steaming mug in one hand. She swatted her son's head with the other hand. "He will lose his job, this one."

I looked at the time. Had I really written for four hours straight? I fixed my eyes on Lee. "You promised me Paris with two gay men on an unlimited budget," I reminded him.

Martin's brows shot up. "Unlimited? Well, in that case . . ."

"The Luxembourg Gardens," Max said. "She needs a place of calm and beauty."

"Yes," said Solange, setting the mug in front of me.

"There are plenty of gardens," Lee groused.

"Yes, but she is looking for her spark," Max said, his eyes bright. "And it was in the Luxembourg Gardens that Cosette met Marius."

"I believe," Lee said dryly, "that she has already found her spark."

"Maybe," I said after a sip of coffee. "But Cosette and Marius? I need to go there. And I do need serene and calm. Is it far?"

"Yes," Lee said.

"Not at all," Max said.

"And there is Paris in a nutshell," Martin said, "depending on whether you live here or are just visiting."

"It's supposed to rain tomorrow," Solange said. "You should walk. Enjoy the sun today, *non*?"

"We will Uber to get to the gardens," Lee announced. "And walk once we're there. Then, if we're still feeling energetic, we'll walk back. Max and Solange, you're invited to join us. But not Jules."

Solange pouted and stooped to pet the dog's head. Jules did not leave Solange's side when she was there, wrapping his stout little body around her ankles whenever she sat down. She sighed. "I would probably only end up carrying him."

"Or making *me* carry him," Max muttered.

She shot him a look. "I need to put something in the oven.

Pot-au-feu. Luckily, it needs to cook for hours, so I will be happy to join you. Perhaps Nicole and Louis can meet us there? They were so lovely last night."

"They're heading back to Rennes today," I said.

"Then perhaps Alan?" Lee suggested. "After all, if you're looking for your spark . . ."

"Alan," I said loudly, "is not sparking anything. Besides, didn't you tell me I'd have plenty of hot men to look at for inspiration?"

"Yes. Strolling through the gardens is a perfect way to see them," Martin said. "We will stop and get food. Fruit and cheese and bread and wine. A picnic. It's the perfect day for it. Invite Alan, Mags. You must. I liked him."

I texted Alan, who met us in the early afternoon, and we all walked slowly amid the quiet couples and laughing children, watching Parisians enjoying their day in the park.

I could have stayed for hours watching the rented sailboats glide around the central fountain, but Solange looped her arm through mine and led me away.

"There is so much more to see," she said. "Much like your Central Park, *non*?"

"*Non,*" Max said. "Central Park was designed to be a wild place, like a natural forest set down deliberately in the city. These gardens are much more formal. There is not much randomness here. It is a very different kind of park."

He was right. There was an ordered calm about the place, from the swept walkways to the carefully tended flower beds. Even the trees lined up, row upon row, their branches meeting high over concrete pathways.

We stopped frequently and ate, then moved along yet another path. As I walked past the former palace, I felt a sense of déjà vu suddenly come over me. I stopped and looked at the formal line of squared chestnut trees behind me, my eyes following their line off to my left. I glanced to the right. Beyond the neat cement walkway stood the gazebo, and farther beyond that were small kiosks.

"This is Sheon," I said.

Alan looked around. "This is *what*?"

"Sheon," I repeated. "The village in my book where Twan is being held."

It was uncanny. I had never been to Sheon, of course, since it didn't exist, but I had a carefully drawn map of it, as I had maps of all my important locations in Delania. Since I'd been battling with how to rescue Twan, I'd spent the morning looking at the map, trying to figure out a game plan.

"Mags," Lee said gently, "Sheon isn't a real place."

"I know it isn't," I snapped. "But . . ." I gestured with both hands in excitement. "See, this right here is the main street. These trees there are all the shops. They're burning, but they're still there. That gazebo is the school, and those little kiosks there? That's where they set up their headquarters."

"Who set up their headquarters?" Alan asked.

"Yeo-Te. He's in one, and the weapons and ammunition are in the other. It's all right here."

"Yeo-Te?" Max asked, understandably confused.

"Yeo-Te is a very bad man," Solange said, and went off on

a very brief but obviously intense rant in French. Max nodded thoughtfully throughout, then looked at me with a smile.

"A very bad man," he agreed.

"And?" Lee asked. "This is important . . . why?"

"I need to figure out how to rescue Twan. He's being held right there," I said slowly.

"In the gazebo?" Alan asked.

"No, silly. That's the *school*."

Solange's eyes brightened. "Oh, are you bringing him back? I love that little boy."

I raised my eyebrows at Lee. "See? Told you." I hurried forward. "Look," I said, pointing. "The duck pond? That's exactly where the lake is, where the villagers fish."

"You mean," Max asked slowly, "the Grand Bassin?"

"Yes. And you come straight up to the village center. I can show you the map."

Max held up both hands. "No, I believe you."

"Good. Now Twan is being held in the school. We need to get him out and away, but it's being guarded." I walked closer to the gazebo. "The best thing to do would be to create a diversion, and that's the problem. It's only Lance and Bella. Someone needs to create the distraction, someone needs to get into the school so that Twan can get out, and then someone needs to cover their escape in case they're seen. Otherwise they'll be shot by the guards."

"But if this diversion is big enough, it will draw all the guards *away* from the school?" Max asked.

"Yes, but . . . how?"

"The munitions shed is the obvious target," Martin said. "If it starts to burn, things will explode, all the soldiers will rush to help, even the guards."

"Excellent. But that will also be closely guarded," I said. "Getting close enough to do anything would get everyone shot."

"I don't suppose," Max said, "there are plastic explosives lying about?"

I shook my head. "Nope. They've got two AK-15s and a Swiss Army knife."

"Grenade launcher?" Martin asked.

"Nope again."

We stood and looked.

"What about that young man, the one who helped them with the stolen medical supplies? He was from Sheon, *non*?" Solange asked.

I made a face. "Sorry. I killed him off halfway through book two."

She closed her eyes briefly. "*C'est dommage*. He was very useful."

Alan had walked toward the Grand Bassin. "Can they get a car?"

I thought. "Maybe."

"Then your hero, what's his name, Lance?" He had an expression on his face I recognized. He was a math nerd at heart and loved figuring things out, and when he worked on a problem there was a certain set to his jaw, a narrowing of his eyes. I smiled. He was working this out for me, and I felt a little rush of excitement as I watched him put it all together.

"Lance can do that thing," Alan continued, "where he fixes the steering wheel of the stolen car, then jams the gas pedal, and the car crashes into the munitions shed all on its own, and he can make it to the school in time to make sure Bella and Twan get away."

Lee snorted. "Maggie isn't Clive Cussler. Her characters don't know how to do things like that."

"Lance does," Solange said calmly. "Remember what he did outside the airport in Greece in the beginning of book one?"

I eyed the distance between the far-off kiosk and the gazebo. "Lance could start the car back behind those trees. There's the dressmaker's shop," I said, thinking aloud. "Bella would be hidden across from the school, behind the burning huts. From there she could see the car make its way toward the munitions shed and make a run for the school. How long . . . how long would it take a car to get from back here to that kiosk?" I asked no one in particular, but I knew where the answer would come from.

"If the car was going, say, thirty miles an hour, with that distance . . ." Alan closed his eyes briefly. "About forty seconds." He opened his eyes and grinned. "Sometimes it helps being a numbers nerd."

"But can Lance run from there to here in that time? And can Bella get to the schoolhouse?" Lee asked.

"Well, we'll find out," I said. "Solange, stand in the middle of the gazebo. You'll be Twan. I'll be here, waiting for the car to hit the shed. . . . Lee and Martin, you'll be the guards. Stand here." I pushed them both into position on either side of the gazebo.

"Wait . . . we're acting this out?" Lee asked.

"Yes," I said.

"Do you do this with all your action scenes?" Lee narrowed his eyes at me. "Be honest, now. You're not just doing this to publicly humiliate me in front of all of Paris?"

"All of Paris isn't here," I told him. "And normally it takes me days to choreograph an action scene, and I end up using salt and pepper shakers all over the dining room table. But I don't have time for all that, and we're here . . . unless you want me to spend the next week trying to figure this out."

Lee shook his head and took up his position by the gazebo. "Fine."

"Good." I looked at Alan, then Max. "I need someone who can run."

Max grinned. "Does running marathons count?"

I grinned back. "Yes. Stand back there. Don't do anything yet, just give me a second to figure this out."

I looked up at Alan. "You have to give a signal for when the car begins its trip across the square. Max, you start running after the car. You'll need to shoot the guards who try to stop the car. But stay low."

He nodded very seriously. "Yes, *mon capitaine*."

"Then, Alan," I went on, "you need to tell us when the car hits and explodes."

"And what if it doesn't explode?" Lee asked. "How can you be sure—"

"Because Lance will set fire to a bale of hay just before he ties down the gas pedal. Now, you two"—I pointed to Lee and Martin—"will start running for the ammo shed as soon it hits."

"Surely," Solange said, "they would see the car and start running right away. After all, it is on fire."

"Good point. Alan, when the car is halfway to the shed, signal Lee. Then they can start running."

Martin raised an eyebrow. "I thought Max was doing all the running."

"Fine," I said. "Pretend to run. I'll start for the school, and Max, you can cut across here and make a sprint for the school as well."

Lee looked around. "Ah, Mags, there are people all around here."

"And you'll never see any of them again. Do you want me to get this scene right or what?"

Max choked back a laugh. "I'll get in position," he said, and moved off.

Alan stood in the middle of the wide pathway, his sleeves rolled up, legs planted slightly apart. From this distance, if I squinted just a bit, he could easily have been Lance himself: tall, with a determined set to his shoulders, hair lifting in the breeze. Solange sat on the steps of the gazebo, Lee and Martin on either side of her. I backed up until I was behind a tree.

"Max, you ready?" Alan called.

There was a pause. "Yes," Max called back.

"Okay." Alan had his phone in one hand, his other hand raised high. Then he dropped it. "Go."

I tried to count, but my heart was pounding so loud I couldn't hear myself. In my mind's eye, I saw it all: the dusty street, the burning buildings behind me, and there, off to the left, the kiosk—rather, the ammunitions shed—surrounded by four men in olive-green shirts, rifles on their shoulders.

"Now!" Alan yelled. The car would appear from behind the row of village shops, moving in a slow, deliberate line. Everyone would know where it was headed. Everyone would try to stop the car.

Lee and Martin left the gazebo, both of them trotting up the walkway. I started running to the school, watching carefully. By now, Lance . . .

Suddenly Max appeared. He was running . . . backward. Naturally, he'd be shooting at the guards around the ammo shed, who would be rushing to the car. Then Max turned around, lifted his hand into the universal symbol for pistol, and pointed at Lee and Martin. Lee grabbed his chest and actually fell to his knees. As I reached the gazebo, Martin threw his arms into the air with an anguished cry.

I bounded up the steps, grabbed Solange by the arm, and led her down the few steps and away from the inferno. Max was suddenly behind us.

"I assume you'll need cover fire?' he asked.

"What do you think?" Solange snapped.

I ran back to the trees where I'd started, Solange and Max behind me.

I stopped and turned. Lee was getting up slowly, laughing. Martin was helping him, and Alan joined them, gesturing excitedly.

"We did it!" I squealed, and I threw my arms around Max's neck. "My hero," I said, laughing.

His arms went around me for a brief second. For all his running around, he wasn't even breathing hard. His eyes were calm, with a hint of a smile, and his arms tightened around me before he stepped back.

"That was fun," he said.

"Oh, God, yes!" It wasn't just fun. It was exhilarating. It was a triumph. It was exactly what I needed for the scene.

"Can we do it again?" Martin asked, trotting up.

"I think I've got it," I said, still laughing.

"Are you sure?" Alan asked.

"Are you?" I countered. "You were in charge of the math."

"Then it was perfect," Alan said.

"And no one even seemed to notice," Lee said, a bit regretfully.

He was right. Despite the odd display, the running and shouting, the apparent assassination in the middle of the walkway, no one seemed to care. The few people who had been sitting and talking had stopped to watch us, then went back to their conversations.

"Did you get what you needed?" Max asked.

"Absolutely," I said. And all the way home, I replayed the

scene in my head, every twist and turn, especially the part where Max had his arms around me, and our lips were inches apart.

We got home in the late afternoon, and immediately my fingers were flying. I was so deep into my own head that I had almost forgotten where I was until I felt a steady, insistent tapping on my shoulder.

"Mags,'" Lee said gently. "Time to come up for air. And food. Solange cooked for us, remember?"

Indeed she had. Pot-au-feu is the French version of pot roast, and it was completely unlike any pot roast I'd ever eaten before. I had two helpings and almost didn't have room for the tiny strawberry tarts that someone had been kind enough to go out and buy. Almost.

I finally sat back at the dining room table feeling incredibly happy. It must have shown.

"That expression on your face," Max said. "I haven't seen one quite like that before. You look practically smug."

I sighed. "My daughter is in love with a beautiful man, inside and out. I'm writing like a madwoman, and I have never in my life eaten such amazing food. So yes, I'm smug."

Lee grinned. "And what you've written so far is some of the best stuff of your career. I was right: Paris is good for you. At this rate, you should be done in, what, two, three weeks?"

I nodded and looked wistfully at the crumbs left on my small, pale pink plate. "Yes. The rough draft should be done in the next three weeks. Usually I like to let it percolate before the first revision. I don't exactly have that luxury under the circumstances, but I may take the extra time after it's finished and go out to Rennes. It's close, right?"

Max nodded. "Yes. Just under two hours by train."

"Perfect. I can fly home the week before the book launch to give myself some time to get ready. Then I can start work on the revisions. That's what . . . another two weeks? The second draft is always harder. It will be tight, but I'll be done by my deadline. I have to be, because after book two is released and the book tour starts, I won't have time for anything."

Lee clasped his hands together. "Sounds like a plan. You can stay here for as long as you are in Paris. Martin and I will be here for another week, but after that . . ."

I glanced at Solange. "That's very kind, but—"

She held up a hand. "Please. I am here by myself all day long. It would be a pleasure to have you around. And believe me, you are not so much work. I cook for myself and Max, what's another dish on the table? You are less of a bother than Jules here. And when you are not writing, I would love to walk with you and show you the real Paris. My Paris, not for the tourists, yes?"

I smiled gratefully. "Thank you. Yes, that would be lovely. I really am getting so much done here."

"Excellent," Max said as he pushed himself away from the table. "I feel like a walk in the evening air. And brandy. Who would like to join me?"

"You'll take Jules," Solange murmured as she rose from the table.

"Yes, *Maman*." He looked at me. "Maggie?"

"That sounds wonderful."

Lee coughed, and I glared at him. "I've been writing all afternoon," I said. "I'm done for the night anyway."

Lee waved a hand. "Fine. Go off then. I just don't want you to lose your momentum."

I shook my head. "No, I need to stretch and reboot my brain. Let me change, Max."

"I have a question," Max said. He turned away from Place Victor Hugo and we entered a side street, darker, with three- and four-story homes crowding the sidewalks. Small pinpoints of light shone through drawn curtains, and from large pots, spring flowers spilled onto the cobblestones.

"Go on."

"This book. This is very important, yes?"

"Yes."

"Finishing it—what will it mean to you?"

I thought. "It will mean the next level of success in my career. The highest level. It will mean financial independence. I won't have to teach anymore. And it will mean I can finally buy a house on the ocean, which has been my dream my whole life. It will mean I'll finally have everything I've ever wanted."

"I see." We turned again. There was only one café, in the middle of the block, the tables out in the street and the low murmur of conversation filling the air. Paris at night was not just bright lights but quiet moments of friends huddled together, sharing wine and conversation. "So why, do you think, has it been so hard for you to write it? If it will get you every-thing?"

I hadn't wanted to think about that. It was something I'd been wondering about myself, for months. I looked up at him and decided to try to find the truth. "Because if I finish this book, and it's as successful as I hope, and I finally have it all . . . what if I'm still not happy?"

His eyes widened in surprise. "You're not happy with your life?"

"I am. Yes. I am. But this kind of success would be the an-swer to all my hopes and dreams. And what if I decide it's not enough?"

"It must never be enough, Maggie. No matter what you do, you should always want more. Not bigger or better or richer, just . . . more. Otherwise you stop growing as a person, *non*?"

We turned another corner and took seats at another one of those tiny, neighborhood cafés, where we ordered brandy.

"And love?" he asked. "Can you be happy alone? Some peo-ple can't."

"I've spent years alone. Well, with Nicole, but . . . unat-tached. There have been men in my life, some of them have lasted a long time, but they always lacked something in the end, and I was never afraid to let them go. I have a good life. I re-ally do. I have a few really great friends back home, I have a social circle that includes other writers, which is wonderful and supportive. Love would be lovely, but I've never felt like a man had to be in my life to feel complete."

"So, it is lucky for you, meeting Alan again like this after all these years?"

"Perhaps."

"And your parents?"

I told him—something I didn't do very often. They had both been killed in a car accident twelve years ago, and the shock and loss had paralyzed me for months.

"After the funeral, I didn't leave the house for six months. Thank God for Nicole. I had sent her to live with Alan, but after the summer was over, she insisted on coming back, and she made me get up every day. She called Lee, and he and Martin came over every Sunday and cooked a big dinner and made me get dressed and sit and talk like a regular person. And then one morning I woke up with an idea for a book, and it was all over."

Jules got up and circled Max's feet, found a better spot, then lay back down.

"Your daughter seems to be an exceptional person."

I felt a warm glow, the feeling I always got when someone else saw Nicole the same way I did. "Yes. And now, she's in love. I can die happy."

He laughed. "Ah, mothers and their wishes for their children. Health and wealth are always on the list. But first and always, love."

"First and always. Mothers know what's really important. Tell me what you'll be doing this week at your conference."

"If I did that, I'd bore you to tears. Finance is tedious and frustrating, and the minutia can kill you."

I laughed. "Okay, then tell me about what you did in Marseille."

"I visited one of my ex-wives. Her mother is dying, and Marie was the best mother-in-law a man could ever have. We had true affection for one another. In fact, she was the reason I stayed married as long as I did."

"I'm sorry."

"She is ninety-three and has six children, twelve grandchildren, and three great-grandchildren. She's the happiest dying woman I've ever seen."

"I imagined you spending the weekend in at attic apartment with a naked redhead, reading poetry to each other."

He stared for a moment, then burst out laughing. "Ah, Maggie, no wonder you are so successful as a writer. You have a wonderful imagination, *non*?"

I narrowed my eyes at him. "Come on, Max. That scenario is not so totally out of the range of possibility, is it?"

He grinned. "No, actually, it's not. But I do not like redheads, as a rule. I prefer blondes, tiny blondes with narrow hips and big, dark eyes who wear severe suits with very high heels."

Well, I did have narrow hips. That was the reason for my nonexistent butt. As for the rest . . . I'd never be a tiny blonde in very high heels. I wondered what it would take to change his mind.

We finally walked back. The apartment was dark, with everyone gone to bed, and as I crawled between the sheets I thought that this was exactly the kind of evening Lance could have used to tempt Bella into his bed way back in book one.

And it probably would have worked.

Chapter 8

Meditations on loss, love, the past, and more love

I got up early again and wrote. Twan was safe. They were heading for the border. With Twan in the back seat of the jeep, sexy-times were difficult, but not impossible. I stopped, thinking I'd done more than enough for the morning. I had a cup of coffee and a light breakfast with Lee and Martin, who were off to see the Paris lawyer, and Max, who was dressed in an impeccably tailored suit for his conference and looked every inch the successful international banker. He was quite impressive.

As it turned out, I felt the urge to write some more.

By the early afternoon, I had finished one scene. It was a difficult, complicated scene, barely two thousand words. I'd written it eight times until it was finally almost just right.

Some days were like that.

My brain was fried, and I was hungry. I had no idea where

Solange was, but I needed to eat, and soon. I glanced at my phone, and there was a text from Alan.

A: What are you doing for lunch?

I texted back.

M: I'm about to eat whatever is left in the fridge, even if it's turning green. Any better ideas?
A: Lol. I'm fairly close. Meet you at the cafe across from your flat in fifteen minutes. Can you last that long?
M: Barely. C u then

In fifteen minutes I managed the world's quickest shower and even put on lipstick. Alan was waiting at a small table outside. He stood as I came up and kissed me on the cheek, and I felt it again, that bit of warmth in my belly. The waiter immediately appeared with menus, and I ordered wine, resisting the urge to tell the waiter to bring whatever was the quickest to cook.

Alan pointed to something on the menu as the waiter leaned over to look, then nodded.

I pointed as well. "And soup? Onion soup?" I knew that I'd get that fairly quickly.

"Nic and Louis are safely back in Rennes," Alan said.

"Yes. So, what did you do all by yourself this morning?"

He looked sheepish. "Don't laugh."

"Never."

"I took my sketchbook down to the river and drew boats."

I smiled. "Oh, Alan, that's perfect." I imagined him leaning over a stone balustrade, pad in hand, his eyes narrowed against the morning sun.

"I like Louis," I said.

"So do I. Very much. He seems smart and personable, and I get the feeling that she doesn't run roughshod over him. She needs a bit of pushback in her life. And he obviously makes her happy, so extra points there. They would make beautiful children."

I looked at him in surprise. "You're right. Are you getting the itch to be a grandpapa? I wonder if that's something she would even consider. Having children, I mean. She's never talked about that."

"The number of things Nicole never talked about could fill half the Pacific Ocean," Alan said. "Although she does seem a bit more expansive these days."

"I told you. Everything has changed for her. She's looking at the world through an entirely new lens. That's what happens when you fall in love." The soup was set down in front of me, thick and rich brown, smelling heavenly of onion and . . . what? Sherry? I slowly brought my spoon to my lips and took a tentative slurp.

Heaven.

Alan laughed. "Watching you eat was always one of my favorite entertainments."

"Gee, thanks."

I ate my soup in silence as Alan watched the people go by.

In the early afternoon, the sidewalks were crowded, and more than once I caught him staring at attractive Parisian women hurrying by looking effortlessly chic. He would focus for a few seconds, then lift his wineglass to his lips, take a sip, and look away.

Good for Alan.

My phone made a noise. A text from Greg—that is, *another* text from Greg. After a week of relative silence, he had been sending me short texts for the past three days, telling me he missed me, asking me to call when I felt ready to talk about us.

I kept texting back that there wasn't an *us* any longer, but apparently he didn't believe me.

"Whom are you ignoring?" Alan asked.

"Greg. I think he's finally figured out how hard it's going to be to find an affordable place to live and figures it would be easier to just grovel his way back into my place."

Alan sniffed. "I always thought he was a bit of a jerk, but I could see the attraction. He was very much a man of action, yes? Unlike your very un-action-loving first husband."

I nodded. "Yes, I'll admit that I found him to be . . . very exciting. He appealed to the romance writer in me. He was also charming and very attentive when he wanted to be. But it was a mistake, and now he's having a hard time with my decision."

Alan sat back. "And you're not. At all. You used to have a hard time letting go of things."

I shrugged. "I'm older now, Alan. And what's the point of getting older if a bit of wisdom doesn't come along with the wrinkles and saggy boobs and gray hair?"

He laughed. "You've managed that part of getting older very well, Maggie. You look glorious."

I felt myself start to blush. "You can thank Max. He's the one who suggested that meeting your ex-husband in Paris warranted a little sprucing up."

Alan's jaw dropped open, and he laughed again. "Well, that may be true. But it's more than your appearance. There's a sparkle in your eyes and, I don't know . . . a bit of electricity around you? It changes the way you look, the way you talk . . . everything."

I grinned. "I'm writing. And it's good. You never had a chance to see me like that, when I'm in the zone. It's the best feeling ever." I shrugged. "Well, *almost*."

Our eyes met. Sex with Alan had been off the charts. For both of us. For me, it was the first time I'd been with a man I truly loved, and that fact changed everything. Alan used to say that I was the first woman he'd even been with who was unafraid, and who trusted him completely.

I felt a shiver at the memory and looked away, and we both laughed as my phone chirped again. I deleted him again and shook my head.

"Well, he is persistent," Alan said. "I give him credit. We have to stick together, we former loves of Maggie Bliss."

I smiled. "That would be a great title for a book."

"Yes, actually, it would. What are you doing for the rest of the day?"

I shrugged. "I'm here to write, Alan."

He nodded. "That's right. But tomorrow? Sacré-Cœur?"

"That sounds perfect."

He stood, then bent down to give me a cool kiss on the cheek, and his hand trailed down my spine, just as it used to when we'd been making love and were finally exhausted and, he'd tell me, he just wanted one last touch.

"Then I'll see you tomorrow," he said, and walked off.

I watched him walk away, then had another glass of wine before walking slowly back to the flat. I was once again left with a warm, familiar feeling. And I was beginning to imagine that growing into something more.

Lee and Martin returned from the Paris lawyer late that afternoon, Lee in a testy mood, Martin laden with boxes that looked like they came from a bakery.

"The lawyer is a pig," Lee said loudly.

Martin rolled his eyes. "The lawyer is doing his job. Things are different here in France. Taxes are more complicated. He's working with your accountant and everything will be straightened out in time."

"In *time*?" Lee said. "It could take days. Weeks. I want this resolved before we leave."

"You can't always get what you want," Martin pointed out.

Lee glared. "This from the man who took an hour picking out the perfect éclairs."

Solange had prepared another meal that smelled delicious, the scent of lamb and red wine wafting from the kitchen. Martin hurried in and exchanged a few words with her, then emerged with a tray laden with cheese and wine.

"Martin, stop feeding this woman," Lee growled. "She can't work in a stupor." He fixed his eyes on me. "You are still working?"

I nodded. "Yes. Because I have to go back and rewrite something. A few somethings, actually."

"This is your first draft," Lee said. "You don't rewrite yet."

"Yes, I do, because what I wrote this morning changes everything that happens from now on, and that means I need to go back a few chapters for the setup." I'd been sprawled on the couch but now stood and stretched. "I thought I was done for the day, but I need to make those changes now, while they're still ripe in my brain."

Solange stuck her head out of the kitchen. "Do you need coffee?"

"No, thanks."

"Do you need for these two annoying men to leave?"

I grinned. "No, Solange. I can work around them."

So I did. I sat and read and rewrote and rewrote some more, and I barely noticed the changing light in the room or the murmur of voices in the background. Finally the smell of Solange's dinner turned my head.

"We're eating?" I asked no one in particular.

Lee sprang to his feet. "Yes, thank God. Solange insisted we wait for you. I told her you wouldn't mind, why, you wouldn't even *notice,* but . . ."

Max was sitting with them, looking tired, scowling down at a file that was open on his lap. He glanced up and smiled briefly.

"I also suggested we wait for you. Lee, you ate enough cheese to last you until Wednesday. How can you claim hunger?"

Lee hurried to the dining room table. "I know what's coming. Your mother is an excellent cook."

That was an understatement. The stew was delicious, and the bread . . . then Martin brought out his éclairs, and by the end of the meal I was so happy I could have burst into song.

"By the way," Lee said, "I passed your room earlier and your phone was chirping."

I got up and hurried in, picked up the phone, and found a series of texts from Alan along with a few pictures. "I'll be going to Sacré-Cœur tomorrow," I said. "Is it worth all those steps?"

"It is magnificent," Solange said.

"You must go to the top," said Max. "And besides, you can take a tram."

"You're supposed to be *working,*" Lee grumbled.

"Didn't Nicole go back to Rennes?" Martin asked.

"Yes, she did. Alan wants to go," I said. "I told him yes."

"Alan is now all alone in Paris and will undoubtedly ask you to do something every minute of every day," Lee muttered.

"And I can say no," I shot back. "I know what I have to do, Lee. Believe me, I know what's at stake."

Max raised an eyebrow. "What is at stake, exactly?"

Lee cleared his throat. "The book business has gotten very difficult," he said. "We have the second book getting published in June. We need to have the third book ready to go by *next*

June. Readers used to be perfectly happy waiting years between books, but not any longer. We need the momentum to keep going. And believe it or not, getting a book from first draft to publication in twelve months is difficult. The publisher is really pushing because they know how important it is. Then there's a possible deal with a cable network."

Max let out a low whistle. "That could mean a great deal of money."

Lee nodded. "Yes, it could."

Max looked at me and grinned. "Your own media empire?" he asked.

I shook my head. "No, I don't think so. But it would mean the beach house."

"Oh, the beach house," Lee moaned. He looked at Max. "When I sold her first book, the first thing she did was go on-line and started looking for a beach house. She's done the same thing every sale for the past twenty-whatever years. This year, maybe, she'll finally get her dream."

Max stood and stretched. He was still dressed in his suit, dark gray and beautifully cut. He looked down at me. "It sounds like a wonderful dream," he said, smiling at me. "I'll walk Jules. A nightcap?"

I jumped up. "I'd love one." I glanced at Solange. "Do you need any help?"

She waved a hand. "Yes, but not you. Go. You worked hard today. No, Lee, you stay right here. *You* can help."

Max and I walked down Victor Hugo, then sat, ordered brandy, and watched the evening settle around us.

"You have been in Paris an entire week," Max said. "What do you think?"

Had it really only been a week? I felt like I'd lived the most important days of my life surrounded by these glorious Parisian blocks. I didn't look down at my feet any longer, worrying about stumbling on the cobblestones. My feet knew the way. I didn't gasp every time I turned a corner and saw a new bit of skyline. I just smiled and nodded—yes, there you are again. I didn't stop at every door, no matter how old and carved or colorful, because I knew I'd see another just down the street.

"I think I love this city," I said. "And I'm usually not a city person. It's not just the beauty. Or the food, although I could make a case for living here permanently on the bread alone. There's an energy here. I can't describe it, exactly. Louis said it was something in the air, and he must be right. Even Alan has caught the bug. My dry math geek of an ex-husband is sketching boats. I'm writing faster and better than I ever have. Paris is invigorating. This is just what I needed."

He swirled the brandy in his glass. "Yes, there is something special about Paris. I live in New York, and as exciting as it is, it is not the same."

"Solange said you also live in London?"

He shrugged. "I'll be selling that place. I bought it to, well, accommodate a friend. But that situation has changed, so it is best to just let it go."

A friend? A woman friend? I felt a prickle of something, tight and bitter. But of course he had a woman. And why not? I had just imagined him with a wanton redhead, spending a weekend naked in bed. But the thought of him being committed enough to have a flat . . .

"Was the friend a she?" I asked, then immediately wanted to crawl under the table and hit myself in the head with my black ballet flat.

"Constance," he said easily. "She died. Cancer."

I felt an unexpected sorrow so strong that it shook me to the core. "Oh, Max, I am so sorry."

He turned to me, his eyes quiet and sad. "She was lovely, and we cared very much for each other. It's been two years and I still miss her. I have found that I'm not very lucky with women."

"And why do you think that is?"

He made a face. "I have a very important job that I love. It takes me all over the world. Women tend to like their partners closer to home. I travel to places at the drop of a hat. It takes a very special kind of woman to be secure enough for that kind of relationship."

I nodded. "I get it. That's what Greg and I had. He was on the road for so much of the year, it was hard to keep the connection. Actually, I could handle his being away." I laughed. "It was his being home that was the hard part. He wasn't really there for me, you know? I was never his . . . first thought in the morning. Part of it was my fault. I let myself believe that taking a back seat in his life was enough. But it wasn't, and he wasn't willing to change, so . . ."

"You should never take a back seat to anyone, Maggie."

"I won't again," I said, and I meant it.

He smiled, and there was a touch of sadness there. I wanted

to reach across the tiny table and grab his hand and tell him not to give up, that the right woman for him was out there, that he wasn't unlucky at all, but hadn't found her yet. . . .

He must have read my thoughts because his smile brightened. "And I imagine you're going to tell me that I deserve a happily ever after. Like in your books."

I felt myself smiling back. "That's exactly what I'm going to tell you. After all, it's what I do. Give people all their dreams tied up with a bow."

We finished our brandy in silence, sitting and watching the people walk by, until Jules rose from under Max's chair and tugged on his leash.

We walked back to the flat without saying a word.

From the terrace of the Basilica of the Sacred Heart you could see all of Paris. Alan and I took the tram up to the top and spent more than an hour just looking at one far-off corner of Paris to another.

The back streets surrounding the basilica were narrow and steep, twisting around small galleries and shops, but we finally sat down for a late lunch. It was a cool and cloudy day, having rained all through the night before, but it didn't matter. Alan and I sat and talked and laughed, and it was almost like when we were first getting to know one another all those years ago.

"This place reminds me of Grant Street," Alan said over coffee.

"Yes! The little place we went to when we first started going out."

"When we finally got out of bed, you mean," he said with a laugh.

We had spent the first few weeks that we'd known each other in a blur of cheap wine and lots of sex. "I was so afraid that we'd have nothing to talk about with our clothes on," I said.

He nodded. "I felt the same way. I was terrified you'd realize I was just a boring math geek who was way too old for you."

"And I thought you'd think I was young and shallow and not nearly smart enough."

"You were beautiful and brilliant," he said. "You still are. We managed to find a great deal to love about each other."

We had. I knew we still loved each other, and we still enjoyed each other's company. But would we be able to build something more? I had been waiting for that little voice in my head to say *yes*.

And as we walked back, his arm across my shoulders, I heard a whisper.

When I got back to the apartment, Max was leaving. A business dinner, he explained as he hurried out. He was wearing a severe black suit that hugged his shoulders and nipped in at his waist.

I was torn. Did I want to take a picture of him and frame it? Or take him to a candlelit room and, with some exotic drum music in the background, peel the suit off of him slowly? As he left I realized that at some point I had stopped seeing him as a generic hero to my nameless, faceless heroine, and he had become a very personal fantasy.

I wasn't sure what to do with that.

Especially since I'd just spent the afternoon trying to figure out what to do with my feelings about Alan.

Things were starting to feel complicated.

Solange watched me as I stared after Max. "Maggie? Lee and Martin are having dinner with friends. It will just be the two of us for dinner. Just soup. Is that enough?"

"Sounds wonderful," I answered. Soup and bread and butter and wine. No Max.

Which was perfectly acceptable. I could have dinner without Max.

I hurried to my room, sat down on the edge of the bed, and began to text.

> M: OK so I think Alan wants us to get back together but there IS a sexy Frenchman and I can't figure out what to do with either of them.

No response. I waited a few more minutes, threw the phone down on the bed, picked it back up, and went back out.

Solange and I ate dinner quietly, and later we walked Jules around the darkened streets. We chatted about simple things, about Alan and Montmartre.

"Montmartre is a lovely neighborhood," Solange said. "I always liked it over there. Very different, but that is the beauty of Paris, *non*? There are so many nooks and crannies, anyone can

be happy here. I love my street and wouldn't trade it for anywhere else, but sometimes, when I walk by those little house-
boats, I get a twinge."

"Yes, I can see that. They're charming."

"Max lived on one for a while. When he was much younger.
With his first wife."

"And what was she like?"

She glanced at me. "She was very young and stupid. She
told him she was pregnant, and he believed her. It was a lie,
and they were divorced after two years. Then there was Celestine. Ah, she was a tiger, that one. Max, he loves women. Not
just the sex, he loves everything about them. After all, he was
raised here, in this little corner of Paris, surrounded by women
of all sorts. Celestine was all fire and passion, and he adored
her. Sadly, fire and passion are not enough. When she left it
broke his heart. Then there was, what do you call it? The re-
bound wife. She was pleasant. I think he needed someone safe
and quiet to heal his heart. But safe and quiet are not so good
either." We stopped at a corner and she sniffed. "You would be
very good for him, I think."

"Solange, I am here to write a book, not become entangled
with a man who lives in another country."

"But Max lives in New York City. That is close to you."

"Well, yes, it is. But I just threw out a man I lived with for
four years. There's probably some emotional baggage there I
need to get rid of. I'm certainly not going to jump into something with Max or anyone else so soon."

"If you threw him out, then you must have been, what's the

word? Detached? Yes? You must have been detached from him for quite a while."

Damn this woman anyway. "Yes, I suppose you're right about that, too. I'd been feeling angry and unhappy with Greg for a while. But part of our problem was that Greg was gone for so much of the time, and Max, well, he's always going off somewhere or other. Why on earth would I want to go through that again?"

"I am certain that my Max is a very different sort of man."

"Yes, I'm sure he is, but . . . Solange, he's not my type."

"Ah." We crossed the street and headed back to the flat. "Well, it is true he is not very attractive."

"What? Are you kidding me?" I thought about those piercing blue eyes, his wide, ripe mouth, the twitch of his chin as he smiled. And then there was the solid warmth of his body that had sent actual chills down my spine in those brief seconds that he'd had his arms around me. . . . "He's certainly attractive, Solange, believe me. Why . . ."

I gave her the side eye and found her smiling.

She changed the subject. "So what is your type? The quiet, helpful sort? Like Alan?"

I shrugged. "I used to think so, but things didn't work out so well for us. And I'm pretty sure I'm not cut out for happily ever after with an alpha male."

"You mean that Greg person? He was undoubtedly a selfish beast. But Alan? Is it possible that you and he will find love again?"

I shook my head. "I don't know. I've been kind of thinking about that. We are not the same two people we once were."

"But all lovers start as strangers. Can you find something new to fall in love with?"

Could I? Was there something in this older, more relaxed Alan that I could discover? He had changed, that was certain. In nurturing his creative side, he had become more open, more engaged. Would it be enough?

I waited while Solange put the key in the massive lock at the front door, and we slowly climbed the steps to the flat.

"I'm not sure," I said at last. "We had a really great day today."

She yawned, putting a graceful hand over her mouth. "I am tired and will go early to bed. I think you need to talk to Alan. I am sure he has hopes. And why not? You are so lovely. Any man would be a fool to have you so close and not at least try to capture your heart."

Any man? Did she mean Max as well?

"Thank you, Solange. You're right. Maybe I'll go to bed early too."

But I didn't. I sat at my computer and tried to write. The words did not come easily. I kept getting snarled in the same loop and couldn't find a way out. I finally gave up after just an hour and looked at my phone.

A: Alan wants to get back together???OMG I'm so happy

C: Wait. Details on the French guy first

A: Forget French guy ALAN!!!

I stared at the screen. Oh, what on earth was I going to say? Or do?

M: Alan will always be my first love. But can't I have
     another love?

The cursor blinked. I washed my face and changed.

C: Is it really that serious?
M: I don't know. That's the problem
A: But Alan . . .
M: Bottom line—French guy is in FRANCE I need
     to sleep. Night guys

I went to bed, where I tossed and turned until I heard Lee and Martin come home and, finally, Max.

And then I slept.

Lee got a message from my editor, Ellen, asking that he call right away. Because of the time difference, and because I was off with Alan at the Palais-Royal, I didn't hear the news until I came back, rather late in the afternoon.

"Ellen says they're delaying the publication of the third book," Lee said shortly. "Call her. She's waiting for you."

I sat down and took a few breaths to steady myself. Delay was not good. Delay would ruin everything. I had her on speed dial, and she, having caller ID, did not even waste a hello.

"Maggie. Love, listen. This is nothing personal."

I felt my heart sink. "What's not personal?"

"We're pushing back book three by a year. We're never going to be able to get the edits done in time. It was tight anyway, and you know how things are always changing."

I tried to keep the panic out of my voice. "Ellen, you know that this needs to come out a year after book two. Otherwise readers will lose interest. You can see the momentum that's building now for book two. We can't lose that."

"This is not my decision, Maggie."

"Well, whose is it?"

She was silent.

"Mark, right?"

More silence.

Mark Carruthers was a big deal at the publishing house, and his ego was proportionately sized to his big corner office. "Mark doesn't think much of women writers, does he?" I pressed. "I bet he's bumping me for another navel-gazing ode to a middle-aged white guy who lost his job and needs to reinvent himself. Probably *written* by some middle-aged white guy. Am I right?"

"Maggie, you know how this industry works."

I looked over at Lee. His face was tight. "This is a bad business decision, Ellen. You know that."

"Yes, I do. But like I said, it's not *my* decision."

"What will it take? To change minds?"

"If the book had been turned in on time," she said shortly.

Fair enough. "What if I send you what I have so far?" I asked.

Lee shook his head. He mouthed, "It's not ready."

"It's not ready," I said, "but it's so good, Ellen. *So* good."

"All your books are good, Maggie. That's why we keep signing more contracts with you." I heard her exhale. "Okay. Send it. I need all the ammunition I can get. The cable option is still on the table?"

"Yes."

"That helps. You'll have it done by deadline?"

"Before," I said. "I'll have a first draft to you by the book launch."

Lee closed his eyes and made a face.

"Okay. I'll talk to you soon."

She hung up. I let the phone drop in my lap. "If they push back the last book, I'm dead in the water," I moaned.

"Nonsense," Lee said.

I glared at him. "Don't you dare go Pollyanna on me now, Lee. You know I need these books to come out one year apart."

"I know."

"They're summer books. They're beach reads."

"I know."

"What can we do?"

"Finish the book before your launch?"

I looked around. Where was Max? If I was going to finish this book quickly, I needed Max. . . .

"Where's Max?"

Lee frowned. "What has Max got to do with anything?"

"I'm just asking. . . ."

"He's in Prague," Solange said. "Some sort of emergency."
She gave me a knowing look. "Very last minute, but he'll be
back by Saturday."

She knew. She'd figured it out. Or had she? Maybe she
thought that I'd fallen in love with the man, which was out of
the question. And here was the perfect reason why: I needed
him and he was gone. The very last thing I needed was another
man in my life who wouldn't be around half the time.

I felt a rise of panic that I beat down with every ounce of logic
I had in my brain. My writing was going along beautifully. Max
had been the reason, but even without him actually in the room,
I could write and write fast. This was my best writing since the
earliest days of my career, when I had too many story ideas and
thought I'd never have the time or energy to get them all down.
This was my job, after all, and I was damn good at my job.

I was going to finish this book, I would have it done before
having to go back to the States for my book launch, and it was
going to be brilliant. With or without Max.

Chapter 9

A revelation or three

*B*ella and Lance were making for the border.

Bella and Lance were making for the border.

Bella and Lance and *Twan* were making for the border.

I stared at the cursor. It was sitting there. It was blinking at me. Taunting me. Saying . . . na, na, n-na, na . . . you ca-an't write . . .

This was absolutely ridiculous. I knew exactly what happened next. They ran out of gas. No—they ran out of water. Wait—maybe a scorpion bit Twan?

No. That was book two.

If I didn't finish this book when I'd promised, I had no chance of bullying my publisher into getting it published next summer and it wouldn't debut at the top of the bestseller list, something I hadn't done in almost eight years.

I got up and made myself a café crème. I needed to be working, if for no other reason than if I *wasn't* working, Lee would ask why, and how could I possibly explain to him that it was because Max was in Prague? I'd written all sorts of books without Max. It didn't make sense. Sure, Lee knew all about the inside-out sweater. He even thought the Mallomars thing was pretty funny. But Max?

How was I going to explain about Max if I didn't understand it myself?

I finally admitted to myself that it wasn't just my writing that I wanted him around for. Our evening walks had become the high point of my day, and when you considered that my day sometimes consisted of the Seine or the Eiffel Tower, well, that was saying a *lot*.

Yes, he was charming. And funny. And sexy—what his shoulders did to a simple cotton shirt should come with a written warning. When he looked at me with those blue eyes, I felt like we were in a bubble, just he and I, and the rest of the world fell away.

What did he think of me? I had no idea. I was probably just that annoying American woman who rose at dawn, muttered to herself over her laptop, and had been in need of a serious makeover. So he was nice to me. Every single person I'd met had been nice to me, despite the urban myth that the French hated Americans.

And now he was in Prague, and I stared at my laptop and wondered what time he'd be back, and what in the *hell* I was going to do until then. Because I didn't think I'd be getting any writing done.

"Are you okay?" Lee was standing behind me, and I practically jumped out of my chair.

"I don't know."

"Listen, I know you're thrown by Ellen's phone call. Don't

be. This is my job. I can fix this for you. Martin says I've been a bear, so we're all going shopping."

I looked at him in disbelief. "What?"

"Well, I did promise you. The best bookstore in the world is here, and you haven't been to the Left Bank, which is full of bookstalls and art. . . . I'll even buy you something."

I stood up. "Am I dying, Lee? You can tell me the truth."

He sighed patiently. "No, you are not dying. At least, not that I know of. But you've accomplished quite a bit, and it's so good, Mags. . . ." He shrugged. "And I need to think about how I'm going to do this. As a last resort, we can always remind them that your contract with them is now done, and there isn't another one for whatever comes next."

I narrowed my eyes at him. "You mean, threaten to *leave*?"

"Only if we have to."

"But . . ." I'd been with the same house for the whole of my career, a rarity in an industry that had seen profound changes in the last few years. My publisher had been sold, resold, rebranded, and risen from the ashes intact. And they had always treated me well. Until now.

"Where's the best bookstore in the world?" I asked.

He grinned. "Get out of your writing clothes. And put on walking shoes. Is Alan busy today? Text him. He can meet us after breakfast."

Shakespeare and Company was just on the other side of one of those fabulous stone bridges, an ancient stone building with nooks and crannies and bookshelves to the ceiling, and all with that heavenly old-book smell. Alan was very patient with me. Well, with all of us. Martin was an intellectual-property lawyer and loved books almost as much as Lee, so the three of us could have easily died and been buried there. I managed to buy only three books, old children's books that were in English with Arthur Rackham illustrations. Lee reminded me several times that I'd have to fly back to the United States with whatever I bought and that books were heavy, otherwise I could have done much more damage.

The book and art stalls were all up and down the river, and between exclaiming over every shabby watercolor I found and imagining Gene Kelly and Leslie Caron dancing along the sidewalks, I had a lovely day.

Which was why, after Lee and Martin left for the flat and Alan and I lingered over a last glass of wine, I didn't mind at all when he leaned over and kissed me, very deliberately, on the lips.

The kiss lingered and I felt it again, that warm glow. His hand reached for mine and our fingers slid back together just as they always had.

The lights of Paris were reflecting off the water as we walked, and boats went by, tourists waving at us from their seats, as we had now become part of the scenery, like the other lovers and strangers who walked beneath the darkening sky. He kissed me again, this time as we stood under a streetlight with his arms around me and his body against mine.

It was a good kiss. Okay, maybe it was a great kiss. And

why wouldn't it be, right there with the Seine at our feet and the whole of Paris backlit behind us? It was familiar, but new at the same time. Was Solange right? Was it possible to find something different and exciting again in this man whom I'd known for more than half my lifetime? The man who had hurt me more than anyone else had, even as he had taught me how to love in the first place?

I stepped away from him and tried to figure out what I was feeling.

"Hey," he said softly.

I lifted my eyes to his.

"My flat is fairly close," he said. "If you wanted to, well . . ."

Did I want to?

Last night I'd been shaken by a possible curveball to my career. I'd felt a certain anger about Max. I'd been discouraged and uncertain and confused and generally a mess. And now, tonight, there was nothing but a quiet ease, a comfort, and a feeling that here, with this man, things would be just fine.

Maybe it was the last glass of wine. Maybe it was being with Alan for days on end now and remembering what it was I'd loved about him all those years ago. Maybe it was standing under a streetlight on a cobblestone street in the most romantic city in the world. Because I almost said yes.

"Alan, I don't think I should be making these kinds of decisions right now."

"Why not?"

Because this is Paris, that's why, and it's not the real world. Because *until* Paris, I'd never seriously thought about the two of us together again. And if Nicole hadn't mentioned the crazy idea in the first place, I never would have.

Because Max. I didn't know what I felt for him or why, I just knew I couldn't stop thinking about him, and I needed to sort that out.

Because I didn't know if *just fine* was what I really wanted for the rest of my life.

"I have to finish this book, Alan," I said. "And I can't let myself be distracted." That was a partial truth, the real truth being that I couldn't let myself get distracted any *more* because, again, Max.

He put his arm across my shoulder and walked me back to the flat, where I spent the rest of the night tossing and turning and trying not to think too much about the possibilities.

"You're not writing," Lee observed the next morning.

"And you're not calling Ellen every five minutes threatening fiery retribution if they push back my publication date."

Martin made a noise and huddled deeper behind his newspaper.

"I'll have you know I sent off a rather scathing email earlier, to both Ellen and Mark, detailing what a disastrous business decision it would be for not only your career but for the publishing industry as a whole."

Solange looked up from her café crème. "Have you taken her to Galeries Lafayette?"

"We shopped yesterday," Lee said shortly.

Solange set down her cup. "Then the answer is no. Are you going to take her?"

Lee made a face. "We have the lawyer again. On a Saturday, so that should tell you how much trouble I'm in."

She raised an eyebrow. "That just tells me how much he's charging you."

Lee exhaled noisily. "Yes. That too. He said he's solved the problem. French taxes are impossible to understand, and this vineyard may end up costing me more money than it's making this year."

Martin lowered his newspaper. "Don't be absurd. It was a simple mistake on your part, a common error that your accountant has now *fixed,* and you'll probably get a small penalty and a slap on the wrist. If we were back home, the IRS would have frozen your assets." He folded up his paper. "Solange, I think that Maggie here has earned a trip to the most glamorous department store in Europe. You need to take her. I'd love to come with you, but someone will have to go with Lee and hold his hand."

"She's not writing," Lee said, rather loudly.

"Mags," Martin asked kindly, "why aren't you writing?"

"Because I haven't seen Galeries Lafayette yet?" I offered.

"Good answer," Martin said.

"I'll write tonight, Lee. I promise." Max would be back sometime today. I wasn't about to provoke Solange any further by asking when, but it didn't matter. As soon as he walked through the door, I knew my fingers would be itching for the keyboard.

At least I hoped. If not, I was in worse trouble than I thought.

Lee glared. "You're going off again. And I suppose with Alan as well?"

I thought. Alan was leaving on Monday, and I hadn't heard from him at all today. "I'll see him before he leaves," I said. "We'll have dinner, I'm sure. What I need is a girls' day out."

"Leaving me with Jules, I presume?" Lee asked.

Solange pushed herself away from the table. "You sound as though you'll have to perform some exotic ritual. He just needs to be walked before you leave for the lawyer. I'm sure you can manage."

So Solange and I went off together, and Martin had not been wrong: Galeries Lafayette probably was the most glamorous department store in Europe. Possibly the entire world. It's possible that maybe somewhere in Dubai or Japan there was something that came close, but I was suitably impressed. I mean, a gold dome topped off the whole place. How do you out-glam that?

"It's best to start at the top," Solange said, "and work your way down slowly. This is like the Louvre. Too much to see in one visit, but we can touch on a few highlights. And eat."

We were on our third break, espresso and macarons, when she finally mentioned Max.

"He should be landing about now," she said, quite casually, glancing at her watch.

"Who?" I asked, totally nonchalant.

"My son. You know, Max? It should only take him a half hour or so to get home. Pity I didn't put anything in the oven. Perhaps we'll pick up some fish. And leeks? We have plenty of wine, but bread . . ." She took a bite of her macaron, pale pink with a creamy white filling. "You write much more when he's around, *non*?"

"Yes," I said shortly. The macaron was crisp when I first bit into it but then practically melted in my mouth, and the almond filling was almost, but not quite, too sweet.

"So, he is your muse?"

"Maybe," I said, taking another small bite.

"He would be quite flattered, you know. He has a very romantic heart for a banker." She folded her hands on her lap. "Or is it Alan? I think you are trying to decide over that one."

I sank back in my chair. "It's very tempting to fall back into old familiar patterns," I said. "And I am starting to find new things about him, things that have changed in him over time. He's much more relaxed and calm. Part of that is because he's retired now. He's painting. He always did, but it's different now, I think. And it's made him different. And I'm sure he has enough money and a thoughtful plan for the rest of his life."

"And would he like you to be a part of that?"

I nodded. "Maybe. I think it would be my call to make."

"But . . . ?" She tilted her head as she spoke, her short hair bright under the crystal chandeliers that hung above us.

But thinking about Max is making me crazy. I can't wait to see him again. I just want to be in the same room with him. Because I need to write. Because I need to finish this book.

Because I need to see that smile, those thin lips curling, those blue eyes glinting at me, full of intelligence and humor and just a hint of mischief. I need to hear that laugh, and see him sip brandy, lounging back in his chair, one leg crossed over the other, his hair sweeping up off his forehead. . . .

"But . . . ?" she repeated.

"But I'm not sure that money and a thoughtful plan would make me happy. Although . . ."

"Yes?"

"He's retired. We would find a place together, and he would be there for me every day. He'd be painting, I'd write. That's a very attractive idea."

"Ah." She nodded. "Unlike, say, your Greg person? He traveled quite a bit. Just like Max."

"Yes," I said faintly. Just like Max.

She glanced at her watch again. "We need to get fish, but we will not find what I want here. Come, I'll introduce you to my fishmonger. His fish are so fresh I swear they swim home behind me in a heavy rain."

The fishmonger was on a tiny crowded side street. He greeted Solange with a kiss-kiss, and they had a long and rather heated discussion before he whisked a large fish off the bed of ice and into the back of his shop, returning a few minutes later with a package wrapped in brown paper. From there it was the vegetable stand, then the bakery, then a small kiosk for hand-packed gelato.

"For Max," Solange explained. "He has a sweet tooth, you know."

Max was standing by an open window when we got home, and when I saw him, I couldn't stop smiling. He turned as we entered, gave his mother a kiss, and grabbed several bags. I followed him into the kitchen, and he grinned at me.

"The best part of going away is the welcome back. My mother always cooks my favorite things," he said. "She took you to the Galeries?"

"Yes. It was fabulous."

"And also to buy fish. You have pretty much covered it all today. How is your writing?"

"It's good. Great. Well, I haven't done any today, but I'm not worried." I put the gelato in the freezer and unwrapped asparagus spears so thin and delicate I was afraid they would snap in my hands. "How was your trip?"

He shrugged. "Boring. And unnecessary. I should have known better, but when I am called, I go." He flashed a smile over his shoulder. "I would have much preferred staying right here. One day I suppose I will become a homebody, but for now . . . ?" He shrugged again.

"Right." I took a breath. "Well, I'm behind on my word count, so I think I'll just go, you know, write stuff."

"Have fun."

I went to my laptop and stared at the screen.

Someday he would become a homebody. But for now . . .

I began to type.

On Sunday morning Max went out early for sweet rolls and fruit and looked relaxed and happy at the breakfast table. "Is there something you'd like to see?" he asked me. "I'd be happy to act as tour guide, especially since I know you've been up for hours, writing."

This, I knew, was for Lee's benefit. Lee made a noise and went back to his single soft-boiled egg.

"It's Alan's last day here," I said. The words practically stuck in my throat as I said them. "We really don't spend much time together in the States," I went on. I wanted to explain. I really wanted to text Alan and tell him to forget it, but we'd already agreed to meet. "I've decided . . ." I stopped to pass Martin more sugar. I had decided to look at the whole Alan and me thing from another angle. What if Alan and I became a couple again? What would *that* feel like?

"Yes. I see," Max said easily. "Enjoy your day."

So that's how I spent the day, pretending that Alan and I were not just friendly exes. Not just tourists walking through the old Jewish Quarter, standing in line for what was called the best falafel in all of France. But *together*.

We were fine. Once again . . . fine.

We had dinner together in a small romantic restaurant that probably advertised itself as the perfect place to propose. I mean, there was even a small man playing a violin walking between the tables. I half expected Alan to have a ring to present after dessert. But the food was superb, and the lemon tart at the very end of the meal melted in my mouth. I knew there were lemon tarts in the States, but were the crusts as buttery and delicate? And the custard so creamy on my tongue?

Alan stirred his coffee and sat back in his chair. We were outside on the sidewalk, and the street was crowded and filled with laughter. There was a cool spring breeze in the air and the faint sound of nearby traffic. "I'm beginning to think," he said, "that Nic's idea wasn't so crazy after all. We've had a lovely time together here in Paris."

"Alan," I told him. "I don't think . . . I mean, yes, we have. You're right, but we're in Paris. Let's face it, there are certain preconceived ideas about Paris, and we could be falling for all of them."

He put both of his hands on mine. "I know. Maybe I'm under the influence. After all, even Quasimodo found love here. But think about us. Please? Would it be so awful, the two of us together again?"

I had thought about it. Mostly I thought about the fact that Alan would not be dashing off to someplace else every five minutes, leaving me by myself. He'd be *there*.

And Max?

But really, was Max an option for me? Why was I dismissing Alan because I was thinking about what my life would be like with Max? Chances were that Max and I would never see each other again once I left France. Whereas Alan would be sitting in a cozy studio somewhere, painting all day, and in the evenings we could sit together, looking at the ocean, sharing a glass of wine. . . .

He brought my hand to his lips. "I know you've got a lot on your mind right now. Just don't close the door on the whole idea. Not right away. Promise?"

I nodded. "I can't promise, Alan, but I'll keep an open mind. Because you're right, it's been . . . lovely. We'll see each other back in the States, okay?"

He walked me back to the apartment and kissed me, and

I felt so much behind the kiss. He was serious about this. He thought we had a good shot at a second chance.

I wrote about second chances all the time, and if this were my book, he and I would be destined for happily ever after.

But no book of mine would have Max taking second to Alan.

That night I curled up in bed and took out my phone.

> M: Alan flew home. He wants me to think about the two of us together again.

The response was immediate.

> C: Well, what DO you think? Tell me about the Frenchman again?
>
> A: Oh this is so lovely
>
> M: What are you two doing? Sitting on your phones? Don't you have LIVES???
>
> C: Honey whatever is happening to me now is not nearly as exciting as whats happening to you
>
> A: So would you get married again or just live together?
>
> C: WHAT ABOUT FRENCHIE?
>
> M: His name is Max and he's lovely and funny and smart and sexy and is also very polite and considerate and I'm probably delusional in thinking there could be anything between us. Good news is the book is going great.

C: Happy about the book. But I think if you feel
   THAT strongly about him, there has to be some
   sort of juju bouncing back at you and you're
   probably not delusional at all
A: Cheri is right. You need some sort of energy to
   feed off of. Are you sure hes just polite?
M: I'm not sure of anything anymore. Talk later

It took me a long time to get to sleep.

The next day, Lee and Martin flew back, leaving me with lots of excellent chocolate. Lee was so pleased with what I'd written he didn't even give me an eleventh-hour lecture.

And that left me alone with Solange and Max. And Jules, who apparently accepted me as one of the family because he would now happily climb on my lap before farting.

Two more weeks. At the rate I was writing, that was all I needed to finish my rough draft. Then a nice visit with Nic to relax my brain before flying home and taking the great dive into revisions.

We had a quiet dinner, and I'd been drowsing in the corner of the couch, almost asleep, when Solange's voice shook me fully awake.

"Going where?" Solange asked sharply.

I sat up. Who was going where?

Max was talking. "I am thinking about Switzerland. You know that little village just outside Martigny? I need to sit and relax, drink quietly, and forget about the world."

I sat up straighter. Max was going away? I knew that he was

taking time off work; he'd told me that the very first day we met. But I'd assumed he'd stay in Paris. After all, who wouldn't want to stay in Paris? If you had the choice of Paris or anywhere else, why would you go anywhere else? Was he mad?

Solange clucked and shook her head. "Then who will look after Maggie?" she asked.

Max looked at his mother suspiciously. "Why," he asked slowly, "can't *you* look after Maggie?"

"Claire-Chantal called this afternoon. She is having bunions removed and asked if I could stay with her while she recovers. Naturally, I said yes."

Max was not convinced, and neither was I. I'd bet she still had a bit of matchmaking on her mind. "And you didn't say, no, Claire-Chantal, I have to stay in Paris and look after Maggie?"

She spread her hands. "I thought you would be here, or I would have refused. But now . . ." She looked at me. "Now, what can I say? Ah, Maggie, you will be here all by yourself. For a whole week. You will take care of Jules, yes? And I'm sure you can cook for yourself. After all, you spent those first few days here alone, and you were just fine, *non*?"

No. Well, yes, but that was not the point. If Max left, would I be able to write? He'd been gone for two days and I hadn't managed a word. Was that a fluke or a sign of things to come? And if I did write, would it be any good? And if it wasn't any good, were there any stores in France that sold Mallomars?

I pasted on a smile as my heart sank to the bottom of my feet. "Solange, don't worry. I'll be fine," I said.

"See?" Max said easily. "Maggie is a grown woman. A very

capable woman. And right now, her writing is brilliant and everything in her world is perfect. Right, Maggie?"

My face must have crumbled just a bit when I answered. "Right." All I could think of was sitting in front of my laptop, my mind blank. The bread would grow stale, the wine would turn sour, and Jules would pee all over the floor before I typed a single word.

Max came closer and sat across from me. "Everything *is* alright, isn't it, Maggie?"

No, I wanted to shout. *I need you.* You don't have to do anything because, yes, I can cook and take care of Jules. What I can't do is finish this stupid, awful, terrible book that's never going to be any good, no matter how hard I try, because if you're not here . . .

"Maggie, did something happen?"

I clenched my jaw and nodded, my mind racing. What could have happened? What could have happened that would keep him in Paris?

His eyes grew dark. "Is it Nicole?"

Nicole! Oh, thank God I had a daughter! I nodded again. Should I squeeze a little tear? Maybe from just one eye? Would that be too much?

He took my hand and I swear my pulse kicked up a notch. "What?"

Oh, dear. Yes, well, I suppose I'd have to tell him something. . . . "When she called today, she said she was . . ." What? What? Dear Lord, I made up these sorts of stories for my friggin' living. Was she pregnant? Terminal illness?

"She's having problems with Louis."

There. That was terrible but not fatal, and I wouldn't have to explain away the baby.

His mouth tightened. "Oh, I am sure she's very upset. And you as well. Ah, Maggie, I can only imagine what you are thinking."

No, Max, I'd bet a million bucks you have no *idea* what I'm thinking.

"Well, they are both intelligent adults," Max said. "I'm sure they'll talk it out."

No, their talking it out was not going to work for me. "He packed up his things."

He raised an eyebrow. "Oh?"

"She was hysterical. I mean, beyond crying. She was..." I pulled my hands from his and waved them in the air. "She sounded really ... depressed."

"That is not good."

I shook my head. How far should I take this? "No, not good at all. I mean, who knows what she might do."

"In that case, you must go to Rennes," he said, nodding to himself. "Yes. Tomorrow."

Damn. I went too far. Now what? "I'd do that, because, well, why not? But there's getting the train, and once I *did* get there, where would I stay? I can't stay with the two of them if there's fighting and he's maybe moving out...."

"Well, obviously not. But I have a good friend, he has a flat there. Right in the Old City. I will call. He will let you stay there, I'm sure."

I fought to keep from shaking my head too violently. "No,

I couldn't impose on a stranger like that. And even if I did, how would I find my way around? Nic told me that everyone doesn't speak English there, not like in Paris, and I wouldn't want to count too much on her in her time of . . . distress."

He sighed. "You're right. Well, there is only one answer."

I let myself relax. He'd come to his senses. He'd stay here in Paris while I pretended to provide long-distance comfort and advice. . . .

"I'll come with you. To Rennes. I can sit and relax and forget the world just as easily there as I can in Switzerland." He stood. "Let me call Gautier. Then I'll get train tickets. We can leave in the morning." He glared at his mother. "I suppose we'll have to bring Jules?"

She looked contrite, but as Max left the room, I saw it.

A twitch of her mouth. A light in her eye.

Max and I were going to Rennes.

All I had to do break the news to Nicole that we were coming and the reason why.

Easy peasy.

Back in my room, I looked at my phone to find Cheri and Alison had both been busy.

> C: Are you any surer today????
>
> A: Maybe with Alan gone you and Max will spend more time together and you'll see what's really going on. But don't get blindsided by Paris. Remember you have to live with your choices in the real world

C: There is nothing wrong with a sexy frenchman in the real world. But you should think about how hard long-distance relationships are

M: He lives in NYC

C: BINGO!!!! Problem solved

Oh, ladies . . . if you only knew.

Chapter 10

Yet another diabolical plan,
and Jules gets a floor show

I called Nicole.

It was way too early in the morning for her and I knew it, but desperate times called for desperate measures. At this point, I was going bananas. I grabbed Jules's leash and headed outside so that neither Max nor Solange would overhear my call.

"Mom? What's wrong? Is someone dead?"

"No. No, honey, everyone here is alive and well, there's just, ah, something has come up and I really need your help."

I could hear the sleep in her voice. "Hold on. Let me get out of bed." There were a few moments of silence. "It's really early."

"Yes, I know, but I took Jules out for his walk to avoid being overheard."

"Sounds devious. Okay. What's up?"

"Max and I are coming to Rennes. We'll be there today, sometime around noon."

"Mom," she asked calmly, "why are you and Max coming to Rennes?"

"Because you and Louis are having problems and you might break up. In fact, you might be severely depressed, and I'm coming to give you solace, and Max is coming with me because I don't think I can finish this book without him."

"Wait." Noises came from her end. She was probably making coffee. Or buttering bread. Or slaughtering a whole pig. "Say this again? This time with footnotes, please."

"I know you haven't been around me while I'm writing for a while, but do you remember how it usually is?" This was a stupid question because Nicole remembered everything, but I felt the need for some sort of introduction.

"Yes, Mom," she said.

"And you know how sometimes if I'm having trouble, I, well, latch on to a . . . thing?"

She sighed. "Is this like that smelly sweater situation?"

"Yes," I said. She had really hated my wearing that sweater inside out and teased me about it for years afterward.

"So Max is your smelly sweater? I get that. But that doesn't explain why the two of you are coming here because I'm breaking up with Louis. Which I'm not, just so you know."

Jules's head shot up as another bulldog appeared across the street. Previous experience reminded me to hold on more tightly to the leash.

"I do know, Nic. But Max was going to leave Paris and go to Switzerland, and I was afraid that if he left, I'd never finish this book, and I panicked and had to think of a reason for him to stay."

"Ah. So you lied and said I was having problems that might result in some serious, not to mention stupid, activity on my part. And since Max seems to be a genuinely thoughtful and caring sort of man, he suggested that you rush to my side. Then you started to make excuses, probably played the helpless-female card, and he then offered to come with you. Is that about right?"

I sighed in relief. Having a brilliant daughter was sometimes a trial, but it usually kept me from having to do a lot of explaining. "That's it exactly. And I'm sorry, because I know this will be an imposition but . . . I really need to finish this book." I tugged Jules around a corner only to find three cats lounging across the sidewalk.

There were a few random noises, a clink that could have been cutlery or possibly swordplay. With Nicole, you never knew. "Well, I don't mind. Honestly. I'd love to show you Rennes, you'll love it here. And I like Max. But you know how I am about lying."

Yes, I knew. She was terrible at it. It wasn't just her complete moral objection to telling a falsehood, no matter how righteous the cause. She was just really bad at controlling her voice and her facial expressions. "Yes. So, I'm thinking if Max asks you about, well, your problems, you could just close your eyes and say you don't want to talk about it. You could probably do that, right?"

"Probably. And Louis is heading out to Berlin today to visit his brother. He'll be gone all week. It's good timing, because Louis isn't a very good liar either."

"Oh, I'll be sorry to miss him. I do like him, quite a bit. But yes, it will probably be less complicated without him around. And you're sure you're okay with my being there?" I started to drag Jules across the street, but a nasty miniature poodle that had previously challenged Jules to the doggy equivalent of a duel was lifting a leg not three yards away.

"Yes, Mom. I have no problem at all with you being in Rennes. But be warned, I'll probably make you buy all sorts of expensive things for the flat that I could never afford on my own."

"A small price to pay for finishing this book. Great, honey. This is great."

"So, noonish?"

"That's when the train arrives. I'll text you when we get to the flat."

"Where are you staying?"

"At a friend of Max's. In the Old City, he said."

"The two of you are sharing the flat? Are you sleeping with him?"

"What?" My voice ratcheted up at least an octave. The poodle stopped doing its business to growl at me, and Jules immediately went on the defensive.

"Well, he is an attractive man, and he's very charming, and I can tell that you like him," she said, quite reasonably. "You both are consenting adults, and you seem to have very strong feelings about keeping him close."

"Nic, honey, any feelings I have for Max have nothing to do with how attractive he is. Or charming." I wrestled Jules back toward the three cats. At least there was a chance they'd back away from him. "You bet I like him. My gosh, what's *not* to like? But this is all about getting this book finished so I can leave Paris with a rough draft and not blow my deadline."

"Okay, but if you wanted to, I mean . . . What about you and Daddy?"

What about Alan and me? "Honey, we talked about things, but nothing was decided. I mean, we hadn't seen each other in years, and to be thrown together in Paris of all places? We both agreed to see each other back home, but no promises."

"I get it. Really, I do. So do you want me to meet your train?"

"That won't be necessary. After all, you're distraught."

"Terribly. But not so distraught that I can't get taken for a really nice dinner."

"I figured that. Oh, and Jules is with us." Thankfully all three cats rose, lifted their tails with utter disdain, and stalked off.

"That is not at all my problem."

"True. Okay, go back to bed. I'll text you when we're settled in."

"Okay, Mom. Love you."

"Love you more," I said back.

But she'd already hung up.

I looked down at Jules. "Are you done yet?"

He finally lifted his leg, and I had to jump away to avoid being peed on in the middle of Paris.

The old center of Rennes looked like a fairy-tale town. Better yet, it looked like a fairy-tale town designed by Disney. I kept waiting for Belle from *Beauty and the Beast* to turn a corner, carrying a baguette and singing about her provincial life.

The streets were narrow and made of cobblestone. Timber-frame houses stood side by side, some of them leaning, paned windows open to the breeze and lined with flower boxes. Max and I had arrived at the train station, taken the Métro, and emerged at a bustling square where café tables spilled onto the sidewalks and the sun filtered down into twisted streets and alleyways.

Max finally took Jules from his travel carrier, folded it up into a neat little pouch, and snapped on his leash. "This way," he said, moving off, Jules trotting beside him. I followed behind, my tote bag draped over my shoulder, trying to take in the buildings, the people, the sounds of the street. . . . I am always *such* a tourist.

It wasn't long before we stopped in front of a sleek glass-and-concrete structure, very out of place in its obvious newness, wedged between a tiny timber-frame shop and an ancient stone wall that soared up at least three stories.

"Part of the old ramparts," Max explained as he picked up Jules, entered a code, and pushed open a glass door.

"The lift is to the left there," he said. "We're on the third floor."

"This friend of yours, is he working? When will he be back?" I asked.

The tiny elevator closed its door and carried us upward.

"He's not here," Max said. "This is one of several places he owns. He uses it as an Airbnb, but as he has no renters . . ." The elevator stopped, Max went down the short hallway to the farthest door, entered another code, and pushed it open.

It could have been any condo in any American city: a large-screen television on one wall, a gray modular couch, and abstract prints on the white walls. But the tall windows looked out over the square and back into another century. Across the way, the windows of all the top-floor apartments were open, curtains flapping in the breeze, and a lone white cat perched precariously on a windowsill.

"You can have the bedroom on the right," Max called. "I'll take this one here."

The bedroom was small and modern. I took five minutes to unpack, wash my face, and fluff my hair before going back into the living room, where Max was staring out of the windows. The light was coming in and he was just a silhouette, shoulders slightly slouched, his linen jacket unbuttoned over a snug white T-shirt tucked into beautifully fitting jeans, a scarf tumbled around his neck.

Oh my God, I thought. What a sexy man.

I pushed the thought away. Hadn't I just told Solange that

I was here to write a book, not get involved with anyone? Hadn't I just explained, very thoroughly, to my own daughter that my feelings about Max had nothing to do with the heart? Or body?

Couldn't I feel my heart start to pound and my throat start to close up and my fingers itch to pull that scarf from around his neck?

He turned to me. "Ready? We can pick up a few things, have some wine if you like. When are we meeting Nicole?"

I had to swallow twice before I could answer. "Not until this evening, so we have a few hours. I sent her the address. She said she knows where we are."

He stepped back from the window. "Good. There's a shop just there where we can get enough for the next few days. I imagine you'll spend your time with Nicole? I will just wander. And I can run in the morning. I am lazy in Paris, but here I can go up along the canal."

"So you really do run marathons?"

He laughed. "Did you think I was joking at the gardens? Yes, I run marathons. Never Boston. I don't much like the cold, and April in New England can be freezing. But New York, every year. It helps to make me feel young."

I could make you feel young, I thought. The whole scene played out in front of me—tumbling onto the couch, pushing the pillows to the floor as we unbuttoned and unzipped while Jules sat watching, a silly doggy smile on his face. . . .

"Maggie?"

"What? Yes. Let's get some things for breakfast. We'll need

coffee and bread and cheese. Maybe fruit, and eggs. Then we can just sit and wait for Nic. That's a much better idea."

He gave me a look. "Much better idea than what?"

Oh, Max. If you only knew.

My daughter did not look distraught. In fact, she was practically glowing as she came hurrying across the square to where we sat at a café table. I watched her as she carefully avoided being touched by any of the many people around her. She dodged and danced through the crowd, waving as she saw us. I leaned over to Max. "She's probably popping Xanax like crazy," I murmured. He nodded back.

She bent down to give Max a kiss on his cheek, then sat next to me, sloughing off her backpack and leaning in for a hug.

"Do you love my city?" she asked.

"Oh yes. It's gorgeous. Amazing. It even smells special."

She laughed. "That's the bakery. Have you had kouign-amann yet?"

"No."

"Wait." Both Nicole and Max said it at the same time, looked at each other, and laughed.

"It's a very Breton thing," Nicole explained. "The best combination of butter and flour and sugar that there is in the world."

Max nodded. "Yes. Just looking at it will force me to run an extra five miles, but it is worth every bite."

They smiled at each other, and I felt something twist in my

gut. Here were two people—the daughter I loved more than anything else in the world and a kind and generous man—and I was using them both. I had to finish my book. I *had* to finish my book. And although they both understood that, I felt a surge of guilt. Nicole, I knew, would walk through fire to help me. Maybe Max would too, but he didn't even know. . . .

"How are you doing?" Max asked her, very kindly.

I closed my eyes.

She did just fine.

"I really don't want to talk about it," she said, her voice perfectly even.

I opened my eyes and took a breath. I wondered how long she'd practiced that line for me.

"Then we won't," Max said. "Now, if I remember correctly, that street right there will become filled with very loud and drunken students in, oh, a few short hours."

Nicole nodded. "You remember perfectly."

"But I also seem to remember that at the end of that street is a very nice brasserie."

"Yes, but I was thinking that maybe Mom could try something different."

I stared. "Different how?"

"There's an excellent Irish pub here," she said.

Max nodded. "Yes, that's right. Maggie, we must go there. All expats. Everyone speaks English, the food is authentic, and it is always great fun. I can watch the soccer match there." He laughed at my expression. "Not to worry. There are many good places to eat. And I will cook for you both. I have one signature dish that my first wife taught me. She was from Alsace, and there is a very famous dish there with bacon and potatoes and cheese. Delicious."

The man could cook. He ran marathons, and he looked fabulous in jeans and a simple white T-shirt, and he cooked. Only one dish, but still . . .

"Whatever you say," I told him.

So I had my first burger in France, and it was quite on par with everything else I'd eaten in France, and there was an obviously very important soccer match going on, so we stayed and Max and Nicole cheered as I sat and marveled at how my daughter had suddenly become a fan of sports. She played soccer as a kid and had been good, but had never been a fan. Yet there she was, jumping up and cheering, calling out the players by name and having a terrific time. I wondered what Max thought of her, since she was supposed to be all upset about her possible breakup with Louis, but he seemed to take it all in stride. In fact, the whole evening might have gone on without a hitch if I hadn't noticed a waitress pass by with a few very interesting items on her tray.

I nudged Nicole. "What's all that?"

"That? It's absinthe."

"Really? The stuff that used to make people go crazy? Isn't that illegal?"

She shook her head. "Not anymore."

"Does it still make people go crazy?"

Max laughed. "It all depends on how far along they already are in the process."

"Can we try it?"

Max held up two hands, as if to ward off a blow. "Not me. I know my reaction, and it is not so good."

"Reaction?" I asked. "What do you mean?"

"Well," Nic said slowly, "it's not your average kind of drink. It tends to hit people in lots of different ways."

I waved to the waitress as she made her way back. "Can I have one of those?" I asked, pointing to the table, which had just received the drink and all its accoutrements.

She nodded. "Just one?" she asked.

"Yes," said Max.

"Just one," said Nicole.

"Really? You're not going to join me? This is a legendary drink. Writers and artists have been talking about this for generations—Van Gogh and Toulouse-Lautrec. Hemingway and Edgar Allan Poe." I poked Nicole in the ribs with my elbow. "Joyce and Lord Byron."

"And do you remember what kind of lives they led?" she asked.

"Oh, come on. What do you think will happen?" I'd already had three glasses of wine, which was usually my limit, but . . . absinthe? I mean, how could I resist?

The waitress set the tray in front of me. "Do you know how to drink this?" she asked. Her Irish accent was adorable.

Max waved a hand. "I'll show her," he said.

He took a tall glass from the tray; it had about two fingers of greenish liquid in the bottom. "First you take the spoon and put it over the top of the glass." The spoon had a long handle and was slotted. "The sugar cube goes here." He used tiny tongs to place the cube on the slots. "Then pour ice-cold water slowly." He took a small pitcher and tipped it, and a slow but steady stream fell over the sugar cube and into the glass.

"Watch," Nicole whispered. "Any second now."

As I watched, the absinthe turned from green to milky white.

"That," Max explained, "is called the *louche*. It is said to release all the botanical bits hidden in the absinthe. Can you smell?" I leaned forward. Yes, I could smell something: fresh and herbal and clean.

He kept pouring water. "Ideally, there should be three to five parts water for every one part of absinthe. So." He put down the pitcher. "There you have it."

I reached for the glass and took a tentative sip. It smelled much nicer than it tasted. I took a bigger sip. Anise for sure. Not black jelly bean licorice, but subtler. Then I took a full-fledged gulp. Very dry. Slightly bitter. I set down the glass.

"Well?" Nicole asked.

"I'm not sure," I said, and took another drink. Then another. By now it was going down smoothly. "I can kind of see the attraction. Will it get me very drunk?"

"Yes," Max said, his mouth twitching. "Perhaps only half?"

"Don't be silly," I said, and proceeded to finish off the entire glass.

Nicole was leaning toward me, watching my face. "When it hits," she said, "you'll know it."

I sat back. "Well, whatever. Finish watching your game here."

"Match," Nicole said. "It's a match."

I focused on the big-screen television at the end of the bar and tried to figure out which team was winning. Just when I thought I'd gotten it all sorted out . . .

"Mom?" Nicole asked. Her face was very close. "Why are you smiling?"

I pointed at the television. "Look at all the men. They're running. And they're all wearing those pretty colors." I put my arm around her neck, drew her close, and whispered to her, "Can you see the colors?"

Max threw back his head and laughed. I *felt* the laugh, the richness and joy, could almost see his delight in the crinkles around those extraordinary eyes, the flash of his teeth behind the red-lipped smile. At some point, I believe the bill was paid, and then we were walking through the cobblestone streets of Rennes. I had my arm looped through Max's and was leaning against him slightly because I was suddenly worried that I might lean too far to the left and fall. After I had one wobbly pitch forward, Nicole took hold of my other arm.

"Will I start seeing more colors?" I asked her.

She did not even try to not laugh. "No, I think the psychedelic portion of the evening is finished."

"Good," I said, concentrating on putting one foot in front of the other. "This is almost like tequila," I said. "But really different."

"That," Max said kindly, "is a very excellent description. Here we are. I've got her, Nicole. We'll see you in the morning?"

Nic said something and kissed my cheek.

"Good-bye," I said, very loudly, and waved. I kept on waving until Max put his hand on mine and lowered it.

"The lift is just here," he said.

The doors slid open. "Like magic!" I crowed.

He laughed. "Exactly like magic."

I leaned against him again. He felt very . . . solid. And warm. No, not warm; the heat coming off his body seeped into my pores, and at that moment I think I felt every one of them. I wondered what his skin was like. I wondered how his hands would feel in my hair, stroking my back, pulling me against his hips. I wanted to see how his mouth would taste against mine.

If only I could move.

We were out of the elevator and there, at the end of a very long and narrow hallway, was a door.

"Is it far?" I asked.

"Not at all," Max chuckled. He pushed me forward and through the front door of the flat, then a quick turn and I was standing directly in front of my bed.

I put both arms straight out from the sides of my body, feeling the space around me. "I got this," I told him.

"Are you sure?"

I nodded for what seemed to be several minutes. Obviously he didn't believe me because he was still there, standing just behind me.

"Do you think I'm attractive?" I asked him.

"Why yes, Maggie. I do."

I lowered my arms and turned around very slowly, because

I don't think I could have done anything quickly at that point, even if I were on fire. "Do *you* find me attractive? Not in a *well, she's got all her teeth and nice ankles* kind of way, but in a more personal, *gosh, I'd love to shag her* kind of way?"

He was smiling and his eyes were very blue. "Why yes, Maggie. I do."

"Then why don't you make a pass at me?" I felt myself shifting slightly forward, and he caught me by the shoulders.

"I would never try to seduce a woman under the influence," he said, smiling more broadly.

"Oh," I said with genuine sadness. "That's too bad." I focused and managed to bring my arms up around his neck, and I sank forward, right into him. My arms tightened, and his lips were so much softer than I'd imagined, and the smell of him . . . Dear Lord, he smelled like a summer night: deep and fresh and earthy. I was drowning in this man, so much so that I didn't even realize he was pushing me steadily away until I felt the cool rush of air where the lean lines of his body had been pressing against me.

"Maggie," he said, his voice very low.

"I love it when you say my name," I told him, and I closed my eyes as I leaned in again.

He stepped back and I heard him clear his throat. "This is a very tempting idea, but like I said, I don't seduce—"

"You don't have to seduce," I whispered. "All you have to do is ask."

"Maggie."

I opened my eyes and shook my head. "Shh. Don't say it."

But he did. "I would never forgive myself if we woke up in the morning and you ran screaming from the bed."

I shook my head again. "That won't happen."

He cracked a smile. "Or if you didn't remember anything."

"Oh, that *really* won't happen."

He pushed me, very gently, and I fell for what seemed to be a very long time before my back hit the mattress. I blinked as I felt myself slipping, very quickly, into something not quite conscious.

He picked up my feet and moved them until I was more or less on the bed, and he eased off my shoes.

"Good night, Maggie," he said.

I don't remember how long it took me to fall asleep, but I do remember my dreams.

They were all about Max.

For the very first time since I'd arrived in France, I did not get up the next morning and write. In fact, when I opened my eyes, I wasn't sure I'd be able to move.

No, it wasn't a hangover. There was no headache. No rumble in my tummy. Just a feeling of being underwater, and although I was breathing normally, moving any of my extremities seemed too much of an effort. So I lay there in the semidarkness trying to remember exactly what happened the night before. It took me a while, but when I *did* remember, I wanted to crawl under the bed and stay there.

Did I really ask Max why he hadn't made a pass at me? Oh

dear Lord. I was never going to drink another thing again. In my life. Ever.

I closed my eyes. Thankfully, that did not require much effort. Did I also tell him he wouldn't have to seduce me at all? That all he'd have to do was *ask*?

As I lay there, I wasn't sure what was bothering me the most: that I'd asked him in the first place, or his answer.

There was a quiet knock on my door. Well, to be honest, thinking that Max would suddenly take off for Switzerland after all and I'd never have to see him again was rather far-fetched.

"Maggie?" He stuck his head around the half-open door. "Are you awake?"

I know my mouth opened several times. I'm just not sure what came out.

"Would you like some coffee?"

Nodding was going to be too difficult, but I think I moved my hand.

He came back a few minutes later with a small tray and a steaming cup. He set it on the end table.

"Should I leave this right here?"

I finally opened my eyes and there he was, leaning over me, trying very hard not to laugh.

"You're enjoying this, aren't you?" I growled.

"Not at all. I'm just appreciating our shared experience. I know exactly how you feel. Believe me, this too shall pass."

"Why didn't you warn me?"

"Would it have made a difference?"

"No."

He straightened. "Come on out whenever you're ready. And a really hot shower will help."

When he left I managed to sit up, drink the coffee, and stagger to the bathroom. He was right. Standing under hot water for about twenty minutes did the trick. I felt almost human again.

Then I had to go out there and pretend I hadn't made a total ass of myself the night before by throwing myself at a man who had the grace to step aside rather than make the catch.

Max was on the couch, his legs stretched out before him, reading. One arm was crooked up behind his head, and he was dressed in blue linen trousers and a white button-down shirt. His sleeves were rolled up and his forearms were, without a doubt, the best I'd ever seen in my entire life.

"I'm sorry," I croaked.

He looked up. "For what? Everyone gets drunk on absinthe. That's the whole point."

I sat down next to him. "Not about getting drunk. About what came after."

He closed his book and clasped his hands together. "Nothing came after."

"Because you are a gentleman."

He chuckled. "Sometimes, yes. But I did not want to do anything that would possibly come between you and Alan."

I blinked. Was I still drunk? "What are you talking about?"

He shrugged. "Obviously you worked very hard at reconnecting with your ex-husband. All that time that you spent with him . . . that meant something, *non*?"

"Meant something? Wait . . . you think that Alan and I are getting back together?" To be honest, I had kind of been thinking along those lines as well, but if Max . . . I mean, if I could choose? I needed to backpedal on that idea, and quickly. "Alan and I are not getting back together. Not now, not ever. No. And I really appreciate the whole gentleman thing going on here. I really do. Very honorable. But, no."

He sat back. "What do you mean, no? I thought you had made up your mind about him."

Yes. I made up my mind this very second. "I decided that Alan and I would always care for each other, but I wasn't going to spend the rest of my life with a man who just gave me the warm fuzzies. If I'm going to ride off into the sunset with someone, there has to be more to it than that."

His face changed. He began to smile and his eyes brightened. He leaned forward, his forearms resting on his knees, his body shifting ever so slightly toward mine. "Really?"

Was he remembering last night? Did he feel that the kiss between us was just a beginning and that things could only get better from there?

"Yes. Really. Look, Alan and I had a great time together, but that was all. There was no . . . fire. Your mother said I should try to find something new to love about him, and yes, there were some things, but it wasn't enough."

"My mother said that to you?"

"Yes."

"What else did she say?"

I looked into those steady blue eyes. "She said she thought I'd be good for you."

The seconds ticked by. "And what did *you* say?"

I took a breath. "I told her I didn't come to France to get involved with a man. I told her I'd just broken up with Greg and probably wasn't emotionally free."

"Ah." His eyes widened and his body shifted again, just a bit closer.

"Max?"

"Yes."

"Now that I'm not getting back with Alan and I'm not drunk, would you like to kiss me?"

"What about not getting involved with a man? What about not being emotionally free?"

"Your mother suggested that I was already, ah, detached. Yes, that was her word. And she was right. I'm feeling completely detached. Now, if you would—"

His mouth against mine felt like it belonged there, like it had belonged there from the very beginning of time. I felt that kiss everywhere. Last night I had been in a fog of lust and absinthe, but here, in the clear and sober light of day, I knew I'd been waiting my whole life for the taste of his lips. And his hands in my hair? My fingertips along the sides of his face? Well, all that was kind of perfect. Nicole was right. We were both consenting adults. And I had some very strong feelings about keeping him as close as possible.

I turned and swung my body over his. He settled down a little into the couch and his hands went up under my T-shirt and against my skin. I shifted my body just enough to feel him getting hard against me. I began to pull off my shirt so I could feel his fingers against my breasts. . . .

The buzzer buzzed.

I stopped. His eyes were inches from mine.

"Don't tell me," I said hoarsely.

"Your daughter is coming over for breakfast," he managed. "I think I'm making omelets."

The buzzer buzzed again.

I practically threw myself to the other side of the couch, pulling down my shirt.

"I need a minute," he croaked, and he got up and vanished into his bedroom. "We will continue this tonight," he called.

"Promise?"

He laughed. "Oh yes. I promise."

I took several deep breaths. The buzzer buzzed a third time, and I calmly got up, pushed the button to unlock the door downstairs, and went to greet Nicole.

Chapter 11

*In which the sun is brighter, the birds
sing louder, and all is right with the world*

After breakfast, Max went running and Nicole gave me her grand tour of Rennes. We walked through narrow streets and past churches and cafés and music shops and clothing stores. I found everything so damn amazing that she finally stopped in the middle of the street, grabbed my arm, and shook it.

"Why are you so happy?"

I breathed deeply. "I'm going to finish my book, I'm in a glorious city, and my favorite daughter is with me. Why shouldn't I be happy?"

"What happened?"

"Nothing."

"You're lying."

I shook my head and started walking. "Nic, honey, I'm allowed to feel happy without something happening."

"Yes, but . . . you were pretty drunk last night. Did you and Max do anything while you were . . . you know?"

"Plastered? No, Max and I did absolutely nothing while I was plastered."

Luckily she didn't ask what we'd done while I was cold sober, because I wasn't so sophisticated that I wanted to talk about my sex drive with my daughter.

I *was* happy. And not just because of the book and Rennes and Nicole. What was happening between Max and me was not just the scratching of an itch that had been pestering me for days now. I knew it would be more than that. I'd written dozens of romantic heroes of all shapes and sizes, but I'd never even *imagined* a Max.

I did not believe in love at first sight. I did not believe in it so strongly that I didn't even *write* about it. Sure, there can be an instant physical attraction—obviously. But love? Without even knowing the person? And barely two weeks' worth of evening walks and shared conversation over brandy in the warm Paris nights did not mean I knew Max. I had no idea what his favorite color was, who his favorite band was, if he liked horses, or enjoyed the theater, or long walks on the beach.

So, this was not love. *Probably* not love. But it wasn't just simple lust either.

I didn't quite know what to do with my confusion. I still firmly believed that I needed him in order to finish my book. But there was something else going on, and I needed to figure it out pretty quickly. When he'd left to go running, he'd whispered for me to take care of Nicole. He still thought we were here on some sort of mission of mercy, and I was feeling guilty about the whole thing.

Nic and I stopped in front of a gallery and I gazed longingly at tiny watercolors of the French countryside. I could buy four of them, I thought, have them framed, and put them in my new beach house.

"I wouldn't mind," Nic said. "You and Max, I mean. I like him."

I tilted my head. "Oh? What about your father and me living out our golden years together?"

She shrugged. "He talked way more about how great it was to see you than you talked about him. I had a feeling things weren't going to work out quite the way I wanted. But Max is a pretty great guy. And he lives on the Upper West Side. Very chichi. Right up your alley."

See? I didn't even know where Max *lived*. How could I possibly be in love?

"How do you know where he lives?"

She shot me a look. "Max and I have *talked*."

"Well, excuse me."

"No, I mean about stuff. Politics, for instance. He's a bit conservative for my taste, but that aligns him pretty much with you. That sort of thing is important."

"Of course." The truth was that anything an inch or two right of anarchy was a bit conservative for Nicole.

"He likes opera."

"I didn't know that."

"And he still reads newspapers."

"I did know that."

"I think you'd be okay together."

"So does Solange. In fact, she's been playing matchmaker from the day I got to Paris."

"Mothers know best."

"Hmmm. When do you think you and Louis are going to kiss and make up?"

We'd been walking again, and she pulled up short. "I thought the whole plan was to keep him with you until the book was done."

"Yes, but—"

"But? As in, but now things are different and you don't have to stay here in Rennes and help heal my broken heart?"

"Well, sort of."

She shook her head. "As in, but now that Max and I are slaves to each other's earthly desires—"

"No! Well, not yet."

"I knew it," she said smugly. "Well, I imagine Louis and I can have a long and meaningful conversation sometime tomorrow, have great makeup sex tomorrow night, break the news to you the next day, and you and Max can head back to Paris by, say, the weekend? How does that sound?"

"There's still so much to see here, though."

"True that. You really must see the Thabor Gardens. Maybe Max can take you tomorrow? I'm working." I knew she had a part-time job as an English tutor to a small group of six-year-olds. "And the museum here is quite good. Breton art. I love going there. The two of you could go in the afternoon while Louis and I are healing the rift in our relationship?"

"Nobody likes a smart-ass, Nic." I reached around her for a quick hug. "That sounds perfect. Max wants to cook for us tonight. That Swiss dish he was talking about?"

"It's called a tartiflette. Potatoes and bacon with melted cheese."

"My God, if I lived here I'd weigh three hundred pounds. I'm amazed at all the thin people."

"They're thin because they walk everywhere. Look at that." We'd stopped again, this time in front of a shop that sold kitchen things. "That's for making galettes. I could really use one of those."

"It's yours," I said. "If you promise to tell me what a galette is."

We pushed our way into the shop. "That's what we'll have for lunch," Nicole promised. "Bonjour," she said to the clerk. "This woman here is going to buy lots of things."

"Yes, I am," I said. "I might even buy something for me."

Max had given me the key code for the flat, so I let myself in and settled in to work at the tiny vanity table in my bedroom. I was halfway through a very tough conversation between Bella and Lance when I felt strong hands against the back of my shoulder and fingers gently massaging my neck.

I leaned my head back. "How was your afternoon?"

I felt his lips on the top of my head. "Excellent. I found a very good Reblochon, which is impossible to find in the States, and perfect oranges from Spain. How was your day?"

"I bought Nicole an entire kitchen full of expensive copper pots, and ate a galette for lunch with cold Breton cider. And I had that kooglemani thing."

"You mean kouign-amann?"

"Yes. It was a religious experience." I turned around, stood up, and put my arms around him. "My second of the day."

He laughed. "You are a woman of many surprises, Maggie. All of them delightful. It is too early to worry about dinner, so go on with your writing if you like. How is Nicole?"

"She was soothed by new cookware. I think they are going to be okay. All young couples go through phases. After all, they are still discovering things about each other. It's a process."

"If they are lucky, they will continue to discover new things until they are old and feeble." He was very close, and I could see the flecks of gray in his eyes and the way the tips of his eyelashes thinned to nothingness. "That is what love is, yes? A voyage of discovery that lasts a lifetime."

I laughed and pushed him away. "I'm supposed to be the romantic here." I shook my head. "Love is still wanting to be with someone even after you know it all."

He kissed my lips gently. "That is true also. You continue to write. I will be out in the square, right down the street. Find me when you're done with your work."

But I never made it down because I was so deep into Delania, I never noticed the room getting darker. The next thing I knew,

I smelled onions and my stomach started rumbling. I hurried into the kitchen.

Max was standing at the stove, a towel tucked into the waistband of his jeans, dicing potatoes. I could have written three books on the spot just about him, in the kitchen, cooking.

"I'm sorry," I said. "I got involved. What time is it?"

He threw me a smile. "After seven. I texted Nicole; she's on her way. She's bringing bread. The wine is open."

I poured a glass and leaned against the counter, watching him. His movements were graceful and precise, with no wasted energy. He knew exactly what he was doing and was doing it very well.

Pretty much a repeat performance of the early morning, when he'd made an omelet so fluffy it had practically floated off the plate.

"Nicole wants you to see the Parc du Thabor, and you must. The roses aren't quite in their glory this time of year, but it's still lovely."

"Yes, she mentioned it. And the museum?"

He nodded and tipped the potatoes onto another pan. When they hit the hot butter, the smell almost brought me to my knees.

"So tell me what you're cooking here."

"Tartiflette." It sounded quite different from when Nicole said it. "It is very traditional in the east, near the Alps. Bacon and onion cooked with wine, then potatoes and cream, topped with Reblochon, which is almost impossible to get in the United States because of ridiculous import laws. Traditionally you boil the potatoes first, but I prefer to fry them up and get them a bit browned in butter, you see?" He tipped the pan. They were turning crisp and golden.

"I see."

"You finish it all in the oven. The bacon and onion bake into the potatoes and the cheese on top gets all brown and melted."

"That is the most erotic sentence I have ever heard in my life," I said, only half joking.

He grinned, put down the spatula, and stepped toward me, backing me against the wall. He took the wineglass from my hand and set it on the counter. He grabbed both of my wrists and brought my hands together over my head and took one more step, pressing against me.

"If you're in the mood for something erotic," he said, his lips against my neck, "we could probably do better than potatoes and cheese."

My reaction was so sudden and intense I couldn't take a full breath. His whole body was pressed against mine, and I was melting against him. His hands let go of my wrists and suddenly were under the cotton of my T-shirt, against my skin, and moving slowly down past my hips. I gripped the fabric of his shirt so tightly I thought I was going to tear right through it with my nails as his hand kept moving south.

"Oh."

His mouth was against mine, which is probably the only reason I didn't scream out loud when I came.

He moved and lifted me up onto the counter as I fumbled

with the zipper of his jeans and tried to kick off my sweatpants at the same time.

"My God," I muttered against his mouth, "you are so hot. . . ."

But it wasn't him. It was the stove. More accurately, it was the spill of butter on the stove that was burning merrily.

He grabbed the towel from his loosened waistband and threw it at the flames. They immediately went out. He grabbed the pan and pushed it off the heat, then leaned over to look at the damage.

"You will be happy to know," he said, laughter bubbling up between his words, "that the potatoes are unburnt."

"Well," I said, before dissolving into giggles, "thank God dinner is saved."

The tartiflette was memorable too.

We began slowly.

Nicole had left, and we cleaned the kitchen, even taking the time to finish what was left of the wine. We sat together on the couch, close enough that I could feel every move he made, and when I began to run my fingers down the length of his arm, he stood up and took my hand and led me back to the bedroom.

He left the light on.

"I have gray hair *everywhere*," I told him in protest.

"So do I," he answered, and pulled the T-shirt up and over my head, his fingers undoing my bra with one quick snap.

"I like a man who knows what he's doing," I said softly as I plucked open each button of his shirt.

"Just wait," he promised, his fingers trailing down the length of my back.

He had a lean runner's body, all smooth muscle and tight skin, and whatever insecurities I might have had about my body melted away, because he obviously delighted in every single bit of it. He was much more patient than I, laughing and teasing with his hands and his mouth—oh, that mouth. If I had been a poet, I would have written odes to that mouth—how soft his lips were, how he bit so gently, how his tongue coaxed and curled until I came so hard I had to grip his hair with both hands. And when he kissed me again, I could taste myself on those lips as I tried to rein in the pounding of my heart and the rushing of blood in my ears, so loud I could barely hear my breath.

And then it was my turn.

"Go slow," he whispered. "I want to come inside you." He stopped and shifted. "Do I need a condom?"

"I'm good if you are," I told him, and then I began to stroke him slowly, with just my fingertips, before I took him in my mouth. He groaned and moved his hips until I drew back and straddled him, sinking slowly. We moved together like we'd been born to it, like we'd been doing this forever, his hands against my breasts and then down along my thighs, finally urging me faster. When I came again he was just done, and we rolled apart, gasping and slick and sated.

I lay on my back, waiting for my breath to slow and my skin

to cool. I thought he was asleep, but he turned toward me, one arm across my breasts.

"I think," he said sleepily, "that went rather well." I heard the laughter in his voice. Even now, in this moment, there was laughter.

"I'll let you know in the morning," I whispered, and he chuckled softly as he fell asleep.

Max snored. He also took all the covers and held them tightly to his chest, and mumbled when I wrestled them away. He did not wake up when I got up to pee, or when I rose at dawn to write.

I took Jules out, picked up a melon and a few more kouign-amann. I was going to eat as much of that pastry as I could while I was in Rennes, even if it was not appropriate.

I heard the shower going when I got back, and for a moment considered stepping in and offering to wash his back, but my phone started going off. It was a text from Nicole.

N: Thanks again for dinner did you have sex yet?
M: None of your business can we take Jules to Parc du Thabor?
N: Not sure. Am I still fighting with Louis?
M: Yes, maybe for one more day.

I wanted to spend a few more days here. I also wanted to go out to the coast to see Saint-Malo and Dinard. I was pretty sure that Max was not going to suddenly take off to Switzerland, and I wanted to see as much of his country with him as I could.

And then what?

"Maggie?" Max stuck his head around the corner. "Did you take Jules?"

"Yes," I answered. "And got breakfast. If you make café crème, I'll slice the melon."

"Melon? Excellent. I'll make a Frenchwoman out of you yet."

He disappeared, and the thought flooded my brain: Would you? Would you please make me a Frenchwoman? Could we live in Paris and see the *Mona Lisa* whenever we wanted? Eat mussels and *frites* at nine in the evening and walk along ancient rivers that murmured softly in the night?

I shook my head. Who was I kidding? I had a life, and so did he. I had to finish my book, and he had to . . . bank.

What were we even doing?

I watched as he measured the coffee into the funnel of the stove-top espresso pot, tamping it carefully, then setting the pot on the stove. He poured milk into a small saucepan to heat up, then noticed the kouign-amann. "This is not really for breakfast," he said.

"I don't care," I answered, and he laughed.

He fixed our café crème in two round mugs and sat across from me, pushing one across the tabletop.

"Max, what are we doing?"

He carefully cut his melon. "I'm not exactly sure. How much longer are you in France?"

"I have to be back in the States by the end of May."

He nodded, as though to himself. "We have time then, *non*? Is it important to you to have an end in sight? Or can we just enjoy each other here and now?" He looked at me then, his eyes bright and very serious.

I took a bite of kouign-amann, savoring the crisp pastry and melting sugar against my tongue. "You're not at all like one of my heroes," I said, licking crumbs from my lips. "You are a very different sort of man."

He sipped his café crème and smiled. "Thank you. But that doesn't answer my question."

"No, it doesn't. I am enjoying myself. Very much."

"Yes. So am I. As I told you when we first met, you have lovely ankles."

And cleavage. He'd also mentioned my cleavage. Was *that* what this was for him?

I felt a twinge. Just for a second. Then I gave myself a mental kick in the butt as I counted back the days. We'd met sixteen days ago. Did I really expect him to think I was the most wonderful woman in the world? Did I think he'd fall madly in love with me, this woman with crazy writing habits and a life so different from his, who practically threw herself at him just a few nights before? I didn't even *write* that kind of thing! Besides, what did I want with another man who would be off somewhere at the drop of a hat, traveling the world without me?

And did it matter? After all, my first thoughts about him were not influenced by the man I knew him to be but rather the man as I'd write him in one of my books, the lover, the fantasy. . . .

Now I knew where we stood. Now I knew what we were doing. I could go forward from here.

"So can we take Jules with us?" I asked. "To Parc du Thabor? Nicole wasn't sure."

"Yes, but we must keep him off the grass. We French are very particular about our grass."

"I noticed that. All the signs in the Luxembourg Gardens. What is that all about?"

He laughed. "We French are a complicated people. I'll try to explain on the way over."

"Good," I said. I stood and gathered the plates, and he looked up at me, his eyebrows raised. "Here and now is good," I said. "Here and now is just about perfect."

There was a beat. "I'm glad," he said.

Jules, for all his interest in sniffing every single vertical object in all of Parc du Thabor and then peeing on it, soon began to drag, so Max picked him up and carried him through to the rose garden, not in full bloom but still beautiful. The whole place was peaceful and a glorious tribute to spring, with tulips and flowers ablaze, and the soft grass turning a darker green. We walked side by side, shoulders occasionally bumping, and Max talked: the history of Rennes, the gardens at Thabor, even a few quick botanical tips.

"You are not talking," he said. "Should I be alarmed?"

"No, not at all. Just thinking."

"About the book? Is there another scene we can act out?"

I shook my head. "No."

"Oh, come on. That was great fun. What are Bella and Lance doing right now?"

"Hiking up the side of a mountain in the dead of night, trying to escape Yeo-Te."

"See? I am sure they are facing many dangers. Perhaps a vicious panther is stalking them? Jules here would make an excellent panther."

I giggled. "No, there is not a panther in sight. Sorry."

"Well, perhaps there should be." He set Jules down and spoke rapidly in French. Jules looked at him. Max repeated what he'd said, and Jules circled twice before he settled on Max's feet, farting loudly.

"That's some panther you've got there," I said with a laugh. "A real threat."

He bent and scooped Jules up. "This dog is totally useless. Let's just pretend he is hot on our trail and we need to escape up a palm tree. See, we can easily climb that one there."

I laughed again. "There are signs everywhere about keeping off the grass. I can't imagine what they'd do to us if we started climbing trees."

We settled on a bench and Max stretched out his arm along the back, across my shoulders. "I was a very good tree climber in my day."

"For a city boy?"

"We often visited the vineyard. We should go there. It is very beautiful."

"Well," I said, quickly devising a lie, "maybe we can. Nic said that she and Louis are talking things through. Another day or two and I'm sure they'll be fine."

"What is the problem between them?"

An insecure, slightly neurotic writer is their problem. "Nic isn't very good in social situations," I said slowly. That was a truth. "She tends to get panic attacks. For a person like Louis who enjoys cafés and parties, it can be very hard."

"But surely he knew this?"

I sighed. "Yes. Just like *I've* always known it. It's still hard. I have to reset myself whenever I'm around her and try to see the world as she does. It can be exhausting." I leaned my head back into the crook of his arm. "We always get along best when we can put some space between us for a while."

"Louis is a philosopher. He'll figure it out."

"I hope so. She's always been so self-sufficient. It's good to see her happy *with* someone."

"And you? Do you need someone to be happy?"

"I've spent my entire adult life trying to figure that out. I've written about that kind of happiness in all its manifestations, and I've lived some of those ideas right out loud. I am very content on my own. I always have been. But there's a certain kind of . . . peace that comes with having someone beside you that you care for and can count on. I'll probably always be looking for that."

"And how will you know when you find it?"

Because I'll be sitting on a park bench, surrounded by sunshine and blossoms and birds chirping, and I'll lean back against the arm of someone, and I'll never want to leave.

"I'm hoping I'll be smart enough when the time comes," I said.

He nodded, and we sat in silence amid the brilliance and grandeur of Parc du Thabor, and I thought that my heart would burst with joy.

We spent the next day at the Museum of Fine Arts, walked along the canal, and saw even more of this glorious little city. Nicole made excuses, so Max and I spent the day alone.

Which felt better than any perfect day I'd ever written for one of my characters.

When I told him I needed to write, he kissed my hand and let me alone. We ate late and spent a third night together.

I could not get enough of him. And not just in bed. Walking next to him as he talked and joked made me happier than I'd felt in months.

Yet I'd lied to him to keep him close and was continuing to lie to him. But I didn't care because now I realized I wasn't afraid to lose him just because of the book. I was falling for this man so hard, I knew that when I finally admitted it to myself I would be a different woman entirely.

C: SO . . . whats new?
A: You've been quiet. That's not good.

M: In Rennes with Nic. Beautiful city I could live here forever

C: Yeah fine. What about Max. Is he with you????

M: Yes

A: Really!!!!

C: And is that a good thing???

M: Yes

A: OMG how romantic

C: Sex yet?

A: Who cares. They're together!!!

M: Yes.

A: OMG!!!!!!!!!!!!

M: I lied to him

A: Well that's not good

C: Will it hurt him?

M: I don't know but I really hate myself for it

C: Girlfriend maybe you should step back?

M: Good advice

And it was, although I wouldn't take it. I kept telling myself that grown women didn't act this way. I wasn't a silly teenage girl with a crush on the quarterback and getting all moon-eyed and goofy because he was paying attention to me.

But I sure felt that way. I was in such a haze I didn't even feel concerned when I got an early morning text from Nicole.

N: Louis is coming home a day early. Will arrive today. Have we made up yet?

"So, listen," I said to Max over lunch. "I think that Nic and Louis are over the worst of this. In fact, she told me that if I wanted to go back to Paris, well, she'd be okay with that."

Max nodded. "Certainly. We can go back to Paris. But if we can leave Rennes, we can go anywhere. Didn't you want to see Saint-Malo? You really should. It used to be a safe haven for pirates. It's a fascinating place. And the channel . . . have you ever seen the English Channel?"

I shook my head. "No, and I'm suffering from extreme withdrawal. I haven't seen an ocean in weeks."

He laughed. "Ah yes, all part of your beach house obsession? Maybe France will convince you to buy a beach house on the same ocean, but in a different country."

Something in my chest tightened. Here and now, I repeated to myself. That had been my mantra, and I was fighting hard to remember *here and now* even as I found myself wanting more.

"I have the last chapter left," I said as we began to walk back to the flat. "If the cable option goes through the way Lee thinks, I can buy as many beach houses on as many oceans as I want."

"And then you will be happy? You will have everything that you want?"

I nodded because I couldn't trust myself to speak.

We were almost to the flat, in the same square we had walked into from the Métro a few days before, when I heard someone call my name.

"Maggie?"

Oh dear God. It was Louis, coming up from the Métro station, looking incredibly handsome, with a leather duffel bag over one shoulder. He ran over to us and gave me a French kiss-kiss.

"Hello. Oh, Max, you are here too. Wonderful. Nicole, she did not tell me you were coming; I am so glad. If I had known, I would have returned earlier."

And with that, I felt the sunlight fade away and something heavy and ugly settle in my gut.

Max looked at me, obviously confused. "Returned?"

"Yes," Louis explained earnestly. "I was in Berlin to see my brother. Just a short trip, he was moving, you see, and I wanted to help. But how long have you been here?"

"Berlin?" Max repeated.

"*Oui.* Ah, here she is. Nicole, what a happy coincidence, yes? Look who I found."

My daughter, coming into the square, looked horrified as Louis ran up, hugged her, and gave her a very affectionate kiss. Then he stepped back, his face suddenly concerned. "What? Has something happened? What is wrong?"

She shook her head. "Nothing, Louis. Ah, Mom . . ."

Max said something in French, a sharp question, and Louis answered, then Nicole said something, and I closed my eyes as the words swirled around me until I heard my name again.

"Maggie? This was all a . . . ruse?" Max asked.

I opened my eyes and nodded.

"So that, what, I would come with you to Rennes?" Max chuckled, and I felt a wave of relief. He wasn't angry that I had concocted an entirely false scenario. I would have been, but I wasn't about to question his thinking.

Nicole looked very relieved. "It began when you said you were leaving Paris. She couldn't have that."

Max was grinning now. "If you had wanted me to stay so badly," he said, a playful glint in his eye, "you could have just *asked*."

"She was in a panic," Nicole went on. "After all, this was all about her book, and she was afraid if you left, well, she'd be stuck again."

Max tilted his head away from me, toward Nicole, and his face changed. Just a bit, but I saw it. And I knew that Nicole had not. One of the things about Asperger's is the inability to read visual clues: facial expressions and body language. It was why she had had such a miserable time in high school, where social interaction was 50 percent nuance. She had no idea that Max had reacted to what she had just said. She didn't see the edge of the cliff, and all I could do was watch as she drove forward.

"She gets a little crazy, my mom," Nic went on. "You see, you were what she latched on to as the reason she was writing so well. Once it was a smelly sweater. One time she paid our cleaning person to sleep over for a whole week because she was on deadline and was afraid if she left . . . well. That whole muse idea? She takes it *very* seriously."

Max looked back at me and his voice was very quiet. "So that was what this was all about?"

I grabbed his arm and pulled him back toward the Métro station and away from Nicole, who looked completely thrown. She had no idea what she'd said. She only knew, from Max's words, that it had gone wrong.

"Max," I began. "Listen—this is complicated."

"No, Maggie. It's not complicated at all. You needed me to be your muse, and you were willing to do anything to keep me around. That seems very simple." His lips pressed together in a thin line. "It makes sense. After all, that is why you came to Paris, *non*? Your book. That is all that matters to you."

"No. Max, that is not true." I glanced at Nicole, who was in a very intense conversation with Louis.

"You came up with this elaborate charade when you heard I was going to Switzerland. You made up the whole thing?" His voice was low and even.

"Not entirely. I just, well, I did lie, but mostly I just let you imagine the worst. I really didn't plan to come to Rennes with you. That was your idea. I was perfectly willing to stay in Paris."

"With me?"

"*Yes*. With you."

"Because without me, you wouldn't be able to write?"

"Well, that was part of it. I mean, yes, it was. But—"

"Is that why you made a pass at me? Because you'd do anything to keep me around?"

I felt a rise of anger. "I was drunk, and you, well—"

"Ah. So, you needed to be drunk but thought it would be worth it? As long as I stayed, right?"

I felt my jaw clench. He was deliberately twisting every single thing I was saying. "You must really think I'm a total bitch if you thought that was what I was doing."

"I didn't think that at all. But *you* asked the question, remember? That morning after we'd made love? You asked what we were doing. Was it because you wanted to make sure I wasn't assuming too much?"

I felt like I'd been hit and immediately hit back. "I wanted to make sure *I* wasn't assuming too much. After all, you were the one that insisted that the here and now was good enough."

"I was not insisting on anything. I asked. It was a legitimate question under the circumstances. After all, you had no plans to stay in France. What was I supposed to think?"

"What was *I* supposed to think, Max? That just because I was in the most romantic city in the world I'd fall madly in love with the first charmer I met? Especially if he was *another* man who would be gallivanting all over the world instead of where I wanted him to be?"

"Don't you dare compare me to Greg," Max said hotly.

"And why not?" I heard my voice get louder but I didn't care. "Greg kept the best part of himself for the bedroom too."

He stared at me. "Do you really think that for me it was all about *sex*?"

"You were the one who brought up my *lovely ankles*. And my cleavage. Are you really going to tell me there was *more*?" I heard the scorn in my voice. As angry as I was, I found myself thinking, *please tell me there was more, please tell me there was more. . . .*

He looked away from me at Nicole, then Louis, then shook his head. "I think I should have gone to Switzerland."

"It's not too late," I shot at him.

He handed me Jules's leash. "Tell your daughter it was a pleasure to meet her," he said quietly. Then he turned and walked away, shouldering his way through the small crowd that had gathered around us, two old people in the street, fighting about love.

How French.

Nicole came closer, her eyes bright, tears close to the surface. "Mom? What just happened?"

Louis let loose a barrage in French, then ended his rant in English. "Couldn't you see it in his face?"

I turned to him. "No," I said sharply. "She couldn't."

"Mom," Nicole asked again, "what happened? What did I do?"

I stepped toward her and swept her into my arms.

"Mom, did I screw it up? I'm sorry, I didn't know . . ."

"Oh, honey, you didn't do anything." I rubbed my hands between her shoulder blades. "You didn't do *anything*."

"I said the wrong thing, didn't I?"

I stepped back, gripping her shoulders. "You told the truth, Nic. It's what you always do because that's all you know *how* to do. It's on me to have expected anything else. I lied to Max and I got caught. End of story."

Her eyes were brimming. "But you *liked* him."

"And I like kouign-amann, but I can't bring it home with me, can I?" I saw Louis standing behind her, looking completely confused and upset. "My apologies to you too, Louis. To make you walk into a mess like this is unforgivable. I am truly sorry. So, listen." I tugged on Nic's arm. "Max will probably appreciate a bit of alone time, so why don't you show me your flat? Please?"

"Mom, go after him and explain," Nic said.

I sighed. That's what I had wanted to do the moment he had turned away, but I'd been mentally talking myself down for the past several minutes. "Explain what? Nic, I do happily ever after for a living, and it was not going to happen for Max and me. We got a happily for now. And the now is over."

It was over. I felt the heavy weight of sadness bearing down on me, something I had not experienced in a long time, not even as I'd walked away from Greg. This man had gotten to me in a way that changed me, and his leaving was going to leave a space in my soul that was never going to be filled again.

"What about the book?"

Right. What about the book? "Let me worry about that." What about the *book*? I could not let panic start to build about the book. Especially not in front of Nicole.

I smiled brightly. "Okay now, where do you two live?"

They lived in a converted stable, behind tall doors that opened to a brick courtyard. Their flat was narrow and deep, with sunlight streaming through the windows in the front and a loft bedroom in the back, nestled up against stone walls and under a pitched, beamed ceiling. We sat in their front door and talked. Neighbors came and went. At some point an impromptu jam session began in the courtyard: someone had a guitar, someone else a mandolin. People brought out bottles of wine and bread and cheese, and I watched as Nicole and Louis danced in the fading afternoon sun.

It was a joy to see them, young and happy, smiling and laughing together. My daughter would have a good life here,

I realized. A life of music and wine and love. I knew that she could be happy here. It was all I'd ever wanted for her.

It was almost dark when Jules started making noises, so I walked back to an empty flat, where I fed him, ate cold tartiflette, and stared for two hours at my laptop before drinking enough wine to finally fall asleep.

Chapter 12

The writing marathon, or how I typed for forty-eight hours without butter or wine

I made it back to Paris all on my own, and it was not nearly as much trouble as I'd thought it would be. I knew I had to buy Jules his own ticket for the train, I remembered where and when to get off at various stations. I even remembered to jiggle the key in the lock of the apartment building. When I finally sat down in the middle of the familiar Paris flat and congratulated myself for a rather flawless performance, I realized I'd done everything right because I'd watched Max do it all the first time. And then I realized that I'd been watching Max's every move since the very first morning.

I knew how he drank his wine, holding the glass with his thumb and middle finger, other fingers stiff and splayed. He tugged at the hair behind his left ear, and he always held out his left hand to Jules when petting him. When he stood, his weight was on one hip, with the opposite leg out to the side. When he lifted his eyebrows, one was slightly higher than the other. And now he was gone and every single thing I remembered about him was suddenly precious.

I went shopping, walked Jules, and felt a twinge of tears as I passed the places where Max and I had shared a glass of wine. Which was pretty much every café in a six-block radius of Place Victor Hugo. Obviously I needed to pull myself together and stop being so emotional or I'd have to stop going outside altogether.

I couldn't be in *love* with Max. I kept telling myself that. So . . . what was this, exactly? Why did I care that he thought I'd only used him for my book? I was never going to see him again, for one thing. Even if he did have a place in New York, and even though I did go there frequently, it's not like I was going to accidentally bump into him. I mean, do you know how many *other* people live there?

He wasn't the only smart and charming and funny man I'd ever met, even with a killer sexy accent. Or just because he wore his clothes with a certain flair and could turn the dullest topic into the best story ever. So what if his eyes were the bluest I'd ever seen, and the sex with him had been beyond memorable and had veered toward award-winning . . . ?

I kept staring at my phone. I could call him. He'd given me his cell phone number when we'd arrived in Rennes, as well as his address in New York. So I could call him. But say what? That maybe it had been all about the book in the beginning but things had changed? Changed to what? And why was he so bent out of shape anyway? After all, *he* had been the one to ask if there needed to be an end in sight. *He* had talked about the here and now.

Double damn him.

Finally, after walking, cooking, eating, cleaning up, and pouring a glass of wine, I sat in front of my laptop.

This was it. Would I be able to write? Or had my muse taken his rugged, wonderful, funny, sexy self to Switzerland?

I closed my eyes. Bella and Lance had reached the end of their journey. They had finally made it out of Delania and were on a boat to Turkey, where a U.S. government plane was waiting to take them back to the States.

To what? Would they even be able to live a life without guns and poisonous snakes and dreadful diseases and all the other dangers they had faced together?

I opened my eyes.

Damn straight they would.

Solange came home late Wednesday afternoon. I heard her voice from the hallway, but it barely registered. My eyes were burning, my throat was dry, and I seriously needed a shower.

But my book was done.

I had spent forty-eight hours in a frenzy, wearing the same sweater and skirt so that I didn't have to waste time changing every time I had to walk Jules or eat. I turned as she walked in and saw her eyes widen.

I probably looked as grubby as I felt.

"Maggie, what happened?" she whispered, approaching me slowly in a slight crouch as you would a dying, wild animal.

"I finished," I croaked. "The book is done. And . . ." I felt my throat close up and tears start. "And it's great," I blurted. "Even though Max left."

She suddenly straightened and drew her eyebrows together. "Left? What do you mean left?"

"He went to Switzerland. We had a fight." I fought the urge to cry. There was absolutely no reason to cry. I had finished my book. I'd done what I came to Paris to do. I was happy, dammit.

She nodded several times. "I see. Maggie, why don't you get up, and I don't know . . . wash your face? Maybe a whole shower?"

"Yes." I stood up slowly. "I took Jules out around eleven, so he should be fine. But a shower . . . that sounds good."

I walked down the hallway, pulling off clothes as I went, and climbed into the huge tub, turned on the hot water, and just stood there until I felt my skin start to pucker. I turned off the water and let myself drip-dry for a bit, then wrapped myself in a few towels and crawled into bed.

When I woke up, it was dark. I pulled on a T-shirt and a pair of leggings, grabbed my phone, and followed the light that was on in the living room.

Solange was sitting in a chair in front of the open window, the cool night air filling the room. There was music playing, an opera, and she was listening with her eyes closed, an expression of quiet joy on her face. What a lucky woman, I thought, to be able to just sit and listen and feel such peace.

Jules made a noise, and her eyes flew open.

"Ah, you must feel better. There is bread and cheese and tomatoes. Can you eat?"

Was she kidding? Could I *eat*? I nodded and sat at the edge of the sofa. Jules hopped up and snuggled in beside me.

I looked at my phone. After two days on silent, there were plenty of messages. Greg had found an apartment. Lee had spoken to Ellen again and I should call him, not her. Nicole was worried and I should let her know how I was doing. Alan just wanted to say hi. He'd arrived home safely. He'd call in a few weeks. And then . . .

> C: It's been days. You cannot just leave us hanging.
>   What in the HELL is going on over there?
> A: I hope you're making good choices, and you have
>   found the man of your dreams

I had. And we had lasted barely a few weeks, and then had gone down in flames. I felt the hurt and anger and sadness start to crawl back up into my chest and fought back the tears.

What could I tell them? That yes, I'd made the best of all possible choices in giving everything I had to Max, and it had all been for nothing?

No text from Max. Why should there be?

"Here?" Solange asked, setting a tray on the dining table.

I pushed away from Jules, crossed the room, and sat. Solange sat across from me and watched me eat for several minutes in silence. Then:

"So, Max told me that you lied to him? About Nicole?"

I started shredding a slice of baguette between my fingers. "Did he tell you why?"

"He seemed to think that you had used him. For your writing. And he seemed to think that his own feelings were . . . what's the word? Ignored?"

"What feelings did he have, exactly?" I muttered. "Do you know what he said to me that first morning? That I had lovely ankles. And boobs. You said yourself he took me to see Nathalie because . . . how did you put it? For his own pleasure? He was fixing me up so he could . . . whatever."

"I doubt that is true. Well, not entirely. I thought that he liked you quite a bit."

I used a piece of baguette to wipe up the last shreds of cheese. "I thought so too. I was wrong, and it's just as well. I'm flying back tomorrow. I made the reservation this morning. I've done what I needed to do. I came to Paris to write and I have, and now I'm going back to my real life."

"Don't you want to talk to him again?"

"And say what, Solange?" I lifted my head to meet her eyes. "I had a wonderful time in Paris. Truly. You have been just amazing. Thank you. Max and I had a moment. Maybe a few. But that's what they were. Moments. You don't fall in love with a person in a few weeks. Not even in Paris."

She sighed. "You should have more belief in what you write about, Maggie."

"I don't write about insta-love. It doesn't happen."

"But you do write about women who are unafraid to go after what they want."

"I wanted to write this book. And I did. That's enough."

"Who are you trying to convince?"

I pushed myself away from the table. "Excuse me. I have to call people." I walked away and into the sumptuous bedroom, with its pillows and marble fireplace, with all the beauty and charm of Paris, and went right back to sleep.

The plane ride back to Newark was uneventful, as was the Uber to Morristown. My apartment smelled stale and felt empty when I arrived. I opened windows and saw that all Greg's things were, in fact, gone.

I checked my plants. Thriving. I called to start the *Times* up as soon as possible. I drove to Whole Foods and was somewhat disappointed. Even their 100 percent organic strawberries seemed lacking.

I bought a small stove-top espresso maker, like the one in the Paris flat, and an aerator to whip hot milk. I sat in my office and had café crème and third-rate croissants and felt generally miserable.

I sent my completed first draft to Ellen and then called Lee.

"What about the pub date?" I asked.

"They haven't changed their minds. Believe me, I've been pushing," he said.

"And the cable option?"

"All they were waiting for was the final book to be done. You may get some good news this week after all."

"I could use it."

"I can't believe you finished, Maggie. I'm thrilled that you did, but why are you back? Weren't you going to see Nicole in Rennes? I imagined you staying in Paris longer."

"I did see Nicole. And Rennes. But—I . . . , well . . . , the book was done. There was no other reason for me to stay in Paris."

"Oh."

"I have to go, Lee."

He sighed. "Okay Mags. I'll talk to you as soon as I hear something."

It was getting late when I texted Cheri and Alison.

M: Im home can you two come over?

I sat and stared at the screen. It just took a few seconds. . . .

A: Why r u back already? U OK???
C: No shes not OK shes here instead of paris where shes supposed 2 B. I haven't showered does it matter?
M: Of course not
A: Do we need wine?
M: I have some
C: Now?

M: Whenever

A: 15 mins

The two of them showed up at my front porch at the exact same time, and when I opened the door and saw them, I hugged them both at once, then began to cry.

Cheri pushed me into the house. "I told you," she said to Alison. "I told you things weren't right."

Since both knew my kitchen as well as I did, they got glasses and poured wine while I sat in my living room and tried not to look like a blubbering fool.

"Well," Alison said, setting the wineglass in front of me, "I'm really glad you did something with your hair. You look great."

"Thanks," I said, sniffing and taking a gulp of wine.

"And a manicure?" Cheri asked, grabbing my hand. "Look at these nails. Girl, you should think about getting this done more often."

"I know. I was told that short nails don't have to be ugly."

"Uh-huh. Right. And who told you that?" Alison asked.

I clenched my jaw, swallowed hard, took another sip, and shrugged like the name meant nothing at all. "Max."

Cheri sat back, folded her arms across her chest, and lifted her chin. "Start talking."

I told them everything. And I mean everything, even the little trick Max pulled on me our second night together that almost made me jump right out of my skin. When I finally stopped talking, the bottle of wine was empty.

Alison shook her head. "Damn."

I sighed. "I know."

Cheri frowned. "What about Alan? You were going to tell us *that* whole story."

"Oh, he was there. And we got along just great. He seems to think that he and I can get back together. Actually, it was originally Nicole's idea that he and I pick up where we left off."

Cheri exhaled loudly. "We need more wine."

Alison sprinted to the kitchen and returned in record time. Glasses were refilled.

"So," she prompted. "Go on."

I sighed. "The thing is, Max travels. All the time."

"Like Greg," Cheri said.

I nodded. "And Alan has retired. He has nowhere to go."

"So is that the only thing in his favor?" Cheri asked.

I shook my head. "No! No. Not at all. Alan is like a favorite blanket. When I'm with him, I feel safe and warm."

"And happy?" Alison asked. "Because, I'm thinking that should be really high up on your list."

"Yes, happy. But Max, well . . ." I sighed. "There's happiness, and then there's Max."

"So he's our man," Alison said.

"Oh God, yes."

"What are you going to do about it?" she asked.

"I don't know," I wailed.

"I do." Cheri pointed her finger at me. "You need to find his New York address, get on the bus, park yourself in front of his apartment building, and just hope he's not as stupid about this whole situation as *you* obviously are."

I felt my whole body slump. "I hurt him. He thought I was only using him. I get that, but what about me? I mean, he was using me too. All he wanted—"

Cheri held up a hand. "Maggie, you have no idea what that man wanted because you heard a few words and drew your own conclusions. Did you even ask him?"

"No, but—"

"Don't you *no but* me," Cheri snapped.

"Maggie," Alison soothed, "what I think Cheri is trying to say is that maybe you were the victim of a Great Misunderstanding."

I sat very still.

A Great Misunderstanding is a commonly used device in romance writing wherein the hero or heroine says something that is completely misconstrued by the other party, and chapters of angst and possible revenge sex happen before the truth is finally known. I hate a Great Misunderstanding and have never used it in any of my books, if for no other reason than if I did, neither Cheri nor Alison would ever read anything I wrote ever again.

"No," I whispered.

"Yep," Alison said. "Do you have his phone number?"

"Yes," I said.

"Don't," Cherie said. "This is too big for a phone call. You need to go to him. Bring wine. Does he like expensive cigars? Maybe have a small string quartet back you up as you plead for forgiveness."

I stared at her, then at Alison. "She's kidding, right?"

Alison shrugged. "Maybe. Maybe not. Yes, he was the one who walked away, but . . . you let him."

I dropped my face in my hands. "I'm an idiot," I wailed.

I felt Cheri's arms around me. "Yes, honey, you are. But you're *our* idiot. And we will help you get through this. Now, when can you go to New York?"

I thought. "I think he's probably still in Europe. He was going to Switzerland."

"Is there someone you can call who would know?" Alison asked.

I shook my head. "His mother, but . . . I don't think she'd be very helpful. After all, she probably thinks I'm an idiot too."

Cheri twisted her lips. "What about your agent? This Lee person?"

I rolled my eyes. "Ah . . . no. I'm sure he might be able to get the information, but he is the business side of my life. Besides, he's got a relationship with Max already, and there's Solange. I don't want to put him in the middle of anything. But . . ."

Nicole. She said that she and Max talked. They seemed to have a genuine affection for each other. Could I ask *her*?

"Maybe Nicole," I said slowly.

"When is her day to call?" Cheri asked.

I nodded. "Monday."

She put both hands on my shoulders and looked me straight in the eye. "You gonna wait until Monday?"

I shook my head.

"You know what you have to do?"

I nodded. I was ready.

I sent her a text, and she called me right way.

"Nicole, honey. Hi. I have a really big favor."

"Yes, and hello to you too. I'm doing just great, thanks, and Louis sends his regards."

I sighed. "Sorry, baby, but this is important."

She waited.

"I need you," I said slowly, "to find out when Max is going to be back in New York."

Silence. "Why?"

"Because I'm probably in love with him." There. I'd finally said it, and never before had so few words sounded so right. "I need for him to know that, and I don't think I should send him a text, as there will also probably be groveling involved."

More silence. There was not even background noise. Was it possible that she was sitting somewhere *just* having a conversation with me?

I cleared my throat. "I think he's still in Switzerland."

"He never went to Switzerland," Nic said. "He went to London."

I took a deep breath to keep my voice from rising an octave or two. "Oh? How do you know?"

"Because I texted him a few times, just to ask how he was

doing. He's all right, by the way. He'll be back in New York Monday morning, but I don't know for how long."

Monday morning. Three more days. I could wait three more days. Especially since I had no other choice. After all, this was, theoretically, the rest of my life I was talking about. What were three more days?

"Thank you, Nicole."

"What about Daddy?"

"Oh, honey. I wish that had worked out. For all of us. But I just can't go back. Not if there's so much in front of me."

Pause. "I like him, Mom. Max, I mean."

"I'm glad, because I hope you'll be spending lots more time with him."

"Me too. So don't screw up, okay?"

I sighed. "Okay, honey. I'll try."

"Good. Love you."

"Love you more."

There was a pause. "I know," she said softly, then hung up.

All I could do was wait it out, and while I waited, I dove into revisions.

Every writer is different. For me, the first draft had one job—to get the story out. The second draft was about the bigger details: making sure the timeline made sense, keeping the characters on track, not letting the sound of the words in my head distract from the actual story. For my revisions, I read each and every line out loud, very slowly. Hearing the words let me find the stupid mistakes, the idiotic typos, and the glaring inconsistencies. I could hear when the dialogue sounded false. I could imagine scenes more easily.

I didn't let the story roll over in my mind. I had no time for that. I read aloud and rewrote and read again. I had sent the first draft to another writer, someone I'd known for years; we'd often critique each other's work. She returned it in record time with tracked changes and suggestions, but then she called me.

"It can always be better, Maggie. But seriously, you could publish that sucker today. It's that good."

Ellen called me. "Mark has decided that you were right. He can't push this back a whole year."

"Thank you."

"He's going to try for the fall."

"No. This is not a book for the fall. You know that. We need next June. I'm sending you the second draft."

"Already?"

"Yes. And I just talked to Lee. We got the contract for the cable deal. He's going over it now. It's ridiculously complicated, but he thinks we'll have it signed by the time book two is launched, so . . ."

She sighed. "Okay. I'll try. You know I'll try. What else are you working on?"

"Nothing."

But that wasn't necessarily true. I was working on me. I got another manicure. I had my roots done. I spent a small fortune in a day spa and was peeled and wrapped within an inch of my life. By Monday morning, I was once again Paris-worthy.

Max's apartment building was a sleek modern rectangle that reached up at least twenty stories and had a very stiff group of men behind the front desk. I was wearing the gray dress I'd bought with Max from Zoë's shop and was so nervous I kept falling off my kitten heels.

"Max Varden, please," I said, noting with some satisfaction that my voice wasn't shaking.

The tallest man behind the desk barely looked up. "Mr. Varden is out of the country until the fifteenth of next month."

"I thought he was due back today," I blurted.

"He was back. He came in late last night and then he left again this morning. I'll be happy to take a message."

My heart sank. My stomach had been in knots all weekend, and I practically hyperventilated myself into a panic attack on the bus trip over, and he wasn't even in the country.

I smiled like it didn't mean a thing. "I'll check back. Thanks."

I crossed the street and went into a very elegant-looking little bar, drank a twenty-three-dollar martini, and went back to New Jersey.

I called Cheri. "He was there and left again."

"Oh, Maggie, I'm sorry."

"He'll be back the fifteenth."

"That's more than three weeks away. You need to keep busy."

"I know. Will you help me?"

We went to the local nursery where I bought eight giant terra-cotta pots, twenty or fifty pounds of garden soil, and little pots of herbs. Cheri and I spent the next few days planting herbs and artfully arranging the pots around my tiny patio. I also spent several afternoons trying to make bread. I even tried making my own butter. I finally decided it would be easier to just fly to France every few weeks and restock.

And then one morning, Alan called.

I'd been thinking about him. I'd been wondering if he would try to call me, or if he realized that whatever he was feeling about the two of us was a result of us walking hand in hand under the springtime Paris moon.

But I had to admit, I felt pretty happy when I saw his number come up on my phone.

"Hi," he said easily. "Are you busy?"

I had just taken every pot I owned out of their respective cabinets and lined them all up on the kitchen counter. I counted five nonstick frying pans with their surfaces so badly damaged butter would probably stick, three stockpots the exact same size but with no lids, and a small, avocado-green enamel saucepan that may very well have been my mother's. Solange had managed to cook incredible meals with just a handful of copper pots and a Dutch oven, and I was determined to follow her example. I had all my shiny new cookware picked out from the Williams Sonoma catalog, but first I needed to purge.

"Trying to organize. I'm going to become a good cook. I hope. How's retirement?"

"Well, I'm traveling a bit."

"Oh, Alan, that's terrific."

"Yes. And since I'm here in Morristown, how about lunch?"

"You're traveling in *Morristown?*"

He chuckled. "If I can't look up old friends and ex-wives, what's the point of traveling at all?"

"Well . . . okay. Give me time for a shower. Where are you?"

"I parked in a garage off the Green. I'm in front of a place called Roots."

I laughed. "You sure can pick 'em. I'll be there in a bit. Walk down to a place called The Office and wait for me at the bar."

"What's the difference?"

"About fifteen dollars a drink."

He was relaxed and chatty, and we spent lunch talking about Paris and Nicole. He asked about the book, and I told him about my marathon sprint to the finish, leaving out everything about Max.

"Well, that's too bad about your fight with your publisher, but the cable option?" He sat back and smiled. "Maggie, that's fantastic! And this means, what? You finally get your cottage by the sea?"

I took a deep breath. "Yes. Finally. I mean, not right away, of course. But . . . yes. Now I have to decide *where* I want to live. The East Coast, for sure. Someplace warmer than here, but not Florida. What about you? Have you decided where you're going to end up?"

"As a matter of fact, I want you to look at something." He pulled out his phone, fiddled a bit, and then handed it to me.

There was a photo of a tiny, weathered house, right on a rocky beach.

"Alan, what's this? It looks adorable."

"It's on Cape Cod. It's small, just two bedrooms, but there's an enclosed porch that would make a great place to paint."

I broke into a smile. "It's yours?"

"Maybe. I haven't put an offer in. But I was thinking. I know you said you didn't want to live someplace colder than Jersey, and let's face it, the Cape gets cold. But this could be a summer house."

I felt my smile break. "Summer house?"

"Yes." His eyes were steady. "I could buy this, and you could buy someplace farther south so we would have a place to go in the winter."

I handed back the phone slowly. "Alan, I—"

He held up a hand. "Now, just hear me out. When we divorced, we had very good reasons, and I think that both of us have had separate lives that were much happier than if we'd stayed together. But those differences don't matter now. You're successful at what you've always wanted to be. And I've stepped away from my career. I want to sit in the sun and paint. Sure, I'd like to travel just a bit, but I'd be more than willing to just follow you. Maybe Nic is right. Maybe now would be the perfect time for us to get back together."

My mind was a jumble. It was so easy for me to remember all the reasons I'd fallen in love with him in the first place. But that was then. This was now.

"Alan, I don't exactly know what to say."

He hung his head. "I was hoping you'd say something about what a great idea this was."

I stared down at his phone. A beach house. Two, actually. And in both of them, Alan would be painting. Not going to Prague. Or London. He would be waiting for me. Every day. It was a rather great idea.

Except . . .

He looked up. "Is it Max?"

I met his eyes. "Max? What do you mean?"

He shrugged. "Anyone with a pair of eyes could see there was something going on between the two of you."

"There was nothing going on, Alan."

He made a face. "Really?"

"Well, okay, after you left, things got more complicated, but . . . we did not part on very good terms."

"Were you in love with him?"

I stared down at my hands. "I think I still am."

"So what are you going to do about it?"

"I'm not sure."

"Well." He signaled for the check, handed over his credit card, and cleared his throat. "I want you to know that if things don't work out, I would love to have you back in my life. In any way."

I felt such a sadness. "That's very kind, Alan. But I don't want to just *be* in your life. I don't want to just *be* in *anyone's* life. I want to be the reason someone gets up every morning. I want to be the fire in their soul. And I want to feel that in return." I held my fists against my chest. "I want to feel it right here."

He stared at the now-empty tabletop for what seemed to be a very long time. "I think that's something we all want," he said very quietly. "And it's something we don't all have the courage to wait for."

"I'm willing," I said.

"Yes. You would be." He looked up at me then. "I hope you get what you're looking for, Maggie," he said, smiling.

I sat up straighter and smiled back. "Oh, Alan. Me too."

Chapter 13

Where we all get our just deserts

The Friday before *Fire in the Blood* was to be launched out into the great, wide world, I sat with Ellen and my team in a tiny, claustrophobic conference room and talked strategy. Yes, I had a team; they had planned the big opening next week, the tour would begin immediately after that, scheduled interviews and radio spots and television spots . . . my head felt like it was going to explode by the end of the day.

"We need a drink," Ellen muttered as we got into the elevator.

"We need two," I said.

As the doors began to close, a voice shouted, and I slammed my palm on the button to keep them open. Who else was skulking around the office this late in the evening?

Mark Carruthers, that's who. Mark Carruthers, who was so sure of his own importance that I'm sure he could not imagine anyone *not* holding the elevator for him.

"This may not be the time," Ellen said under her breath as he paused before the open doors.

"Hello, Mark," I said brightly. "Come on in, there's plenty of room."

He smiled broadly as he stood beside me, and even bent down to give me a kiss on the cheek. "Great to see you, Maggie. And so excited for your book launch. Lots of good things planned? I know it will be amazing."

"Yes, but this year's launch doesn't concern me. I've seen the presale numbers. Amazon alone is probably going to earn me back my advance. And have you heard? The cable deal just went through. Lee is hammering out the details right now. Only one season, but, hey. Three books, right?"

He showed the palms of his hands. "But romance is, well, not quite sci-fi. Or even mystery. You never really know how a book like yours will resonate with an audience."

"You're right, Mark. An attractive hero and heroine, hot sex, adventure, danger, a few thrills, and true love . . . I mean, look at *Outlander*. God, I sure hope those poor kids can keep it up."

The elevator stopped and the three of us stepped out. I didn't dare look at Ellen. I kept my eyes on Mark, whose eyes had narrowed.

"You do know that I don't have another contract with you," I said. I adjusted the tote bag on my shoulder as though this were just another office conversation. "I have nothing at all for what I'm working on next. Not with you, anyway." I couldn't believe the words as they fell out of my mouth. Was I actually threatening my publisher?

He tilted his head. "Now Maggie, we've been together for years."

"Yes, we have. And if you push the release of my third book to next fall, instead of next summer where it absolutely needs to be, it will be your last book."

He glanced around. The lobby was not terribly crowded, but the dozen or so people who were there were all publishing people, and they were all looking in our direction. He dropped his voice. "Maggie, you know how things work. It takes time to get a book together. And you did miss your first two deadlines."

"But I made this one. In fact, the revisions are on Ellen's desk right now, *ahead* of schedule. The cover is done. All the promo has been in place since the first release."

"Yes, but edits—"

"Pretend I'm that porn star who slept with you-know-who. You managed to get her book on the shelves in a matter of months. Maybe you could get that editor to help out?" My mouth was so dry I felt my tongue sticking to the roof of my mouth. Was I really saying all this? Lee would kill me if he heard me right now. He had always gone to bat for me. He was the fighter, and he'd always done right by me.

But this last book was too important. And this last book had cost me the most. I wasn't about to let anyone or anything keep it down.

Mark looked down at the sleek marble floor, his lips puckered. Finally, he nodded. "Okay."

I did not let my knees buckle from relief. I did not throw my arms around him and squeal with delight. I lifted my chin.

"Thanks. Maybe you could make my launch. It's right down in Union Square. I hear they throw a great party."

A real smile now. "Maybe."

I turned and sauntered away, through the revolving doors, and out into the Manhattan evening air. Ellen, coming up behind me, was practically apoplectic.

"I can't believe you talked to him like that," she gasped.

I put both my hands on her shoulders and leaned my forehead against hers. "I can't believe it either."

And then we both started to laugh.

I was rearranging my new copper pots when Lee called.

"Did you really attack Mark Carruthers getting out of an elevator and harass him about your third book?"

"No. That is not correct."

"I got five different texts, all describing the same encounter. What happened, Mags?"

"I just reminded him that this book is the last one I'm contracted for. And that there was the possibility it would be the last one ever."

I could hear him muttering under his breath, then there was a long exhale. "That's my job, Maggie."

"I know. Which is why I used *your* idea."

"I was talking to Mark. We were reaching an understanding."

"Good. But now the issue is resolved." I'd been walking around my kitchen, but finally sat down. "I know I overstepped. I'm sorry. But . . . you know what this book means to me, Lee."

"Yes. But Mags, it could have gone very wrong."

I took a breath. "Well, I was figuring the odds were in my favor. Since my love life had already gone so very wrong, it made sense that something somewhere would go right."

He cleared his throat. "Well, I wouldn't know about that. And I don't want to, although I've had to threaten Martin with near death to keep him from driving over there to get the whole story about you and Max."

"Tell him to wait. The story may not be over."

I hung up, hugged my new sauté pan to my chest, and looked at the calendar hanging on my wall. The days until the fifteenth were marked off in red.

Ten days to go.

The Barnes & Noble in Union Square was not my favorite bookstore in the world. After all, I'd just recently browsed Shakespeare and Company in Paris, France. But for a book launch, it was pretty spectacular.

Copies of *Fire in the Blood* were stacked everywhere. Banners displaying its distinctive cover hung on every floor. The cover was done in deep greens and black, a faintly tribal, Middle Eastern–looking design, with the font in deep red.

My name was above the title. I loved that.

First, I was to have a bit of a chat. Meredith Walters, author extraordinaire and longtime friend, would be with me, feeding me questions and facilitating the Q&A. Then the signing would begin. We were starting early, and the store would be open until eleven. Minions from the publisher, as well as Ellen and her assistant, were on hand to keep the flow of books coming. Lee and Martin were there, sitting in the front row. Cheri and Alison had come in on the bus with me. We'd eaten an early dinner, and they were going to sit on either side of me at the table, feeding me coffee, chocolate, and new Sharpies.

Every seat was filled. And not just with women. I was thrilled to see couples, even single men. It wasn't just about capital-R Romance anymore.

Right at seven, we began. Meredith fed me all the right questions: How did Delania begin? What was it like to create an entirely fictional country? What was the secret of good sexual tension? After about an hour of give-and-take, she looked out at the audience.

"I know what you're all dying to hear about, right? The *third* book!" she called out.

There was a thunder of applause and I felt my face get red.

Meredith gave me a look. "So . . . tell us. What was it like to finish this story?"

I took a breath. "It was the hardest book to *start* that I've ever written. And the easiest to finish."

Meredith leaned forward. "Don't stop there."

I glanced at Ellen, who looked intrigued. "I had to ask for an extension of my deadline. Twice. I was seriously stuck. But once I began to actually sit down and write it all out, the words flowed." I met Meredith's eye. "In the zone. Totally."

Meredith laughed and looked at the audience. "That's

writer-speak. It means that she didn't change out of her pajamas and lived on coffee and stale cookies for weeks."

More laughter, then she turned back to me. "Tell us—what
got you there? In the zone?"

"I found inspiration. Of the highest order."

She arched an eyebrow. "Oh? A place? A person?"

I laughed. "Both. I was in Paris, and I met someone who
changed the way I looked at my life. Between cobblestone
streets, incredible art, and long café conversations, I was . . .
unstoppable."

"Your muse?"

I nodded. "Exactly."

"And the third book is coming out when?"

I looked at Ellen, who gave me the thumbs-up. "Next summer."

I wish Mark Carruthers had been there, because the place
exploded with applause. Ellen was actually jumping up and
down.

As the noise died down, Meredith grinned. "Perfect. Because
we all know that the Delania books are the perfect summer
reads. Now, who has a question? Just raise your hand and Amy
here will bring you the mic."

I loved Q&A. I got emails all the time from my readers, asking questions and telling me things about my books. But seeing
them in person was a totally different experience. Most of the
hands in the air were women, and the questions were all pretty
routine.

Q: Was Bella a real person?

A: Of course. She's me, only younger, taller, with perkier boobs.

Q: Is Lance a real person?

A: If he were, do you think I'd be *here*?

Q: If you weren't a writer, what would you be?

A: A lifeguard at the beach.

Q: Have you ever been in a situation like Bella's, where you had to live rough for weeks?

A: My idea of rough is having to walk more than two blocks for wine.

Q: What's the most important thing to you?

A: My daughter and her happiness.

Q: Is it hard to write the action scenes?

A: Not at all. I have people act them out for me. No, don't laugh. That's true.

Q: You write about young couples. Do you think you'll ever be inspired to write about an older hero?

My heart stopped. I knew that voice. I'd dreamed about that voice. There, standing way in the back, was Max, his beautiful French accent echoing through the sound system.

I stood up slowly. I could barely see him. His head was tilted slightly; I couldn't see his face or read his expression. But the fact that he was there . . .

"The most romantic man I ever met was an older hero."

Meredith looked over in Max's direction. Lee and Martin were both turned in their seats.

"In fact," I went on, "if I had the chance, I would spend the rest of my life writing about him."

He sat down. I had to grip the edge of the chair to keep from running off the stage and down the aisle. I looked at Cheri.

Her eyes were huge. *Is that him?* she mouthed.

I nodded and motioned with my hand. She shot up and ran to the side aisle and began working her way to the back.

"Okay then, let the signing begin," Meredith said loudly. She stood and grabbed my arm. "You okay?" she said in my ear.

I kept taking slow, deep breaths. "Yes. Let's get started."

I walked down off the stage and sat at the table and tried to keep a smile on my face as the line began to form. And then it began. I was on autopilot. Smile. Take the book. Read the name on the Post-it and repeat the name. Small talk. Sign the book. Thank you.

Next.

Cheri slid in next to Alison, shaking her head. "Sorry," she said. "There were too many people. I couldn't get to him fast enough."

It didn't matter. I knew exactly how to find him.

Smile. Sign. Repeat. At one point I looked at Alison. "Is this the longest signing ever?" I asked her. She and Cheri had been helping at my book signings for as long as we'd been friends.

She shook her head. "No, honey. But I bet it feels that way."

Lee crouched down behind me. "Why was Max here?"

"I don't know," I answered truthfully.

"Did something happen between you two I don't know about?"

"I'm not sure, Lee. What exactly do you know?"

"Nothing!"

"Then yes, something may have happened."

"I don't want to know."

"Make up your mind, Lee. Better yet, have Martin call me. Now, can I maybe sign this book now? Please?"

When we were finally done, I was so exhausted I thought I could drop my head on the table and sleep right there, except the caffeine from the coffee and the chocolate had my blood racing. My neck and shoulders hurt from the stress, my hand was cramped, and my face hurt from smiling all night.

Ellen came up to me. "We have a car to take you back home."

"Thanks." I motioned to Alison and Cheri. "Can my friends come with?"

She nodded. "Sure, Maggie. Just tell the driver. He'll take you wherever. Great job, by the way. And you're ready for the rest of the week?"

The rest of the week meant three more store signings, a luncheon event on Long Island, and a reading on Saturday morning. "Yep. I'm good."

"Did you know that guy? The French guy?" she asked. She didn't often get personal, but she did have a reason to be curious.

"He was my muse," I said as I gathered my purse.

She whistled under her breath. "Lucky you."

"Oh yeah."

The car was sleek and black with more than enough room for the three of us in the back.

"What, no minibar?" Alison asked.

"No. Sorry. Hey . . . what's your name?" I asked.

The driver looked at me in the rearview mirror. "Joe."

"Good. Okay, Joe, I have an address uptown I need to go to first."

He shrugged. "Whatever."

I gave him Max's address and clutched my purse in both hands.

"So, what's the plan?" Cheri asked. "'Cause I don't see wine or flowers or a string quartet."

"I'll just tell him the truth."

"And what is the truth, exactly?" Alison asked.

"That I fell in love with him and I miss him and I'm miserable and an idiot."

Cheri nodded. "That sounds about right."

"So, what should we do? Go with you?" Alison asked.

I shook my head. "No. Stay in the car. Circle the block a few times. I'll either be back on the sidewalk to be picked up and taken home, or I'll send you a text and you go without me. Hey, Joe, if I stay in the city, you'll get my friends home, right?"

He nodded. "Right. Someplace in Jersey?"

"Yes."

"Whatever. I get paid no matter who I'm driving."

I sat back and closed my eyes. "I'm so tired. And I think if I have to smile one more time my face will crack. What if he closes the door in my face?"

"Would he have come all the way to Union Square if he didn't want to send a very direct message?" Cheri asked. "I mean, if I were living in his neighborhood, I'd *never* go that far downtown."

You'd think that traffic on a Tuesday night after eleven would be light, but it seemed to take forever to get to his building. Cheri looked up and whistled softly under her breath.

My heart was in my throat and I felt the blood pounding in my ears. It was fight or flight again, but this time flight was not an option. There would be no walking away. I would fight until the very last breath. "Okay, guys. Wish me luck."

Alison gave me a quick squeeze. "Honey, you don't need any luck. I bet he knows exactly who he's getting."

I got out of the car and went into the lobby. There was a different set of men behind the desk, the night crew.

"Mr. Max Varden."

One of them looked up. "Ms. Bliss?"

I nodded.

"He said to go on up. Top floor."

I stepped into the elevator. He had left my name. He had hoped I'd come.

The friggin' top floor?

I stepped out into a long hallway, and the door at the end opened.

There was just his voice. "Maggie? Come on in."

I felt like I was that guy in the movie *The Green Mile,* walking in slow motion, hearing the sound of my heels on the marble floor of the hallway. I went through the door, and in front of me were floor-to-ceiling windows, the whole of New York City was spread out before me.

"Wow," I whispered.

"Thank you," he said.

I turned slowly. He looked so good, his button-down shirt crisp and white, his hair a bit longer, spilling onto his collar.

"I, ah, hope this isn't too late," I began. I tore my eyes from his face and tried to pretend we were having just a simple conversation. "Quite a view. Almost as good as Paris." My fingers were kneading the leather of my purse as I clutched it to my chest.

"Yes," he said. "It is almost as good as Paris." He reached over and took hold of my purse and gently pried it out of my clenched hands, setting it on a small table. "And no, it's not too late."

"You weren't supposed to be back until the fifteenth," I said.

"How do you know that?" he asked, frowning.

"Because I came by to see you and that's what they told me. That you were out of the country until the fifteenth."

His face, which had been somewhat guarded, softened. "Really? You came here?"

I nodded. "Yes. See, Nic told me you'd been to London and then you were coming here, so *I* came here, but you'd already left again. In the morning. Early."

"The desk didn't tell me I'd had a visitor. You didn't leave a message."

I forced myself to look away from him and instead out at the dazzling lights of Manhattan. "No, I didn't leave a message. What I had to say needed to be said in person." I glanced around.

Dark blue walls, sleek hardwood floors, beautifully framed photographs of Paris on the walls . . . his apartment was stunning.

I looked up at him. "You came back early?"

He smiled. "Yes. You see, I had a very important book launch to attend." He shifted his weight from one foot to the other. "You had something to say to me?"

I made my hands into fists at my sides to keep them from running up and down his chest. "I had a speech planned out."

He raised his eyebrows. "A whole speech? I'm flattered. About what?"

I cleared my throat. Yes, I had a speech. I'd been running it over in my head for days. Why was it that now, looking into those blue eyes, feeling the heat of his body radiating toward me, I couldn't remember a single word?

"Well, it was . . . you know. About how yes, you were my muse. And yes, I felt like I needed you in order to write my book. I mean, that was important. In the beginning, anyway."

I swallowed. Now what? What could I say to him? All those carefully thought-out words and phrases left my head completely. All I could think of was how I'd missed him, how important he had become, how much I wanted him in my life. "Somewhere it all changed, Max. It stopped being about the book and it was just about you." My mouth felt dry and I hoped my voice wouldn't crack. "It was all about you. The way you talked, and your laugh. You were all I could think about. How when you smiled at me, the rest of the world faded away. How you rolled up your shirtsleeves, just that one turn, and the way your fingers stuck out as you held your wineglass." The words were coming faster now, and I could hear the shake in my voice. "It was all about you. You and me. Us. Is there an us, Max?"

"There was always an us, Maggie," he said, very softly. I could hear the faint tick of a clock and the pounding of my own heart.

He took a step toward me, but I stepped back. Here was the question I didn't want to know the answer to. "Why did you ask me about the here and now?"

"Ah." He nodded as though to himself. "Yes. That was probably a poor choice of words."

I reached out and shoved him in the chest with both hands. Hard. "Ya think? That's what did it, you know. I thought, I mean, I was thinking about how I could possibly keep us going forever, and you made it sound like once I left France . . ."

He grabbed my hands and held them against his chest. "You said that here and now was perfect. Those were your words. What was I supposed to think?" I could feel his heartbeat thrumming against my palms. "And then when Nic said I was just . . . well . . . my ego couldn't take the possibility that maybe I was completely mistaken about you."

My eyes were on his.

"I adore you. You know that, don't you? You are such a . . . force." He stepped closer. "And I knew there was so much at stake for you. Your book. It meant so much. Then there was Alan and Nicole. I didn't want to make anything harder for you. I didn't want to add the burden of what-if."

I shook my head. "That was not a burden, Max. That was a gift. Because I was falling in love with you."

His eyes lit up. "My mistake. I should have realized you were woman enough to take on the whole world. Which is why I went to see you tonight. Because I love you too, and I had to find out if there was any chance . . ."

I leaned forward to kiss him. My hands went up and around his neck, and his hands were around me, and we were back, and my head was spinning, and we were laughing, our foreheads touching, our eyes locked, and in that moment, anything and everything was possible.

I kissed him again, and I let the whole of my body stretch against him. "I need to send a text," I told him.

His eyebrows shot up. "Now?"

"Yes, now. My two best friends in the world are circling the block in case I end up back on the street and need to go home to Jersey."

He threw back his head and laughed. "My God, Maggie. Now, *that* should be in your next book."

I kissed him again.

Then I texted Cheri:

Looks like another successful launch

I threw my phone on the floor. "I have about one hundred events to go to in the next two months," I said, my fingers busy with his belt. Why did men insist on belts anyway? Couldn't something with snaps do the same job?

"I have to get back to Dubai by Thursday morning, and then I'm in Japan for two weeks." His lips were on my neck as he patiently unbuttoned the back of my dress.

I pulled back, searching his eyes. "That's right. You're . . . away."

He nodded. "It's my job, Maggie. I'm good at it. It's important and it takes me away, sometimes for days at a stretch." He smiled. "But you can handle that because I promise you, I will always come back to you. Better yet, you can come with me." His smile broadened. "After all, you can write anywhere, I think. All you need is your laptop, a comfortable pair of sweatpants, and coffee, *non?*"

I felt another explosion in my chest. "Come with you?"

"Only if you wish. Either way, *any* way, is fine with me. There can be no holding back for me, Maggie. I choose to love you, and you will drown in that love. Do you believe me?"

I felt the answer deep in my heart. No, in my soul. Yes, I believed him. I smiled back. "You may have to prove it to me."

"Not a problem. At all."

"We have tomorrow. No, I'm in Staten Island. But I could come back tomorrow night." I pushed him down on the couch and knelt to pull off his jeans.

"Have you bought the beach house yet?" Snap. Goodbye bra.

"No. Will you come with me to look?" I climbed on his lap.

"We'll get one together. We'll go back to France. We'll have a beach house on every beach we can find."

"Perfect. That sounds perfect." I looked over my shoulder at the sparkling lights of the city spread out before us. "Are we going to make love right here, in front of the whole of New York?"

"Can you think of anything else quite as romantic?"

"Not right now. But give me time. After all, it is my job."

And then we stopped talking altogether.

Acknowledgments

First and always, I need to thank my agent, Lynn Seligman, for believing since the beginning.

I (literally) could not have written this without my daughter, Alley, who first showed me Paris, and her lovely husband, Gautltier.

Huge hugs to Nisha Sharma, all-around amazing person and critique partner extraordinaire.

Over at St. Martin's Griffin:

A huge shout-out to all the talented people who worked behind the scenes to bring this book to life.

I humbly bow down before Leslie Gelbman.

And to Alice Pfeifer, thank you for helping me on this journey. It has been the dream of my lifetime.

About the Author

3 Chicks That Click

DEE ERNST grew up in Morristown, New Jersey, and attended Marshall University in Huntington, West Virginia, where she majored in journalism, thinking it would help her launch a writing career. She miscalculated, gave up writing entirely, and began a long career as a bookkeeper. Dee is now back in the Tri-state Area, happily married and finally fulfilling her dream as a writer.